D0464645

My
Week
with
Him

Also by Joya Goffney

Excuse Me While I Ugly Cry

Confessions of an Alleged Good Girl

JOYA GOFFNEY

HarperTeen is an imprint of HarperCollins Publishers.

My Week with Him

For information address HarperCollins Children's Books, a division of HarperCollins Publishers, 195 Broadway, New York, NY 10007.
www.epicreads.com

Library of Congress Control Number: 2023930476
ISBN 978-0-06-325474-9

Typography by Molly Fehr
23 24 25 26 27 LBC 5 4 3 2 1

First Edition

For my big sister—my hero, my teacher, my biggest inspiration. Without you, there would be no me.

@AntTheProdigy: Nikki! Not sure if you know who I am, but you follow me, so maybe? I'm loving your videos. I especially love your voice and your look. My boss, THE Derek Atkins, is putting together a girl group for his label, and I think you'd be perfect. Auditions are on the 18th and another round on the 25th. Not only do I think you could make the group, I think you have a lot of lead-singer potential. Think you could make it to LA? Let me know!

Friday

(the first night of spring break)

7:56 p.m.

Riley somehow manages to snap along to the music, despite the red claws attached to her fingers. My mother would never let me paint my nails such a grown-woman color or keep them so long and pointy. But Riley's parents are lax, and she's quite honestly super spoiled.

She has a full-on orange-and-pink color-coordinated room, as if she snatched the whole thing straight out of a Target catalog. *And* she has her own attached bathroom and walk-in closet. Even Mal doesn't have a walk-in closet, and his house is the closest I've ever come to stepping foot in a castle.

"Daeja!" Riley shouts from her bedroom.

"What?" Daeja shouts back from the bathroom.

"Come here, babe. *Please.*" She's spinning in circles, letting the tulip skirt of her red dress flip and flap in the wind. Riley looks really good in red. She's told me why before, but I can't remember. Something about her skin tone. She's a mixed girl with brown, shoulder-length curly hair—white dad, Black mom.

Daeja grumbles about doing her eyeliner, but she still comes out grinning. It's obvious how beautiful she finds her girlfriend.

I'm sitting on the floor with my back against Riley's bed frame, painting my toenails white, while they dance together. We're supposed to be pregaming for Mal's annual Spring Break Bash tonight, but my head isn't really in the game. . . . Probably because I'm not *going* to the party tonight.

Riley's mom comes waltzing in, wearing fuzzy slippers and a really sweet-smelling (expensive) perfume, and holding a half-full glass of white wine. "Girls, look at this." She holds up her phone.

Riley struts over in her eight-inch heels, not even the tiniest bit scared of what her mom will say about her outfit. Daeja follows.

"Six Flags wristbands are on sale," Mrs. Ross explains, before Daeja and Riley can even read the screen. "We could go have some fun over spring break. And then when summer rolls around, we could have, like, a graduation last hurrah there, with all your school friends. Nikki, you too," Mrs. Ross says enthusiastically.

I smile over my shoulder, knowing my mom isn't about to pay for a Six Flags wristband. Hell, I probably won't get through this week without her yelling at me about getting a job. But still I say, "That sounds like fun."

"I don't know," Riley says, popping out her hip. "Over

spring break, sure, but I hate going to Six Flags during the summer. It's too crowded and hot. My skin *hates* too much sun."

"Your skin hates everything."

"It's not my fault that my skin is sensitive," Riley snaps at Daeja.

Mrs. Ross ignores their bickering, being as used to it as I am. "Rie, is this what you're wearing to the party? It's *so* cute. My baby's growing up too fast."

When I glance over my shoulder again, Mrs. Ross is gazing at her daughter, on the brink of tears. My eye catches Daeja's. She looks just as confused as me. Can't even imagine having a mom like Mrs. Ross. I could get away with so much shit. Life would be good.

"And Daeja, this outfit is everything," Mrs. Ross compliments her.

Daeja's wearing black jeans, baggy and formless, with a fitted black tee. Her skinny, two-strand twists all fold to the right side of her head, hanging over the shaved part. She looks really put-together, like she tried harder than usual.

Then Mrs. Ross looks at me. "Oh," she says, with her free hand rushing up to cover her mouth. "Nikki, *sweetie*, you look absolutely gorgeous. You are definitely gonna catch a lot of eyes tonight."

"Oh, I'm not going to the party. I'm—"

"But she might stop by," Riley interrupts. "That's why Daeja did her hair and why I did her makeup." Riley throws me a look, like *keep to the plan, idiot.*

Damn, I almost forgot. "No, yeah. I'll probably stop by," I say. "Yeah, for sure, for sure."

Mrs. Ross studies me for a second, then she nods slowly as if she understands something new about the situation. "Well, either way, I love this dress on you, and I think *Malachai* will too."

I immediately snap my gaze over to Riley, who's currently trying to sneak back to her bathroom. "You told her?"

"It's nothing to be ashamed of," Mrs. Ross cries, sitting on the bed, close to where I'm leaning. "Trust me, I get it: Mal is cute, rich, and he's very respectable. I think you two would be great together."

"We're just friends, Mrs. Ross," I say, finishing up my toes. Not even waiting for them to dry before standing up. "We've been friends since eighth grade," I add on, hoping this will be the end of the conversation. "Besides, he already has a girlfriend."

Mrs. Ross shoots up from the edge of the bed, nearly spilling her wine on Riley's pink rug. "Since when?"

"Since he did a huge promposal in front of the entire school for some random cheerleader," Daeja says, then goes back to the bathroom to finish her eyeliner.

"What's the girl's name?"

"Cynthia," Riley answers for me.

"Last name?"

"Valle."

"Valle?" Mrs. Ross repeats. "I know that family. Her dad is Brazilian, right?"

"Yeah, I think so."

I *really* don't want to talk about this. "Riley, you said you were going to let me try on some earrings, right?" I say, attempting to turn the conversation around.

Riley ignores me and keeps filling her mom in on everything about Cynthia Valle and how Mal practically stopped the whole school day to prompose to her two weeks ago.

I retreat to the bathroom, past Daeja doing her mascara in the mirror. I can still hear Riley and her mom chatting about me in the bedroom, but at least there's a slight muffle from the rap music blaring over Riley's speakers.

"You were absolutely no help," I hiss at Daeja.

She runs the mascara wand through her lashes, slowly and carefully. "I wasn't *trying* to help."

"Clearly."

"I just think you should stop by the party tonight, seriously, Nikki . . . and make him look at you."

"Why would I want him to look at me?"

She laughs, and her breath leaves a small radius of fog on the glass. "You know why. You look hot. And he'll regret ever dissing you."

"He didn't *diss* me," I say for the umpteenth time tonight.

She scoffs. "At this point, it's not even a matter of *if* he dissed you. It's how many *times* he's dissed you. From the whole prom thing, to how he couldn't even be happy for you about the audition, to the fact that he's dating Cynthia now—a girl he barely knows." Daeja drops the mascara and puts on her nonprescription glasses. "I never liked Mal," she says.

"Yeah, I know."

"And I can't wait to see his stupid face when you're performing at the BET Awards or at Coachella or something. You should come tonight—it'd be a good preview for him."

I try not to flinch. Because I'm not supposed to care. When Daeja heard that I was finally done with Mal, she jumped for joy. I've really liked having her on my side about this California thing. I don't even care that the only reason she's on board is because Mal is deathly against it. I just appreciate her support.

Mrs. Ross finds me sitting on the toilet seat, and then Riley appears behind her. The two of them crowd the doorway and give me no space to run. "Nikki, Malachai is stupid," Mrs. Ross assures me.

My jaw hardens. I'm tired of talking about Mal. I'm tired of hearing his name.

"That's normal for boys your age," she says. "Sometimes they're just stupid."

Riley nods. "Mal is stupid all the time."

"He's a *straight A* student," I say, looking at the two of them, perplexed. "Mal is far from stupid. He knows what he wants. And anyway, I'm fine with it. I can see why Mal likes Cynthia. She's really pretty and . . . she's not a bad person."

"She's not *great*, either," Daeja says, giving me a disgusted look.

"She's terrible," Riley counters. "A serious bitch, Mom."

"Yeah, I know her parents," Mrs. Ross says, A-OK with her

daughter cussing in front of her. I can't even imagine.

"It doesn't matter. I don't care," I say, standing from the toilet to face the mirror. All three of them watch my reflection, and none of them look convinced. "I *don't*," I say, rubbing my glossy lips together.

Mrs. Ross slowly shakes her head at me, sympathetic. "Oh, *honey* . . ."

8:13 p.m.

Riley thankfully steered her mom out of the room. And Daeja left, too, saying she was going to grab another beer.

"*Hope you find a way away. Baby, you're my sunny day,*" Vontae raps from the bedroom, while I stare at myself in Riley's mile-long bathroom mirror. I can see so much of myself. At home, my mirror is square and tiny, dotted with white toothpaste splatters, and only really there to make sure I don't forget what I look like. But here, the row of vanity lighting at the top makes the edges of my reflection glow. I look like I'm not of this world. I look *admittedly* sexy.

Black lace exposes portions of my midriff. My ass kinda hangs out of the spandex shorts underneath, while the corset top pushes up my boobs in a way that it doesn't when Riley wears this dress. I told her it doesn't fit me right, but she's convinced it looks better on me than it ever looked on her. She's tall and thin while I'm shorter and a bit curvier.

I imagine how Mal would react if I actually showed up to his party like this. He's never seen me in a dress, or really anything that isn't a ten-dollar outfit from Goodwill.

Riley steps back in. She's fixing a pair of gold hoop earrings to her ears. "Nikki, I'm sorry. I know that was shitty."

"I don't need your mom pitying me like that, Riley."

"She wasn't pitying you. She really wasn't. She just . . . We've all seen how Mal looks at you, and how he *talks* to you, and how he drops everything for you—"

"He does not drop everything for me." I roll my eyes, tired of hearing that exaggeration from everyone I know.

"Well, fine, but he does a lot for you." She crosses her arms over her chest. "He does *boyfriend* things for you—and y'all aren't even having sex."

"Ew, Riley."

"I'm just saying, boys don't usually do that kind of shit for free."

"What shit? He doesn't do anything for me, but like . . . sometimes he does my homework."

"Nikki." She purses her lips. "Don't act like he didn't drive all the way to Cactus and back to pick you and your little sister up for school for damn near a week. He was late to practice for you. That's serious, and you know it."

I look away with a slight smack of my gums. I was hoping she wouldn't bring that up.

"Which is why I get it—I get why you're trying to do this LA thing." She glosses her lips in the mirror, then she rubs them together. "I think it's *crazy*. But I get it."

"I already told you, Riley. None of this is about Mal. I'm going to California because it's my *dream*."

She exhales through her nostrils. Props a hand on her counter, then turns to me with a smile. "Okay. I believe you."

She doesn't *look* like she believes me.

"All I'm asking is for you to drop by his party tonight, before you get on the road."

"Why? So he can see me dressed like this?"

"No, so you can *talk* to him. I'm happy for you about the audition, but just talk to Mal first. Don't go to California for the wrong reasons. If this really is about your dream, go say goodbye to your best friend before you road trip across the country, Nikki. At least say goodbye."

8:27 p.m.

I'm coming back to Texas after the audition. I'll be back in just a couple of days. And it's not like I've said two words to Malachai in the past two weeks. Why should I say goodbye now?

He's not stupid—he knows exactly what he wants for his future. He wants to go to prom with the prettiest girl in school, graduate, and go to college with her in Dallas . . . and leave me here in Bumfuck, Texas. His burnt-out best friend. And I'm supposed to just smile and say congratulations. He never told *me* congratulations.

My song slowly comes through Riley's computer speakers. She's playing it from Spotify, adding to the half a million plays it's already gotten since I dropped it a few months ago. When my vocals come in, I mime singing and focus solely on my performance. I push myself. Make every motion sharp. Make every single body roll full and intentional.

"Yes, honey!" Mrs. Ross shouts. "Give me more face."

I toss in more sultry expressions. Mrs. Ross smiles and nods in approval.

Just one last rehearsal in front of my girls, then I'm out. By the end of the performance, though, Riley gasps and jumps to turn off the music. With my heart racing and my breath heavy, I ask, "What's wrong?"

"You're not performing barefoot, are you?"

I look down at my white toenails. This whole time I've been imagining this dress, this performance, these pristinely painted toenails with black open-toe dancing shoes . . . the ones I completely forgot to grab from home this morning.

"You told me not to buy shoes, remember?" Riley says, sharpening her gaze.

I nod, hands on my hips, dread washing over my entire body. "Yeah. About that . . ."

"Nikki, you had one job!"

Riley supplied my dress and my makeup—including the perfect shade of foundation for me—while I was supposed to bring the shoes. I told her I had the perfect black pumps at home, because I felt so weird having her buy shit for me. It's one thing when Mal does it, but Riley?

"Well, what size do you wear?" Mrs. Ross asks. "I might have some you can wear."

"Mom, Nikki wears an eight." Riley and her mom both wear seven and a halfs.

I rush to grab my phone and keys off Riley's bed. "I'll just run home and get 'em. No big deal."

"Except, isn't your mom home?" Daeja says.

I glance at the clock on my phone. "I'm pretty sure she went grocery shopping after work. I'll beat her home."

"And what if you don't?"

"Then I'll go to Cal—" My eyes jerk to Mrs. Ross's. "I mean, I'll go to Mal's party without the shoes," I say, like it's obvious. "They're just shoes."

"I knew I should have gotten a backup pair. If only we wore the same size!"

"Riley, everything will be fine. If I have to go barefoot, I will."

She makes a disgusted face.

"I'll text later," I say, slipping my feet into my busted-ass sneakers, holding on to the draping black tulle skirt so it doesn't drag on the ground.

Riley rushes over and pulls me into her arms. She smells like the same expensive perfume her mom is wearing. "Please stop by Mal's. Talk to him," she whispers to me.

I roll my eyes and say nothing.

Mrs. Ross joins the hug. "You look gorgeous, Nikki. And if Mal can't get his act together and realize the mistake he made, then he doesn't deserve you."

I sigh and say, "Thank you. Thank you both."

Daeja remains seated on Riley's bed. She's not a hugger—neither am I. "Seriously, Nikki, be careful. If your mom sees you dressed like that, you're done."

"I know." I nod at her. "I'll catch y'all later."

Hell, I know better than *her* how done I would be. If my

mama found out I lied about "staying at Riley's all weekend," and that I was actually going to an audition in California, she'd probably resort to violence. Which is why it's a good thing she went shopping after work today. I mean, hopefully that was still her plan.

On the way to my car, I grab my phone to call Vae, but she doesn't answer. I call her again. The girl has never been good at keeping up with her phone—which is so *strange* to me. It's hard to catch me without my phone, but Vae will leave hers on the charger for days. I figure it's because she doesn't have time for it. She's so close to being valedictorian that things like spring break have absolutely no power over her. It's not like she has a social life. . . .

After the fourth missed call, though, I start to worry. What if Mama has her trapped at home, in a line of questioning? Vae knows everything about my plans this weekend because I tell her everything, but dammit, she's really bad at lying to Mama.

As I'm racing across Dumas to get back home to Cactus, I'm hoping to God that Mama isn't behind me. Hell, I hope she hasn't left Walmart yet.

Sometimes she takes so long grocery shopping that I think it must be her escape, because even after what feels like hours of her "being at Walmart," she never comes home with more than a few bags of food.

Twenty minutes later, I turn into my trailer-park neighborhood, prepared to dip if I spot my mama's car, but the driveway is empty. And the house looks *dark*.

After school, Vae told me she had a ride home with some kid from the marching band. I didn't think too deeply about it, because of who I know her to be. She's not one to hang out with friends. She's definitely not one to be secretive or sneaky.

Disappearing and not answering her phone? That's some shit *I* would do.

The neighborhood is relatively quiet, considering that it's the weekend. Usually, I can hear Tejano music from two streets over and smell weed everywhere. So much weed that it almost covers the shit smell of the factory down the street. But tonight, I guess, *everyone's* taking their festivities outside of Cactus.

I have to admit, though, the silence is ominous. Like the calm before a storm.

As I'm running to the front door, my phone vibrates. *Vae?* Nope, it's just a text from Riley—a shit ton of pictures she snapped of me after she finished doing my makeup. I stagger up the steps, mesmerized by the images. I look like I belong on magazine covers—like *Ebony* or *Essence.* A brown-skinned beauty. Maybe it *wouldn't* be such a bad idea to let Mal see me all dolled up like this.

But even the thought of his name puts a bad taste in my mouth. This isn't about him. It's about my dream.

As soon as I get the door unlocked, I race to my mama's bedroom. Flip on the closet light. I spot some dusty dress shoes that look like she bought them twenty years ago, a few shirts that have fallen off their hangers, but not the black pumps.

It's probably a good thing I didn't mention to Daeja and

Riley that the shoes I plan to wear are my mama's favorite (and only) pair of name-brand shoes. Daeja would have fought tooth and nail to find an alternative.

Dammit, I know she's on her way home.

I text Vae: **Do you know where Mama keeps her shoes? You know the ones.**

Please answer me. Please answer me. She texts back: **In a box, under her bed.**

My heart settles. *Finally*, she responded.

After sweeping my hand under Mama's unmade queen-sized bed, I find a black Calvin Klein shoebox. They're open-toe, black and shiny without a scuff in sight. I pull my tennis shoes off and slip into the black high heels. They fit a little tight, but they're cute while not being too tall to perform in.

And Mama will never even know they're gone. She tries saving these for special occasions, but the last "special occasion" was when Grandma Bobbie died. I'll be doing her a favor, knocking off some of the dust, taking them out into the world for the first time in months.

I sprint to the door, relishing the *click, click, click* they make against the linoleum in the kitchen. But as I slip outside with my dirty sneakers in hand, I'm too late. There's a car parked in the driveway, the headlights like a spotlight on my scantily clad body.

8:56 p.m.

My racing heart beats like a drum in my ears. It's drowning out my rationality.

What's Mama gonna do to me?

What *won't* she do to me—dressed the way I am, while also wearing her shoes?

They were a gift from a man she dated a couple years ago. An African man she worked with at the factory. Let Daeja's mom tell it, the two of them were in "love." It was weird and gross hearing Daeja detail it to me. Mostly because I can't imagine my mama being in love with anybody. Not even me.

But I think Amadi did, at least, make her happy—as happy as anyone *could*. It wasn't like she was suddenly prancing around the house in a tutu, singing love songs. She was just a little more understanding with me and Vae. A little more open and human and sometimes even *nice* to us.

They'd go on dates once a month. Out to Amarillo and

back. Vae and I met Amadi, and we'd see him every so often, when he'd knock on the door to pick Mama up, but he never slept over. She went to his house a couple times, but all in all, she pretty much shielded him from us. Like maybe she thought we'd run him off or something. She had nothing to worry about. We didn't hate him. I think Vae and I were *surprised*, more than anything. That Mama was capable of being soft with someone.

Anyway, he died three years ago. From an untreated, infected wound he got on the line. So crazy to think you could die from something that happened at work. Vae and I didn't go to the funeral. Mama didn't ask if we wanted to. She just told us where she'd be all day and then left, dressed head to toe in black—including the shoes he bought her for Christmas.

The ones on my feet right now.

As I'm slowly closing the front door, I'm waiting for her to come barreling out of her car, screaming her head off about my outfit, but I've been staring into those headlights for at least ten seconds now and nothing has happened. Not a single door has opened.

I lean in, narrowing my eyes. There's someone sitting inside. Wait, no, that's two people . . . and they're *kissing*?

Oh my God. Is that *Vae*?

I've barely ever heard her talk about a crush, but now she's staying out late and kissing boys in our driveway? This must be what distant relatives mean when they say they feel old looking at how much I've grown.

As I make my way down the rickety porch steps in Mama's heels, I notice the color of the car and the make of it—a bright red Camaro. *Damn*, Vae. Not only is she staying out late and kissing boys, but she's kissing boys who drive really nice . . . Wait.

I know that car.

My eyes widen at the familiar license plate frame on the front bumper—burnt orange, covered in tiny white longhorns. Adrenaline pumps through my veins. I can smell the inside of the car from here—men's body spray mixed with Black & Mild cigars. I used to wear that smell in my hair and all over my clothes. I used to wear it proudly.

All those girls. All those names I watched Sarge drag through the mud, and I thought I was somehow . . . different.

Vae.

I drop my tennis shoes on the side of the rotten porch steps and take off. The heels of Mama's shoes get caught between the rocks of our driveway. I nearly twist my ankle. But I manage to land against the passenger-side door, yelling, "Vae, stop!"

She pulls away from Sarge's lips, fear in her eyes.

"What are you doing?" I ask through the glass. "Where have you been with him?"

She glances at Sarge and says something to him, then slowly opens her door.

"Huh, Vae? Answer me. Where did he take you?" I grab her arm as soon as she's on her feet, then slam Sarge's door behind her. "Have you been drinking?" I go in for a sniff, but she pushes away from me.

"Stop," she hisses. "You're embarrassing me."

"Embarrassing you?" I say, astounded.

How can she not see the gravity of this situation?

But then again, I guess she wouldn't. The grossly untrue rumors Sarge spread about us having sex had mostly cleared out when she got to high school. And I sure as hell didn't tell her about him. Not with how judgmental Vae can be.

"You don't know who he really is," I try to explain to her.

"Nikki, seriously, you're *yelling.* Let's just go inside."

But then Sarge whirs down the passenger-side window. "Bae," he coos to her, "everything okay?"

I can see what it does to her, hearing him call her *bae.* She turns to him with a soft expression and nods.

"Call me later?" he says. She nods eagerly, and he backs out of our driveway with his windows down. As he gets closer to the street, he says loud enough for both of us to hear, "*Daaaamn*, Nikki—looking that good, you can call me *too.*" He laughs. Cackles.

My sister is quite obviously in love with him, yet he openly hits on me, and then he fucking laughs about it, like Vae doesn't mean *shit* to him.

She stiffens and narrows her eyes at me.

Just as Sarge is about to back his car onto the road, another car blocks him in.

Mama's home.

9:00 p.m.

Mama gets out of the car. When Vae looks at me, we share the same terrified expression. "Fuuuuck," I hiss under my breath. This is worst-case-scenario shit. Absolutely worst-case scenario.

Not only am I caught dressed like an extra grown woman, but there's a boy backing out of our driveway. And Vae is clearly drunk (clear to *me* anyway).

Mama stops at Sarge's open window. And for a second, I'm happy he got caught here, 'cause if anybody will set him straight, it'll be my mama.

"And who are you?" she says, but she doesn't let him answer. "What are you doing in my driveway, young man?"

"Uh, yes, ma'am, I was just dropping off your daughter," he says, and we can barely hear him from here. Funny how far that laugh of his carried, but he's not so loud now that my mama's all up in his face. *Li'l bitch.*

"Get the hell off my property," Mama says sternly. "And don't come back."

"Yes, ma'am."

Then her fiery eyes cut to us—her two helpless baby fawns. Her slow footsteps toward us look tired but determined. Especially with Sarge's headlights flashing across her back. He moves around her car and peels out onto the street, never to return, I'm sure.

"What are you wearing, Shaniqua?" She's smiling, on the verge of laughing. "Where do you think you going, dressed like that? Or I guess"—she points over her shoulder toward Sarge's car, disappearing down the street—"I guess I should ask where you're coming from."

"No, he—"

She cuts me off. "You must think I'm stupid. You think I don't know what 'staying at Riley's' means? Riley's mama just wanna be friends with her daughter. I know she don't keep an eye on y'all. And I had a *feeling* you were meeting up with boys, but . . ." Her unbothered smile scares me to the bone. "I thought it was just Malachai. Never in my days did I think you had multiple boys with their nice cars, and their nice houses, running you up and down the street."

"He wasn't here for me," I say, like a cry, begging her to believe me. She thinks I'm something I'm not. She thinks I'm having sex with rich boys to get stuff from them—that's always been her theory about why Mal has kept me around for so long. But "staying at Riley's" usually means that I'm staying at Riley's.

"If he wasn't here for you, then what was he doing here?" she asks.

"Vae," I call to my little sister, in disbelief. I mean, like, why hasn't she *said* anything? Why hasn't she set Mama straight yet? She's just staring at the ground, facing north, like she's not even involved in this.

I motion to Vae. "He was here dropping her off."

Mama glances at Vae, standing in the driveway in her school clothes. "Stop lying." Mama rolls her eyes back to me. "That boy wouldn't be here for Vae."

"If you smell her hair and her breath, you'll believe me."

Vae looks at me sharply, like she can't believe that I'd sell her out like that. But *I* can't believe she hasn't stood up for me yet. She knows this whole thing will be worse for me than it will be for her. Vae isn't a stranger to Mama's ways. She typically rides for me more than she rides for Mama. But at the same time, Vae looks out for *Vae*. And she likes being the favorite daughter. So hearing Mama put her down is a much bigger deal for her than it is for me.

"Actually, *yes*, he was here for me," Vae says. "But I was forced to catch a ride home with him from band practice . . . because Nikki never showed up. She was too busy trying to get to LA this weekend."

10:30 p.m.
(much later into the first night of spring break)

Okay, so. I guess I'm homeless now?

10:45 p.m.

My fingers drum against my steering wheel to absolutely no music. Only me and my thoughts. I haven't stopped drumming my fingers since I left Cactus. My nostrils haven't stopped burning.

As I turn the sharp corner, into a middle-class, suburban neighborhood, my phone vibrates in my cup holder. Vae.

I turn my eyes back to the windshield, swallowing the acidic sewage tunneling up my throat. Let's add Vae to the list of people in my life who I'm completely done with. But while I'm at it . . . should I take Mal *off* that list? I'm not sure yet. I'm here, at his house, crashing his party, because I can't fucking *see* straight right now.

Despite what happened between us two weeks ago, I just . . . need my best friend right now.

11:03 p.m.

Each side of his street is packed. I've never seen this place so crowded—not even at one of his previous spring break bashes.

Takes me ten minutes to find a spot on the next street over. But I don't get out immediately. I adjust my rearview mirror so that I can see myself, to see if I look like how I feel. I don't. My face is still intact—I look beautiful. I look like someone who doesn't deserve the hand she's been dealt. But I'm not about to sit here and feel sorry for myself. I have an audition in California with a world-renowned producer and world-famous hip-hop sensation Derek Atkins. Once I leave Moore County, I'm never coming back. No matter how much everyone thinks I'll end up just like my mama—pregnant and stuck working at the meat factory for the rest of my life—I'm not coming back to this sinkhole of a town. I swear that.

I push open my door and leave my phone and all of the ignored texts from Vae in my car. Then I start walking the block.

Mama ripped her shoes off my feet the second she saw them—took some of the white toenail polish with them—so I'm back to wearing my sneakers. At least my feet won't hurt by the time I get to Mal's house.

Honestly don't think I've ever walked this path before. Anytime I'd hang out at his house, we mostly stayed inside. Playing video games. Doing homework. Even when we did nothing together, we were never bored enough to go outside.

Come to think of it, the very last time I was in this neighborhood was two weeks ago. I don't typically go three days without being at his house for something or another. It's so close to the high school, it just makes sense to chill there until my mama is due home from work. But nothing had felt comfortable between us since he'd gone off and expressed his love for Cynthia. We'd been carrying out the motions and holding in a lot of our words for days. So, for me to just show up at his house that day was . . . unexpected.

But I had good news. I had *really* good news. I had decided to put our differences aside and drove to his house, smiling so big that the edges of my mouth hurt. Until he opened the door with Cynthia at his hip. The way he looked at me, it felt as if now wasn't a good time. Like maybe I was interrupting something.

Suddenly my good news felt like a secret . . . a secret I should keep from him too.

Things had changed between us, but I hadn't been ready for that when I drove to his house that day. I hadn't been ready to accept that we would be like this *forever.*

That's why I can't really figure out what I'm doing here right now. I had good news that day and he all but shat on my dreams. What makes me think he'll give a shit about my bad news *tonight*?

I spot Riley's car on the way up Mal's street. I wonder what she and Daeja will say when they see me—having sweated out my edges and still wearing my busted-up sneakers. Even better: What will I say to them? If I tell them what happened at home, I already know they'll try to stop me from going to California, as if that's not my only option now that I'm homeless.

Slow-rolling 808s pass through my body as I stand outside his front door. I can hear laughter and chatter on the other side. Everything feels slow—my thoughts, the blinking of my eyes, my pulse.

I really, really expected tonight to go differently. I thought I'd drive to California, get to LA tomorrow and hopefully make it in time for the audition, and the whole time my mama would think I was at Riley's. I'd come back (with a record deal) either Sunday or Monday, like nothing happened. But now that coming back to Texas isn't an option, I might as well stay in Cali. Right? So long as I get into the group, I'll be fine. I'll be better than fine. I'll be rich and famous and shit.

Then the front door opens. Loud music and Cynthia's best friend, Aneeshah, come pouring out at me.

"Oh," I say, drawing backward.

Aneeshah gives me a quick once-over, her eyes hesitating on

my dirty shoes. "Are you okay?" Her gaze makes it back up to my eyes. It looks like she's forcing herself to be "friendly" with me. It *always* looks like that when she and Cynthia talk to me, especially since Cynthia started dating Mal.

"Yeah, I'm fine. Thanks." I move around her and go inside, where lights dance and flash across the walls. Music blares from the main speakers, sounding like incomprehensible mush, as I approach them from behind. I forgot Mal said he was hiring a professional DJ for this party.

I make it to the edge of the living room, and *holy shit* this place looks amazing. I'm used to the couch being in the middle of the floor, facing the television that's mounted above the fireplace, but he moved it—along with the heavy oak end tables and the matching ottoman—right next to the kitchen doorway. The living room floor is filled with bodies, some of them dancing, but most of them just hanging out in groups. Regardless, the strobe lights make everyone look like they're in slow motion.

I take a step onto the crowded floor. I can't really see my shoes or anyone else's. I immediately bump shoulders with a sophomore girl. She looks surprised, then she glances at my outfit and looks floored. "Ohmygod, I love it," she says. I don't remember her name, but I smile my thanks, making my way through the bodies. I don't know where I'm going, and I don't know why I'm here.

I haven't even made it halfway through when I'm bombarded. "What are you doing here?" Daeja shouts over the music.

"And why are you still wearing those shoes?" Riley points her whole hand at my feet.

"Oh, I . . ." I never figured out what I was going to tell them.

Daeja studies me closer. "Wait, Nikki, what happened? Did your mom catch you?"

"No," I say like a reflex. "She wasn't home."

"So then, why didn't you get the shoes?" Riley asks.

Daeja cuts in, "And why are you even *here* right now? I thought you were on your way to California three *hours* ago. You're losing a lot of time being here."

"No, I know, I just . . ." I shake my head because you know what? I hadn't even thought about that. About how much time I wasted banging on my front door, begging my mother to open it. *God*, I should have never gone home. Damn the shoes—never shoulda been there.

"Is Mal around?" I ask, getting to the heart of the matter.

Then both their eyes droop, as if they've realized something simultaneously.

"Oh," Riley says.

"You're having second thoughts?" Daeja asks.

"No—"

"It's about her *love* for him," Riley says with doe eyes. "She doesn't want to go all the way to California mad at him. She wants to open up and be honest with him."

I wrinkle my nose. "Riley, stop. I'm not in love with Mal." I hiss the L word and his name. They both look at me, unconvinced.

Daeja asks, "So then, why are you here, Nikki?"

I don't *know.* That's what I've been trying to figure out. But I can't tell her that. I can't tell her what happened at home. My eyes roam across the tops of everyone's head, looking for him. But then I see Cynthia before I see him, and she's sitting in his lap. There's that pang again. That feeling that I shouldn't be here.

Mal has always been good at defusing my bombs, though. All those emotions bubbling up to the surface, clouding my eyes and my mind and my judgment—he clears them away. Especially the ones about my home life. Every time I've ever run away, I've always come straight here, straight to Mal's house.

But this is different. This time I got kicked out.

As I make my way through the crowd in his living room, I'm doing my best to hold down my emotions. But it's getting really difficult, because every time I look up from the hips and shoulders I'm brushing past, I catch him mid-flirt with Cynthia. And the closer I get, the more I can see the smile on his face, flashing in and out of my view in time with the strobe light.

He's surrounded by his friends and his football buddies—all of whom are watching a group of senior cheerleaders dirty dance with each other. But Mal's not watching them. He's watching Cynthia.

When I stop in front of him, he doesn't even look up. It's Dex who notices me first. "Yooooo, Nikki." He checks me out with his mouth open. "You look . . . *wow.*" And I have to be honest with myself—it's how I wish Mal would react to seeing me, but he still hasn't looked away from Cynthia.

She's a light-skinned mixed girl with sandy brown curly hair and light eyes. She's wearing a cute miniskirt, crop top set—having put much less effort into her appearance than me—and she still looks exceptional. I peer down at my shoes. I almost wanna laugh at how ridiculous they look beneath this dress. Figures that this would happen to me. Fancy isn't something I was born into, or something I can pretend to be. Everything about me screams poor.

Dex finally elbows Mal in the side. "What the hell?" Mal complains, before following Dex's gaze to me. I stop breathing the second our eyes meet. "Nikki?" he says, taking a quick glance over my outfit. Cynthia looks at me, too, but with much more stank on her face. "What's going on?"

I can't actually hear him, because the couch is sitting right next to a speaker on a tripod, but I know how to read his lips. I know how he thinks.

He can see the exhaustion on my face. "Wanna talk?"

I nod, not even thinking about it. Honestly, I didn't expect him to be so merciful. And maybe that's why I'm here—just to see if there's still a chance . . . for us.

NOTE TO SELF: Fill up gas tank before leaving town tonight.

What if I made it all the way to New Mexico or Arizona, and then broke down? I can't even imagine what I would do. Get out and thumb my way to California? Either that or I'd have to bite the bullet and call Mal to come rescue me off the side of the road. *Again.*

My fuel gauge is broken. One day it just got stuck or something, and now it always says I have half a tank. It's harder than you might think to keep up with that shit on your own. A lot of times, I don't know how much gas I have until I'm sputtering on the side of the road. It happens more often than I'd like to admit, and every single time, Vae has called Mal to come scrape us off the road. She's so damn sneaky about it, too, because she knows how much it pisses me off.

That time Riley was talking about? When Mal "dropped everything for me" and chauffeured me to school and back every day for a week? That was Vae's fault. We weren't even close to being out of Cactus. I pulled over, turned my flashers on, and slammed my head back against the headrest. "Dammit." After a long sigh, I turned to Vae in my passenger seat, about to suggest that we walk back and catch the bus, because we were early enough where that was still an option, but she was *already on her phone*.

"Mal. We're stuck again."

"Vae!" I snapped at her.

She hung up without another word, because I'm sure Mal said "I'm on my way" without question.

"You can't keep doing that."

"What else are we supposed to do?" she asked.

"Catch the bus."

"Yeah, I don't want to walk all the way back home just to catch the bus."

"Well, you can't call Mal every time something goes wrong. What are you gonna do when he goes to college in a few months?"

"What are *you* gonna do, Nikki?" she asked quietly. She was biting the corner of her lip, worried. "What are you gonna do after you graduate? Are you really gonna work at the factory with Mama?"

"No," I said, knowing for sure I would never settle for that. I've seen what that place has done to her. How mean it's made her. How it's fucked up her body and her mind.

"I'll be fine," I told Vae, as if I was sure everything would work out. "I'll figure it out."

She watched me for a while, then she turned back to the windshield, and we waited in silence for Mal to come rescue us *again*.

Fifteen minutes later, his black-on-black Dodge Charger pulled over behind my piece-of-shit car. I watched in my rear-view as he got out, wearing dark jeans and a tightish black T-shirt and black tinted sunglasses. He looked like a movie star.

Vae got out and met him between our cars. He grabbed her backpack with a joking smile. He was probably giving her shit for how it was ten times bigger than her. Mal was the only person—outside of me—who could make Vae smile like that. She's quiet and small like a tiny church mouse and she keeps to herself a lot, but somehow Mal has made his way into her comfort zone.

Mal lugged the backpack onto one of his shoulders and ushered her into the back seat of his Charger. Then as he opened his trunk, to put her backpack with his athletic bag, I turned off my flashers, grabbed my keys, and got out.

That day I was wearing baggy Goodwill jeans, a T-shirt I'd gotten for free back in junior high in support of our shitty eighth-grade football team—it had a hole in the left armpit—and dirty sneakers that were coming apart at the soles. My hair was pulled back in a bun that was probably already coming apart, and I was wearing just enough makeup to cover the scar on my jaw and the pimple on my chin.

I went around the back of the car and joined him at the trunk. Mal watched as I threw my backpack beside Vae's. Then I looked up at him, my breath heavy with exhaustion. I was exhausted from lack of sleep and lack of answers to so many questions, from breaking down on the side of the road all the time, from having to be such a burden to him all the time, from never having enough money for anything, from fighting with my mom, like, every day.

He could see the exhaustion in my eyes. He reached over

and playfully pinched my nose. "You okay?"

I just stared at him, trying to find his eyes behind those dark sunglasses. When I didn't say anything, he pulled the glasses off and showed me his concern. I started crying. Just out of nowhere. Because I knew Mama was at work, pissed at me. And Vae was in his back seat, worried about me. And he had missed practice for this, and we were all about to be late to school *again* because of me.

He pulled me into his chest. He was warm and solid and he smelled good, like his Old Spice soap and the matching deodorant and that single spritz of Acqua di Giò on his neck.

"You're okay. I promise, you're okay."

I wanted to spill everything to him. I wanted to apologize for being such a hassle all the time. The words were clawing their way up my throat, but all that came out were croaks and moans.

Then he said, "I'm always going to be here for you. No matter what."

No matter what?

Did he really mean that?

11:16 p.m.

He leads me up the stairs, past the dancing shadows on the wall. The music muffles behind us. And when he opens his bedroom door, the bedside lamp is already on. He waits for me to walk inside before swinging the door shut. I slowly cross the dimly lit room. Then I sit at his desk, cross my legs, and face him.

"So?" he says, taking a few steps in my direction, looking at me like he doesn't recognize me. He doesn't sound eager to hear what I have to say. So it's really hard for me to open my mouth.

"I know it's been a while—"

He raises his eyebrows, like what I said is an understatement. I guess when it comes to how often we're usually around each other, two weeks of no talking feels like centuries for us.

My lips are stuck again.

"Nikki, what's going on?" he says, demanding an answer.

"There are a million people downstairs right now, totally unsupervised. And my parents are probably watching the cameras. They'll kill me if they see that I'm not down there—"

"Okay, okay. It's just that this is really awkward."

"Yeah, probably because you've been acting weird ever since me and Cynthia started dating."

My breath catches in my throat. And just like that, my lips clamp shut again. I really shouldn't be here right now, should I? He doesn't care. He proved that to me the last time I came to his house. Why do I keep giving him chances to hurt me?

It's over. I should just go. . . .

11:19 p.m.

I'm running down the stairs.

I told Mal that he was right. That he should get back downstairs and enjoy his party. I told him I'd get out of his hair and leave. But I didn't say goodbye. And I didn't tell him where I was going tonight, either. I don't need to tell him, because I don't need his permission. I'm leaving and I'm never coming back.

Daeja meets me at the bottom step. "Come with me," she growls, pulling me through the crowd, past people who I barely take the time to distinguish from each other, because it's not like I'm ever going to see them again.

Daeja pulls me into Mrs. Brown's office. Riley follows us in, turns on the light, and closes the door. I've only ever been in here twice in my life. "We shouldn't be in here," I say. I can't even believe Mrs. Brown left it unlocked, knowing how many teenagers would be in her house tonight.

Daeja searches my eyes. "Nikki, what happened at home?"

I'm caught off guard. "What are you talking about?"

"Vae just called me in tears, saying that your mom kicked you out. She's convinced you're going to California and never coming back."

Oh. So she knows.

I'm trying to keep a hold on the bile that came up at the sound of Vae's name. Then, calmly, I shake my head. "She's overreacting. I'm coming back."

Riley leaves my side to join Daeja, both of them inquiring with their eyes before they can get the words out of their mouths. "What happened?" Daeja insists.

"Nothing happened. Seriously." I shrug nonchalantly. "I mean, Mama came home and caught me, but I didn't get *kicked out*. Vae is exaggerating."

They don't look like they believe me. Half of me doesn't want them to. Half of me wants them to be as pissed at Vae as I am. She's the whole reason I got kicked out in the first place.

Never coming back to this sinkhole of a town.

"I need to get going." I turn and open the door of the office.

"Wait, Nikki," Daeja says. "You're coming back, right?"

I sigh, really hating this part. "Of course I'm coming back. But I need to get going if I'm gonna make the audition. Like you said before, I'm losing a lot of time." The lies come easy. It's the smile I tack on at the end that's shaky. "We'll talk later."

When I walk out of the office, back into the chaos and the

noise of the party, they follow, begging me to stop. "Nikki, seriously!"

Then Riley asks, "What about Mal? What happened upstairs?"

"What about school? You're two months away from graduating."

"What about . . . *us*?" Riley says.

It's that part that makes me stop. "This isn't about y'all," I say, spinning around. "This isn't about *Mal* . . . I don't even know why we're having this conversation. I'm *coming back*."

"And when you come back, where will you live?" Daeja asks.

That's the question, isn't it.

"This is crazy." Daeja spins on her heel and takes off through the crowd.

Riley stares at me, like I pierced her heart. "You are coming back, right?"

"Yes," I say again.

"You promise?"

I nod, blinking slowly. "I'll text you when I get there. Okay?"

She doesn't say anything. She doesn't believe me. But I have to go. I'm losing too much time.

11:32 p.m.

Waylon Jennings wrote a song about leaving Cactus—I read about it on the Cactus Wikipedia page. I found the song once on YouTube, and after listening to it for about ten seconds, I was like, "Cool," then I never looked into it again.

But now I'm kinda wishing I knew what it was about. Was he just leaving Cactus? Or was he *escaping*? What I'm doing right now feels more like escaping, and nothing about it has been easy—cutting the ties on my back that were holding me facedown in the dirt. Telling myself I don't need anyone ever again. Knowing that I barely have enough money to *make* it to California, much less stay in California.

Never coming back to this sinkhole of a town.

"Nikki, wait!"

There's another one of those ties, trying to pull me back. I hurry, because my car is right there. I get to the door and unlock it as his footsteps pound the pavement behind me.

"Nikki, stop!" he begs, voice cracking on *stop.* Then he's right next to me, and he's shutting my car door so I can't get inside. "You were just gonna go to California without saying shit to me?" he asks.

I sigh, staring through my window at my runaway bag. So, Daeja ran and told Mal? Wow.

He leans against my door, so close I can smell his cologne and his beer breath. The heat of his body is melting my resolve. "That's what I mean to you, Nikki? Not shit?"

Keep quiet, Nikki. Even if he's wrong, I tell myself to keep quiet, because I'm not sure how to form the words around my pride.

"Nikki, you know how much I hate it when you make that face."

"What face?" I say, like I don't already know the answer.

"The face you make when you're trying to hide your feelings from me." He studies my eyes. "What happened at home? Please, let's go back inside and talk about this." Then he reaches out and grabs my hand—the one holding my keys.

I planned to talk to him. That's the reason I even came here. But then Cynthia shook her magic dust all over him, and he couldn't give two shits about me. The anger comes roaring back.

"There's nothing to talk about." I rip my hand out of his grasp. "What are you even doing out here, Mal? Does your girlfriend know where you are?"

"Just please come back inside," he says, not acknowledging

my question. "You can stay the night with me."

"Did *Cynthia* say I could stay the night with you?"

"Nikki, stop."

"Why?" I laugh. "This was going to happen in a few months anyway. Time to rip off the Band-Aid. You're going to Dallas, and I'm going to . . ."

He nods. "Going where?"

"It doesn't matter. We can't be in each other's lives forever."

"I'm not *asking* for forever. Just tonight."

"Yeah, well, I don't have tonight. I'm losing time."

I open my car door and rush inside. But when I start the engine, he opens my door again, looking in at me. "Stay with me this week. My parents will be in Mexico all spring break. Stay with me, and if you still want to run to California at the end of the week, I promise I won't try to stop you. Just do me this solid. Give me this week."

"Can't," I say, putting the car in drive. "Can you close my door, please?"

"What about school? Huh? You're about to graduate. And what about Vae? What about me?"

I roll my eyes, looking up at him. "What *about* you? We haven't talked in weeks, Mal. I wasn't even planning to come to this party tonight."

"Then why did you?" he asks, eyes searching for anything to hold on to. "Earlier, you wanted to talk to me. So let's go talk."

"The time for that has passed. You made your choice. Cynthia was clearly more important." I scowl, because dammit, I sound bitter. I'm not supposed to care.

"Nikki, I know things have been really messy between us, but I have never stopped . . . caring about you. I *need* you. You are the best friend I have ever had."

"Mal, you don't need me. You've got a bright future ahead of yourself—scholarship to UT, a beautiful girlfriend, supportive parents. I have *nothing.*" My body fills up with the fear I've been pushing down all night. Fear of going to California alone . . . and never coming back to this sinkhole of a town. "I have nothing," I say again.

"You have me."

I look into his eyes, big and bright, and down to his lips, *wishing* that was true.

"Go back inside," I say. "I'm sure Cynthia is worried." Then I shut my door and lock it. He tries pulling on the handle, shouting through the glass. "No, Nikki! Wait!"

I give him one last lingering look. Then I let off the brake.

NOTE TO SELF: Look up that Waylon Jennings song and see if the lyrics are instructions.

Because I'm having a really hard time leaving this shithole of a town.

@nik_nik_nikki23: Hey Ant! Change of plans. I'll be at the second audition instead of the one today. Nothing's wrong. Just some family business to take care of.

Saturday

7:02 a.m.
(after the longest night of my life)

His house always smells like vanilla and brown sugar—like homemade cookies. I found out during one of my many runaway stays in his guest room that it comes from the abundance of wall plug-ins his mom has been hiding around the house.

This particular time that I ran away, Mal and I were juniors. His mom was home when I pulled up.

The way her eyes started to water when she saw me on her doorstep, with my runaway bag hanging off my shoulder, made *my* eyes water. I hated it, but at the same time I *craved* it. Like the first drops of water in a march across the desert, I craved how much she felt for me—a girl she had no responsibility for—a girl who wasn't her daughter. Why couldn't my mama feel like that for me?

"Nikki, come in. Take your shoes off." As I shut the door behind me and slipped out of my sneakers, Mal's mom watched me with a sad, forced smile, like she was doing everything she could to make me feel comfortable. "You're just in time to weigh in on this week's debate."

"What happened this time?" I said. "Did Mal insult your drapes again?"

"You know better than to bring that up." She smiled at me over her shoulder as she entered the light of the living room. That was when the smell hit me.

"Wait, Mrs. B, are you baking cookies or something?"

She laughed. "As if you'd *ever* find me trying to bake. If I so much as turn on the stove, Hutch and Mal are immediately down my throat, reminding me what happened on Thanksgiving six years ago. I'm sick of it."

I had heard the story of that dreadful Thanksgiving—I'd heard it every single November since Mal and I met in eighth grade. Between the undercooked turkey, the chunk of Mrs. B's finger falling onto the cutting board, and the *fire*—she really shouldn't be allowed near the kitchen. The sheer amount of people in attendance who called 911 that day is spectacular in and of itself.

"No, sweetie, what you're smelling are my new plug-ins. I may have gone a little overboard, I can admit."

"No," I said, laughing. "It smells like a whole-ass bakery in here, but that could never be a bad thing—in my opinion."

"*Exactly*," she said, laughing too. "I concentrated a lot of them in the front hall, since that's where Mal seems to always leave his stinky shoes. I would much rather my house smell like a whole-ass bakery than a stinky boys' locker room."

Mrs. B led me over to two outfits spread across the back

of the couch. "Okay, so, here it is—the latest debate in the house—which outfit to wear for my new headshots."

I scrunched up my face a bit, unimpressed with the topic. "Which way did Mal vote?"

"I'm not going to tell you that. I already have Mal's opinion. I want *your* opinion, because your opinion matters a lot in this house—I hope you know."

After a couple surprised blinks, I looked at the outfits closer. One was a silky pink V-neck blouse paired with gray, straight-legged slacks. The other was a silky blue closed-neck blouse paired with a mustard skirt. I pointed to the blue-and-mustard combo.

Mrs. B put her hands on her hips. "That's two against two." Then she smiled at me. "You and Mal chose the same one. Hutch and I like the pink one."

I smiled, giving me and Mal's choice another once-over. After staring at the two outfits for a while, Mrs. B turned to me with a careful look in her eyes. "You wanna talk about what happened at home, sweetie?"

"Everything's fine," I said automatically, without even thinking about it. I mean, what was I supposed to say? With the amount of times she'd seen me walk through her front door, holding my runaway bag, Mrs. B was definitely not under any impression that everything was "fine" at my house, but she also knew I wasn't up for talking about it.

"Nikki?" Mal came sauntering down the stairs. Then he saw my runaway bag. "What happened?"

"Nikki's staying with us tonight," Mrs. B said. "What do

you kids want for dinner? How about pizza?"

I smiled at her, turning out of Mal's inquisitive gaze. "Pizza sounds amazing."

Mrs. B always knew exactly what to say. And this house has always felt so open and welcoming, and like my opinion actually matters here. I mean, how lucky is Mal to have a mom who asks for his opinion? I guess that's why I always come here when my world comes crumbling down.

A single tear rolls down the side of my face, but I wipe it away fast. Now is not the time for this. Grayish light is starting to peek through the front windows. Mal will be coming downstairs any second now.

When I got back last night, the front door was unlocked, and the party had cleared out. I walked in, lay restless on his couch, thinking about last night. About Mama and the last thing I said to her. About *Vae* and the last thing I said to *her.*

As I'm starting to allow myself to feel guilty, I hear movement upstairs. I lie still as stone, clutching the couch blanket beneath my chin. Then I hear his bedroom door creak open.

I've been thinking a lot about the last thing I said to him too. The scene has been hard to put out of my mind. The way he looked so desperate, pounding on my window. The way his voice was weak. I have no idea how to face him now.

Then his feet are on the stairs—one, then two, then three steps downstairs. He gasps at the sight of me, bundled up on the couch. "Holy shit . . . *Nikki*?"

7:39 a.m.

Hutch Brown keeps a beautiful kitchen, mostly all on his own. Mrs. B and Mal typically avoid the space, especially while Hutch is cooking. First time I experienced how serious he gets was actually last Thanksgiving. Mama wasn't up for cooking or even pretending to celebrate it, so I went to Mal's house and brought back some food for me and Vae.

I had never seen such an *organized* Thanksgiving before. Nor did I expect to see so many random white people.

"Cheese or pepperoni?" Mal asks. He catches me reaching my finger up to greet one of the pots hanging above my head.

I meet his eye, doing everything I can to not look at his bare chest, but then I quickly move my eyes back to the pan. "Both, please."

When he turns back around, my eyes float down to the bottom right corner of his back, down to that tattoo of a crown he got for his eighteenth birthday—the one I had to hold his hand through, because he's always been afraid of needles. I watch him pull the boxes of pizza out, and then he loads up two plates. For me, one cheese and one pepperoni; for him, double pepperoni. He places mine in the microwave first, then he turns and catches me staring.

We haven't exactly talked about . . . well, anything yet. He was pretty speechless after finding me on his sofa this morning. The only thing he was able to say was "Breakfast?" and I followed him into the kitchen.

Now, here we are, both of us silent, pizza bubbling in the microwave.

"So, you're . . . ?" He narrows his eyes at me, like he's looking for something. "You came back?"

As much as it was the obvious question, I'm still not quite ready to talk about . . . *well*, anything.

"Vae told me about what happened last night." He crosses the kitchen to stand across the bar from me. "I know you got kicked out, but you don't need to be scared. You can just stay here—you know that."

"This isn't your house. This is your *parents'* house."

"And you know they'd be okay with you staying here," he says to me in disbelief. "You want me to ask them?" He pulls his phone out of his pocket. "I'll call them right now."

"Mal, stop." I reach across the bar, grabbing his phone out of his hand. And when I do, more than just our fingertips touch. I'm acutely aware of the fact that I'm still wearing Riley's dress from last night and that he's still very much shirtless.

My eyes fall to his phone in my hand, and his eyes do too. "You can't tell anyone I'm here. Especially not your parents."

"Why not?"

"Because the second you do, I'm going to pack up and leave."

He rests his elbows on the counter, leaning closer to me. "You came back here just to leave me again?"

"You said to give you a week, and that at the end of it you wouldn't try to stop me from leaving. Remember? I'm only here taking you up on your offer. The second audition is next Saturday, and I plan on being there."

He sighs, straightening his back as the microwave beeps. "Okay, understood. So it's my job to convince you to actually come back afterward." Then he spins to go retrieve my pizza.

"I mean, I don't know that you can. . . ."

"Don't underestimate me, Nikki. I'll figure out what it is." He puts my pizza on for another few seconds.

"Figure out what *what* is?"

"By the end of the week, I'm going to figure out what it'll take for you to stay with me—then I'm going to make that shit happen."

NOTE TO SELF: What would it take for me to choose to stay in Texas?

I don't know. I guess a home.

Even if my mother did allow me to come back, though, I wouldn't.

Even if Vae's dad talks Mama into being a rational human being, like he always does, I'm not going back to that house. I swear that.

7:57 a.m.

I eat like I haven't eaten in days. I always eat like this when I feel comfortable. Unfortunately, with how comfortable I get with Mal, it isn't until grease is running down my chin that I realize how sloppy I must look.

I rush up from the table and run across the kitchen to grab a paper towel. After wiping my face and my hands, I raise my eyes. I catch him with his mouth full, staring dead-on at my body.

I'm barefoot and my smooth legs are draped in tulle, with my toes painted white. I pause, caught by surprise, waiting for his eyes to finally meet mine. When they do, my stomach evaporates.

"You can have my bed tonight. I'll take the air mattress in the guest room," he says.

"That's not necessary. I'll take the guest room, like always."

"You're staying for the week, right?"

"Yeah, as long as you don't *tell* anyone."

"Well, that air mattress sucks. Take my bed."

"Whatever, Mal," I say, because this fight isn't worth having. I don't even know if I *am* staying the whole week. I'm still not sure what the fuck I'm doing here.

"And if we're keeping this a secret, then you should probably move your car into the garage. Where'd you leave your keys?" He jumps off his bar stool. "You wouldn't want someone like Daryl showing up and finding your car parked in my driveway."

I laugh through my nose. "Right. Daryl. Or do you actually mean *Cynthia*?"

His eye twitches, and then he takes a couple steps backward. "No, actually. I broke up with Cynthia last night. So."

My cocky smirk slips away. I stare in silence before turning my eyes back to my feet.

"So, like I was saying, where'd you leave your keys?"

NOTE TO SELF: Calm down, Nikki.

Yes, this new bit of information is a game changer (he broke up with Cynthia?!), but you gotta stay focused.

8:45 a.m.

After washing my face with the Browns' expensive skin-care products, I pat my newly softened cheeks and force a smile at my reflection. I tell myself that I'm staying for an entire week in the house of the boy who makes my heart stop—and he just broke up with his girlfriend.

Why? Why'd he do it?

I come out of the guest bathroom with my runaway bag on my shoulder (my dirty clothes stuffed in a Walmart bag), and as I'm passing his bedroom, I can hear the water still running in his attached bathroom. I head down to the living room and check my phone for the first time since last night.

Vae: **I never should have done that. I don't know why I did that.**

I didn't think Mom would kick you out.

She's a lunatic, and I don't want to be alone here with her. Please text me back.

Yeah, she is a lunatic, but you made your choice. That's what I *want* to send back, but no. Saying nothing will do more damage.

I move on to my group chat with Riley and Daeja. Riley asked, **Did Mal catch you before you left?** Then not too long after, Daeja said, **Holy shit, Nikki. The second Mal got back inside, he broke up with Cynthia.** Riley: **WTF???!!!!!**

I scroll between the three texts repeatedly, focusing heavily on Daeja's. *The second Mal got back inside, he broke up with Cynthia.* Was it public? Does *everyone* know? And are people saying that it's my fault?

Instagram doesn't give me any answers. Mal's and Cynthia's profiles look exactly the same as any other day (not that I'm stalking them or anything). I ponder it while he showers, and I think I know how to ask him without looking thirsty, but then he walks downstairs shirtless, and all of my thoughts go out the window. I've seen Mal shirtless *countless times*, but for some reason, it is really stealing my breath today.

"Yo, did your water stay hot the whole time?" he asks, jogging down to the bottom step.

I shrug. "Yeah, sure. I don't know."

He makes a face, scratching his fingers through the top of his hair. "I think our hot water heater might be taking a shit."

A stray bead of water drips from his ear and crawls down his neck. My eyes follow it down to his clavicle. By the time I meet his gaze, I realize he's bold-faced watching me check him out.

"Uhhh," I say, trying to find my way back to Earth. "That sounds expensive."

He nods and stops in front of me, thankfully ignoring my ogling. Then he holds out a hand. "I found a new horror game a while back. Wanna go play?"

"Have you been waiting for weeks to play it with me?"

I smirk, and he rolls his eyes. "You know I have."

Malachai Brown does not play horror games unless I am in the room with him.

I grin, grabbing his outstretched hand. He helps me up from the couch and starts backing toward the stairs. "It's an indie horror about a house intruder."

"I love those."

"I know you do."

We hit the bottom of the stairs, completely lost in each other's eyes, when the doorbell rings. Our heads swivel to the front door.

I don't know who that is, but something tells me they're here for me.

I follow Mal to the window beside the door, covered with luxurious white drapes—Mrs. B's drapes that Mal ruthlessly insulted. "Shit, it's Vae's dad," Mal says, letting the drapes fall back in place. "What do I tell him?"

"That I'm not here."

"He's gonna have more questions than that."

I hiss, "Open the door, before he thinks something's up."

Mal scowls as I press my back flat against the wall. Then he opens the door and puts on way too big of a smile. "Hi, Mr. Daryl, sir."

"Malachai, you seen Nikki?"

"I *have* seen Nikki, yessir." He's smiling stiffly.

"When? Last night?"

"Yes—yessir. Last night at my party."

Daryl takes a deep, audible breath. "Vae says she hasn't seen or heard from Nikki since last night. Has she texted you today?"

"Um," Mal says, nervously shifting his eyes over to mine.

I point sharply to the open door.

"I texted her, but she hasn't answered mine either," Mal says.

Daryl sighs. "God, I swear. Yolanda and that Nikki. Why can't they just get along?" Then he huffs, like he's exhausted with me and my mama's shit. "Let me know if you hear anything. You got my number?"

"Um, no, but I have Vae's. I'll text her."

"Yeah, all right. Thanks, man." Then I hear his footsteps on the porch.

Mal shuts the front door. "Good thing we put your car in the garage, huh?"

I stand with my back against the wall until I hear Daryl's truck speeding away. Daryl made it seem like me being homeless is half my fault. Like the arguments I have with my mama are just "growing pains" or something. I've seen what healthy looks like. I've felt it from Mal's mom. What does Daryl know, anyway? It's not like he lives with us anymore. He doesn't know what that woman has turned into.

Mal can see the calculations in my eyes. "Nikki, what's wrong?"

I pull out of my thoughts. "Huh?"

"You looked like you were a thousand miles away just now."

I shake my head briskly, dropping eye contact. "It's nothing. I was just thinking."

"Nikki."

"What?" I push away from the wall, then start toward the stairs.

"You know how much I hate it when you make that face."

"What face?" Then I start jogging up the steep, softly carpeted stairs in my socks.

He follows behind me, his voice jiggling. "That face you make when you're lying about your feelings."

"That's an exaggeration. I'm not *lying*."

"Nikki, just talk to me. You're leaving in less than a week. What does it even matter?"

I make it to his room. All the lights are out, but the morning sun is bright, pouring in through his huge square window. As he shuts the door behind us, I plop down at the bottom of his bed, crossing my legs on the mattress.

"I don't know, Mal," I say, staring down at Riley's pink nail polish already chipping away on my fingernails.

"Is it about Daryl?"

"It's what Daryl *said*," I whisper.

Mal crosses the room to close both of his curtains. Now it's completely dark.

"Did you hear him when he was like, *why can't they just get along*?"

He fumbles around, looking for his mouse to wake up his computer and light up the room. "Yeah. As if you have any control in the situation *whatsoever.* What he should be doing is asking your *mom* where you are. Asking your *mom* why you run away so often." He plops down on the bed beside me—*right* beside me.

The way he gets pissed off about my mama is the reason I always go to him with this stuff. Mal is rich, but he isn't spoiled. His parents give him the world without pause, but he never milks them for more, and for some reason I find his respect for them so attractive.

He's still ranting about her when my lips turn up and my eyes soften. He catches me smiling, and when he starts to return it, I turn my eyes back to his computer screen. "We should play," I say. "I could really use a laugh right now."

And a distraction from his shirtlessness, and how dark it is and how close we're sitting together. If I'm truly *never coming back to this sinkhole of a town*, then I definitely need to stop leaning into him.

2:27 p.m.

Vae's haunting gaze wakes me out of my sleep. She looked almost inhuman last night, standing behind Mama, watching everything go down without setting *anything* straight.

"Tell her, Vae," I begged. "Just tell her the truth."

But Vae didn't say a word. She was making that face she makes when she closes up her heart and turns everything around it into ice—guess it's the same face Mal is always talking about. But with Vae it's different. The way she can switch herself off and turn into an unfeeling zombie is truly scary.

Probably why I'm having nightmares and shit.

His bedroom is completely dark now, and I'm seemingly alone, wearing Mal's duvet with my head on his pillow. The last thing I remember is watching him endlessly search a bedroom in the horror game—just to avoid running into the killer upstairs—me getting bored, and lying down, telling him to wake me up when shit got interesting. I guess it never did.

I sit up in the dark, wondering what time it is, when Mal's bathroom door suddenly opens. Light pours out along with his shadow. "Nikki?"

The first thing I notice is the black duffel bag on his shoulder. Then I notice that he's wearing a shirt and jeans, his gold chain and diamond studs. He's *dressed* dressed. Alarm bells sound in my head. "Where are you going?"

I can't really see his face since the light is behind him, but I know by the way his facial muscles lift that he's smiling. "*We* are taking a trip to Colorado. I already got all the reservations and everything sorted out."

I toss the blanket off my body. "What, really?"

"Yep." He walks over and opens his bedroom door, letting in more light from the hallway. "I feel like we could both use some time away from this place."

A smile tries to form on my lips, but I fight it off. "So we're just gonna up and go to Colorado? And you already made reservations? That sounds expensive." I'm spinning out, because half of me is excited and the other half feels guilty about him spending that much money on me.

"It'll only be expensive if we don't show up. Otherwise, it's worth it." Then he tilts his head at me. "Nikki, I know besides California you've been wanting to go to Colorado more than anything." He shrugs. "Just say yes. Who cares about the money at this point? This is our last week together. Grab your bag and let's hit the road." Then he walks out of the bedroom, like the matter is settled.

I try to slow the rush of blood and excitement in my veins. I've never been out of Texas before. And right now, getting far away from this town sounds like exactly what I need.

NOTE TO SELF: Remember how the roads look when you're leaving Texas.

If Mama holds true to her promise, I'll lose my phone service today. May end up learning how to use a paper map.

4:43 p.m.

The air feels like soft breaths against my face. He drives slow while I hang out the window, half my upper body riding the waves. The music throbs and beats against my forearm as the sun beats against my forehead.

We're nearing the border between Texas and New Mexico. So far, all I've seen is nothingness. Just plains and churches and rustic industrial structures of some sort—mills, refineries, whatever. I've never been so close to New Mexico. I don't know why I imagined it would look different, like it'd have lusher trees and greener pastures.

Then the song inside the car cuts off, and all I hear is wind. He tugs on the back of my shirt. "We're here!"

My eyes land on the blue sign welcoming us to Texline, Texas. I crawl back inside the cabin, plopping back into the passenger seat. My eyes twinkle when I look at him.

"We're leaving Texas, Nik-Nik! Are you ready for this?"

He eats up my excitement like the corner piece of a birthday cake.

Living so close to the border, it's strange if you've never been across it, but Mal has never looked at me weird when I've told him about all the shit I've never done. He knows how huge this is for me.

NOTE TO SELF: On the way to Cali, remember to get out and stretch.

Legs get tired, being all bent up like that for hours and hours.

Longest drive I've ever been on was to Dallas to visit Grandma Bobbie. Usually happened at least once a year. Occasionally Mama would schedule it so we'd be there at the same time as Aunt Mari and our cousin Marley, but typically Mama tried avoiding them.

There was a McDonald's at the halfway point. Three hours in and we'd stop to stretch and pee and eat. But one time when I was sixteen—the last time I saw Bobbie alive—Mama didn't wanna stop. She packed snacks and water and tried to drive six hours straight.

Around the four-hour mark, though, she caught a charley horse so bad in her calf, she had to pull over. The cramp left her limping, and it kept coming back, so I ended up having to drive the rest of the way without a license or a permit. I knew how to drive—I've known how to drive since I was twelve—but I'd never driven in a real city before. Driving around Cactus does not count.

I was terrified. And for most of the way, Mama was not helping. She couldn't understand why I was so scared—my thirtysomething mother who has also been driving since she was twelve, and had at least two decades of experience, couldn't understand why I was afraid. She kept saying, "We've driven this way for years. You still don't know how to get there?" But it's not like I was paying attention. Most of the time I was either on my phone or messing with Vae.

Once I had exhausted my voice, begging her to be sympathetic, we got into Dallas—the hard part, with its crisscross highways and one-way streets. Mama could see how nervous I was by how hard I was slamming on the brakes and how jerky my lane changes were. And I guess she grew a heart.

"Shaniqua," she said, "you know how to drive. So just *drive*, and if you make a mistake, people on the road will usually help you. And if they don't, me and Vae will scream out our windows and shoot them the bird. You're fine. You're gonna make a right at the next light."

It was unorthodox, her method of consoling me, but it was also . . . unexpectedly perfect. I laughed. And Vae said, "Yeah, we'll cuss them out for you, Nikki!"

"*I* will cuss them out," Mama corrected her. "You just nod and mean mug 'em."

"Deal," Vae said.

I kept laughing, a wave of relief calming the muscles in my legs and in my fingers, wrapped tight around the steering wheel. I laughed until tears blurred my vision.

It's not that Mama doesn't know *how* to console me. She just usually chooses not to.

4:47 p.m.

Texline only takes up a small piece of the road. We get from one end of town to the other *very* quickly, but it feels like it takes forever. The whole time I'm watching Mal—the way he steers with one hand, and the way his other hand rests on the console. I gaze at the Apple Watch on his wrist and the class ring on his finger, until he catches me staring.

"Nikki," he says.

The sun cuts across the bottom half of his face. After a half second of holding my gaze, he glances at the road, and then right back at me. "Watch this." He lets his window down like mine, amplifying the wind rushing through the cabin. Then he fiddles with the controls on his car's touch screen. As soon as the song starts playing, he meets my eye. It's my song.

A smile rushes my lips so fast, I don't get a chance to overthink it. He always raves about my music, as if I'm as good as the greats: Jhené Aiko, Alex Isley, Cleo Sol. He's crazy, because I'm definitely not that good. I *just* started learning how to produce music. I'm no FKA twigs.

Regardless, though, this particular song of mine is my absolute favorite. So I lift myself out the window again and scream the lyrics. Mal's screaming them too.

This was one of the first songs I showed him. I remember, he came back raving. "Nikki! How have you been keeping this from me? I'm low-key pissed that this is the first time I've heard your music." Then he started reciting my lyrics, which was just the nail in my coffin, because, sure, Vae had her favorites that she'd sing along to, and sure, she was supportive, but it was different. Vae always thought all these impossibly great things about me—I'm her big sister. But Mal? He had no obligation to give a shit.

We scream the lyrics now, out of our open windows. "You left me here alone. I could say that yesterday meant nothing and be wrong."

I let the wind whip away any negativity still soaking in my bones, any weirdness between me and Mal, any feelings at all about the home I come from. I'm here, and I'm so excited to be here—with him.

"Goodbye, Texas!" I shout, carefree. The wind whips tears out of my eyes as we grow closer to the New Mexico sign. When Mal pulls over, I barely wait for him to park before I open my door and jump out. The sign is so much bigger than I expected. *New Mexico Welcomes You.*

My grin is soft. "Mal, this is awesome."

He gets out of his black-on-black Dodge Charger, like a movie star, like *always*, and it never fails to snatch my breath away. I watch him, turning to a ball of mush, as his shoes crunch on the sparse rocks. He's holding his phone up at me. "Nik-Nik is in New Mexico—out of Texas for the very first time! Tell the people how you feel."

"You better not be going live," I say.

"I'm not. I swear. Come on. Tell the people how you feel."

A dually truck rushes past us, crossing the border from Texas into New Mexico like it doesn't mean shit. It probably doesn't to that person.

"I feel like . . . I don't know, Mal. Like I'm standing on the moon or something."

6:05 p.m.
(Mountain Time)

New Mexico is so different from Texas. It's dry, and there are hardly any trees—just desert shrubs, like green chunks of hair, splotched over mountains. And the road just seems to cut through them, while the rest of the land is so flat that you can almost see the Earth curve. The sky hangs so low to the ground, it feels like it's on top of you.

I keep saying "wow" and Mal keeps looking over, pleased that he could do this for me.

We ride for half an hour through New Mexico, then he pulls over out of nowhere—parking in front of some place called Alejandro's.

"What are we doing here?"

"Aren't you hungry?" he asks with an excited smile. He looks like he knows something I don't. "I've never been here before, but Cody told me this place has some of the best green chile tamales he's ever had. You're not about to turn down some authentic New Mexico green chile, are you?"

I laugh as he takes off his seat belt. "I've never had it, so what would I know?" And as I'm taking off my seat belt, I get a really good look at the place—the dirt parking lot, the rusty vehicles parked out front, the rust on the building itself.

My face must show my apprehension, because he gets out of the car and comes around to my side. Bends down so that his head is lower than mine and grabs my hand. "I won't let anything happen to you. I promise."

Looking into his eyes makes me feel like I'm onstage. Exposed and vulnerable. I blink away from his smoldering gaze. "It's not your job to be my hero."

"While we're here, it is," he declares. Then he tilts his head to the side. "Come on. Let's go eat."

He doesn't let go of my hand. Not once.

Inside is really dark, and the floor is dusty. It doesn't look like a restaurant. It looks like a bar or a pool house. Definitely the kind of place where you have to seat yourself. And all the people are quietly drinking in groups of two and three. All of them have tan skin; most of them look wrinkled. We definitely stick out.

An elderly Latino man serves drinks and talks amicably to people I'm sure he's known for decades. Mal and I sit on two empty stools, and it takes the man at least five minutes to acknowledge us. "How y'all doing today?"

"Good," Mal says.

"Ever been here before?" The man eyes us curiously while

passing us menus. We shake our heads, and he nods. "I recommend the chicken fajita tacos, myself—with the green chile—but not if you don't like spicy."

"I love spicy," Mal says.

"What about you, young lady? You like spicy?"

I give a slight grimace. "Not really."

"Well, then for you, I recommend the cheese enchiladas. Can I start you folks off with a drink? A Coke?"

"Two beers please," Mal says, confidently.

The bartender smirks. "Sure thing, son." No ID check or anything.

Okay, so maybe I misjudged this place. It's pretty cool once you're in it. Nice atmosphere. *Really* good food. I get the enchiladas, as was recommended to me. Mal gets the tamales, giving the bartender his whole story about Cody trying them first. Now we're chowing down. "Good?" Mal asks, licking his fingers.

I nod, swallowing, then chasing it down with a sip of draft beer.

Before I can properly answer, though, he stands up and walks across the restaurant. I watch, confused, while trying to clean my face with a napkin. He goes over to a grand piano that I didn't even see until now. It's hiding away in a dark corner. Looks like it hasn't been touched in years.

He beckons me over with a smile. I immediately get performance anxiety. I shake my head no, but he insists.

"You play piano, young lady?" the bartender asks, wiping a spot on the bar.

I turn my head, cheeks burning up. "Not really. I've never had lessons."

"Who *has*?" he says with an encouraging smile. "Go on. Show us what you got."

Mal left space on the bench for me, but not much. Our legs are touching. So are our hips. "Any requests?" I ask, rolling my eyes up to his.

"'Yesterday,'" he says.

"We just listened to 'Yesterday' in the car."

"Yeah, but I wanna hear it live. I've never heard it live."

I stare at his eager eyes, then glance around the restaurant. There are a few curious stares, but most people are at least pretending not to look. I take a deep breath, set my fingers on the starting keys. The vocals come in right after the first chord. That's why it's so hard to start.

But then Mal stretches his arm around my back and grabs on to the inch of bench beside my back pockets. He crowds me with his heat and his smell and his voice in my ear. "You are too talented to be scared. You got this."

My heart slows and my stomach feels airy.

It seems Mal knows how to console me too.

I press down on the keys softly. And I sing even softer: "Forgive me, I was so wrong when I thought you cared. Yesterday was a mistake, when I thought you cared if I was there." I raise my voice louder, and press the keys harder. "So I won't come along with you anymore, because you don't want me to. Forgive me, I really thought you wanted me there with you."

Mal starts humming along with me, curling his arm around my waist. And just like that, I forget that there are people around us. He is the only thing I feel. The only person I'm singing to. The only person in the bar.

I lean my head against his shoulder and sing, comfortably and confidently, right into the hook. "I could say that yesterday meant nothing and be lying. Yesterday, I felt like we were bonding, truly felt like we were vibing, and I thought that you were happy. But nooooo."

I release a shaky breath, so proud that I hit all the notes so cleanly. And I'm so incredibly *relaxed*. I can tell he's proud of me too. He raises his eyebrows and widens his eyes in anticipation. I watch him as I finish the song. Watch him smile and lean closer. Until I hit the last note.

The piano rings out into silence for a few seconds, then we're surrounded by gentle applause, rocketing us back into the club. Back to reality.

"Woooo, Nikki!" Mal joins in, pulling his arm away from my waist to join the applause. I smile, looking around the restaurant. They all look so impressed. The bartender is holding up two more beers, offering them as a reward.

I didn't know my voice could do that to people.

NOTE TO SELF: Views on YouTube is just a number.

This kind of reaction to my *live singing* is everything a musician dreams about. The claps. The smiles. The beer on the house.

I can have this all the time if I can make it to that audition and impress Derek Atkins just like this. I'm so close to having my dream. I can't let that go. No matter what happens with Mal or with Mama, I have to get to LA on Saturday. No matter what.

7:31 p.m.

The closer we get to Colorado, the more I can see it over the horizon—just white peaks, glowing in the falling darkness. "There it is!" I screech.

Mal laughs, letting down the windows, and my God, it's actually cold—which is surprising, because it was, no lie, ninety degrees in Texas when we left this morning. But fifty in Colorado feels a whole lot different than fifty in Texas. In Texas, when it gets cold, it takes on a physical form that gets in your nostrils and rests, uninvited, on your skin. But here, fifty degrees is gentle—which, I'm sure, has to do with the elevation or whatever.

It's pretty dark outside now, but I'm still scouring my window for all the sights. Every time I see the silhouette of a mountain in the distance, I feel like I'm on another planet. Real mountains are breathtaking. Huge.

I stare silently out my window, until his phone starts ringing.

"Mom" shows up on his central touch screen. He doesn't even disconnect his Bluetooth before answering. "Hello?"

Mrs. B's voice booms over the car speakers. "Malachai, where are you going?" Mal rushes to turn the volume down. "Why does my tracker say you're in Colorado?"

"Mom," Mal says, hiding his sigh, "some friends and I are taking a quick road trip. Do some skiing and sightseeing. Is that okay?"

"You know, son," his dad says, "it's customary to ask permission *before* doing the thing. We would appreciate it if you asked first."

"Move, Hutch," his mom hisses. "It's fine, sweetie. I was just calling to make sure you weren't getting kidnapped. . . . You're not getting kidnapped, right?"

I look at Mal with an amused smile on my face.

"Pineapples, Mom."

She lets out her breath. "Thank God. Aren't you glad we came up with those code words?"

"Yes, Mom," Mal says, monotone. He complains about his parents being too overprotective, but the boy is lucky to have parents who care.

"Anyway, baby, which city are you stopping in? Because if you're going to Vail—"

"We're not going to Vail. At least not tonight. I was planning to stop in Colorado Springs."

"Oh, okay," she says. "Well, let me book you a room, baby."

"Mom, it's okay. I got it."

"Save your money, son," his dad says. "If your mom is still willing to baby you, I would take it if I were you."

"Shut up, Hutch. I will *always* take care of my baby."

Mal looks at me with thin-pressed lips. I have to stop myself from laughing.

"I'll text you the reservation," she says. "Be careful, please, my love. And text me when you get there."

"I will, Mom. Thank you."

"Oh, wait!" she says, before he can hang up.

His shoulders sink. "Yes, ma'am?"

"I've heard some things about Nikki . . . that she's run away again?"

My heart stops.

He looks at me. "Um, yeah. I've heard that, too."

"So, she's not with you?"

Mal checks my face again before saying, "No. I haven't seen her since the party, and she won't answer my calls."

"*Jesus Christ.* I'm getting worried, son. This isn't like her. Usually when she's having problems with her mom, she comes straight to our house. I wonder why she didn't come to us this time. Is it because we weren't home with you?"

Mal interrupts her incessant worrying. "I'm sure she's okay. Nikki is strong."

"She shouldn't have to be so strong, though."

I swallow a lump in my throat and turn back to my window.

"She's run away so many times, I've had to stop myself from calling CPS."

"Mom, I'm sure everything is fine," Mal says, trying to rush her off the phone.

"I hate it, Mal. How does a mother birth a child and then just . . . ?" She sounds tearful.

I can't see anything out of my window anymore. All I see is my reflection. That's the only thing about Mal's parents that makes my skin itch. Every time I'm around them, they remind me just how unlucky I am.

Mal disconnects his phone from the speakers and talks his mom down, while I try not to listen. Once he hangs up, he instantly looks at me. "Nikki, I'm so sorry."

"No reason to apologize."

He glances at me, then back at the road, then back at me. "There's that face again. I should give it a nickname." He glances at the side of my face, but when I refuse to give him my eyes, he turns back to the road.

8:55 p.m.

We park outside a massive hotel. It looks like the whole city could get a room here.

"Are you kidding me?" I look at him like he's crazy. "I thought we would hit a Motel 6 or something. What is this"—I turn back to my window, peering at the stacks and stacks of lights—"a castle?"

"Listen, I hate this place with a passion," Mal says. "The people here look at me like they've never seen a Black person before. But I'm not about to turn down a free room with room service *and* a hot shower, are you . . . ?"

He grabs his keys and phone and opens his door, while I weigh my options. When I don't get out too, he bends down to look at me, eyebrows slightly raised, but with eyes that are amused. "You coming?"

I've never stepped foot in a place that beautiful. Doesn't look like the type of place that would let a girl like me through the doors.

"Hey," he says, asking for my attention. He's looking at me with gentle, smiling eyes. My expression melts. "It's gonna be fun. I swear."

My runaway bag is on my shoulder. He's carrying his own duffel bag, full of clothes, shoes more expensive than my entire wardrobe, and some of the alcohol left over from his party. We walk into the main lobby, and I do everything I can to not gasp. Damn, this place looks royal. The gold trimming, the burgundy carpet, the leather chairs and real-ass plants.

The main desk has about three blond chicks manning the computers. Mal leads me that way, and I start to sweat. I mean, look at us—two Black teenagers with no adults in sight—dressed how we're dressed. Surely, they're about to "politely" ask us to leave, right?

As if he can read my mind, he reaches back and grabs my hand. His fingers are warm and surprisingly soft. I thought a sports-boy, obsessive-weight-lifter dude like him would have calluses. My fingers fold in between his as we approach the desk.

"Hi, I'm Malachai Brown, checking in under Melanie Brown."

While he's getting the key, I glance around the hotel. It's weird, but I feel like the people here look different from the people back home, like their faces and their skin color. Or maybe it's just how overwhelmingly white it is.

Our room is on the eighth floor. When we walk in, though, I realize it's actually a fucking *suite.* The bathroom has a shower even fancier than the one in Mal's bathroom at home, mirrors that must be brand-new, because they look impossibly clean, a living room on the left and a giant king-sized bed through the doorway on the right. *Damn*, this is what Melanie Brown buys for her rebellious son when he's road-tripping to Colorado without her permission? Must be nice. . . .

Mal sets his bag on the floor, then spins around, arms open. "But you gotta admit, this place is nice as hell. Right?"

"Sure is." He watches me expectantly as I walk past him. "Just one bed?"

"Oh, you can have it," Mal says quickly. "I'll take the couch."

"Mal, your mom got this room for *you*. I'll take the couch."

"I only offered you the bed to be nice, but if you insist on taking the couch, trust me, that's fine." He grabs his bag and starts walking toward the bedroom. "I've slept here before, and this is, by far, the most comfortable bed I've ever slept on. If you don't want it . . ."

I roll my eyes with an annoyed smile. "Okay, fine. I'll take the bed."

"Uh-huh, that's what I thought." He spins around. Then his phone rings. "Fuck. It's my mom again."

I drop my bag on the bedroom floor. "I'm gonna use the restroom."

He nods and then answers the phone.

9:01 p.m.

When I come out of the ridiculously elegant bathroom, the rest of the suite is silent. "Mal?" I look around the empty bedroom and the attached living room. I thought he'd still be on the phone with his mom, knowing how long she can go, but I don't hear a peep.

I grab my phone from where I threw it on the bed and just as I'm about to call him, I see three missed text messages.

Daeja: **Nikki, please tell us you made it to Cali okay? Just let us know you're okay.**

Riley: **You promised, Nikki. Please, just talk to us.**

I try to control my guilt by concentrating on the text from my backstabbing sister: **Nikki, it's seriously getting scary now. I know Mom hasn't cut your service. Please just talk to me. I think I can get Mom to change her mind.**

My guilt skyrockets.

I hate knowing that Vae is scared. It's the one thing I'm

supposed to look out for, as a big sister, especially with how prone Vae is to panicking. I almost break and respond, but then I remember the look in her eyes—her cold, dead stare.

Other people would describe Vae as quiet and sweet and meek. But I know better. When Vae gets mad, Vae gets mean.

But still . . . after all the nights she's lain in bed with me, talking about how karma would take care of Mama, and how the two of us would always be there for each other, I guess she meant so long as I didn't piss her off.

I roll my eyes and drop the phone on my mattress. Then my screen lights up with a message from Mal: **You gotta come see this.**

I text back: **Where are you?**

Go up the stairs, right across the hall from you—there's an exit door between the eighth and ninth floor.

I grumble all the way to the door. I really don't want to be walking around this hotel by myself . . . or at all, honestly. And I hope he has the room key because I sure as hell don't. I open the exit door confidently, but then pause at the sight. It's a huge balcony with several hot tubs and a hundred multicolored standing lamps.

The night air calms my nerves, not to mention the view. It's dark, but I can clearly see the mountain across the street and the trees surrounding it. What a dream, just to wake up to mountains outside your window. I can't even imagine.

"Pretty cool, huh?" Mal asks when I approach. He's sitting on the edge of one of the empty hot tubs, legs swimming in the steamy bubbles. Two towels lie folded on the ground beside a bottle of Peach Cîroc, bathing in a bucket of ice. He bends over, picks up a shot glass for himself, and hands me the other.

I grab it, confused. "Mal, I didn't bring a swimsuit."

"So?" He bends down and opens the mostly full bottle of vodka, then pours himself a shot. "It's spring break. Our underwear is just as good as swimsuits when it's spring break."

A couple blond girls laugh a few hot tubs down, but otherwise, the rooftop is bare. The multicolored lamps against the shimmer of the hot tub water makes the whole rooftop look like an underwater party.

"I didn't want to have to do this to you, Nikki, but truth or dare?"

I shift my eyes back to Mal, annoyed. "What are we—back in eighth grade?"

"It's the only way I've ever been able to—"

"Get me to do what you want?"

"No." He smiles. "To get you to talk to me." I roll my eyes, and he laughs. "Stay in Texas, and I'll never say the words *truth or dare* ever again."

I scoff. "Fuck that. If I *win*, you can never say those words for as long as we live."

"How do you win truth or dare?"

"If you refuse to do what I say, then I win. And vice versa."

He frowns. "Fine, but my offer still stands."

"Yeah, I won't need it. I'm going to win."

NOTE TO SELF: This is a dangerous game—I know from experience.

It started as soon as he moved here.

At Dex's fourteenth birthday party, a group of promiscuous boys and girls started a game of truth or dare that devolved into a game of dare or dare and ultimately ended up as a kissing and groping game.

Someone dared me to kiss Dex. I remember how embarrassed I felt, and how embarrassed Dex looked. I said, "No, I'm not playing." I claimed that I was just watching. And the birthday boy played along, said that he was just watching too.

Dex and I have always had a rapport. Sometimes that rapport got flirty, but it was never serious. Over the years, he'd say things like, "I got a seat right here for you, baby," and he would motion to his lap. I would say things like, "You could never handle me." And he would check me out and say, "Try me."

It was fun and meaningless. I've never had *real* feelings for him. At least, not since intermediate school.

Then Mal came along and stole everything. My heart. My attention. My desire. Later that same night, someone dared Mal to kiss me on the cheek. I added the appropriate amount of surprise to my expression, but I didn't deny him. I didn't deny that I was playing, and he didn't either. He kissed me at the center of my right cheek, and that was it. My heart has belonged to him ever since.

9:32 p.m.

"What's the real reason you came back last night?"

I smile. "You remember the rules, don't you, Mal?"

"We made those rules up when we were in eighth grade."

"But they still stand! If you can't pose your question with 'Is it true,' then you can't ask that question. That's too bad." I tsk. "But don't worry. Your question was a waste, anyway."

"How was it a waste?" He looks like a sculpture in a garden—chiseled chest, dotted with hot tub water and decorated with that chain of his.

"Sorry. I think it's my turn now. Truth or dare, Mal?"

He laughs, impressed. "Okay, that's how we're playing this?"

"This was *your* idea. *Truth or dare?*" I repeat.

"Fine. Truth."

"Is it true you broke up with Cynthia in front of everyone at the party?"

"Whoa," he howls.

"Daeja and Riley texted me about it. So I thought maybe you did it publicly."

"It wasn't *public*." He looks up at the stars. "Okay. So. After you left—"

I lean against the edge of the hot tub, settling in for story time.

"I was really pissed. I thought you were fucking *gone*." He drops his eyes to mine. "When I went back inside, I was trying to get to the kitchen, where it was quieter, but *Cynthia* and *Dex* and *Daeja* wouldn't stop following me. Asking me stupid questions like *why was I so upset that you left*. So I broke up with her."

I brace my arm against the siding, waiting impatiently for him to keep going. When he doesn't, I ask, "And what was the reason? Why *were* you so upset that I left?"

He smiles at me slyly. "If you wanna know that, you'll have to use another turn. Truth or dare?" he fires off, splashing water in my direction. I'm sitting on the side of the tub, still wearing all of my clothes, while he's now fully submerged in the water, only wearing his underwear.

"Ummm." I swallow and decide to use my safety. "Truth *and* dare."

He gives me a disapproving face. "Weak."

"It's called strategy."

"Yeah, well, you only have two of those left—"

"I'm well aware. Go on, ask me something."

His eyes look at me like I amuse him. Like I *intrigue* him. "Okay, Shaniqua."

I raise my eyebrows at his use of my government name. The only person who still calls me Shaniqua is my mother.

"Is it true that you once played a game of fuck, marry, kill where you had to choose between me, Dex, and B-Mac—"

"I swear I'm gonna kill Riley!"

He busts out laughing. "Welp! I think I just got my answer to that question."

"No, you didn't," I say, embarrassed. "You might have gotten false information. Go ahead. Tell me what you were going to say."

He starts his question over. "I heard you chose to kill Dex *and* B-Mac, then you said you'd fuck and marry me."

Oh . . . It seems he *does* have the right information.

"Okay. And what is your dare?" I ask.

"I don't feel like I need to give you a dare. I think I already know it's true."

"I haven't confirmed or denied *anything.* What is your dare, Malachai?"

"I dare you to strip down to your underwear, *Shaniqua*, and get in this hot tub with me."

My skin burns red hot. I hate hearing him use my full name. But at the same time, I love it.

"Okay," I say, standing up.

"Okay, what?"

I nod, reaching for my shot glass and the vodka. "I'll get in with you."

"Seriously, Nikki? You refuse to admit it?"

I throw the shot back and hook my fingers around the waistband of my shorts, ignoring his question. "Truth or dare, Mal?"

His eyebrows rise as his gaze zeroes in on my fingers. He throws his arms over the sides of the tub, opening his chest to me. "Truth," he says.

I'm so grateful Riley painted my toes, because in this moment, I feel so uncharacteristically dainty and pretty. I bite down on my smile, then shimmy out of my shorts and kick them to the bottom step. Without making eye contact, I pull my shirt over my head.

Now I'm standing in my underwear in front of Mal. It's cold and way too quiet. I look up, and his eyes are roaming. He looks like he's trying to remember everything about my shape and my skin.

Flames spread down from my cheeks to my neck. "Is it true that you only dated Cynthia to make me jealous?"

NOTE TO SELF: These locs are about to get f'd up in this hot tub water.

You look cute now. But tomorrow is a different story.

9:54 p.m.

He's been stalling.

"*Wow.* You ain't holding back. Okay." He nods to himself. "Wow. So yeah. I guess one reason I dated her was to make you jealous."

Excited butterflies tickle my throat and my tongue.

"But mostly, after you turned me down for prom, I figured I should just move on."

And just like that, the butterflies go poof. "Wait, wait." I close my eyes and hold up my hands. "I didn't *turn you down* for prom."

"Yes, you did. I said we should go to prom together, then you said—"

"*Exactly.* I was sitting on your couch, covered in beer and pizza sauce, and you said that we should *go to prom together.* That's not asking. That's suggesting. What you did for Cynthia—*that* was asking someone to prom."

He closes his mouth, looking at me while his mind races a mile a minute.

Just a few days after I "turned him down," he managed to gather the entire school before lunch, just to surprise a girl he knows from the student council with a magical and *very public* promposal.

"I mean," I say with a painful laugh, "how did you think watching that would make me feel?"

"I *know* you, Nikki. I know you don't like all that extra shit."

I slowly roll my eyes up to the black sky. "It just would have been nice. The way you asked me felt like you were asking as a friend."

His narrowed eyes slowly open to what I'm saying. "Well . . . I'm sorry. I didn't know you'd want that. I truly didn't mean to make it seem like I didn't care."

10:49 p.m.

I've been holding on to this question ever since he asked me about that embarrassing game of fuck, marry, kill. "I heard through the grapevine that your football buddies were ranking chicks in the locker room—best ass, best boobs, prettiest face. Is it true that you said I was a ten across the board?"

His expression is one of complete and utter horror. "Where'd you hear that?"

"It doesn't matter."

He shakes his head. "Fucking Dex."

"Yes, it was Dex," I confirm with a laugh. "Now answer the question."

He shrugs. "Sure. Yeah, it's true."

My eyes widen. "Wow, so I'm a dime, huh?"

"Stop," he says, laughing.

"You think I'm a ten across the board? Wow."

"Yeah, and?"

When our gazes meet, his eyes are done joking. He's more than serious about his attraction to me, and the tension between our skin is starting to boil the water, more so than the jets. I lick my lips and look down at the chain around his neck.

"Truth or dare, Nikki?" he asks.

I look over his shoulder, at the mountain in the background, thinking of all the crazy things he could dare me to do right now. "Dare," I say.

His eyes flicker down my neck to the bubbling water on my chest. "I feel like you're too far away. I dare you to come sit next to me."

The way his eyes beckon me closer, my body turns light and hot, like a balloon floating on water. I give up control and float to his side of the hot tub, to where our arms are touching and our knees accidentally keep brushing.

"That's better," he says in a low tone.

I smile, looking anywhere but at his face. "Um, truth or dare, Mal?"

"Truth." He turns his head, searching for my eyes.

"Is it true that you want to fuck and marry *me*?" I ask with a sly smile.

"We should make it a rule that you can't do that."

"No changing the rules in the middle of the game. Is it true?"

"No . . . I'm too young to get married," he says, while running his fingers through my long faux locs, floating in the water.

I swear to God, the water is getting hotter by the second. Or maybe that's just my body.

"Truth or dare, Nikki?"

"Dare," I say.

"I dare you to kiss me."

I look up, stunned. "Wait, what?"

He widens his eyes at me. "Did I just win?"

"No. No, I was just—"

"It's okay if you don't want to. It just means that I won."

"You didn't win," I say.

"Okay, well, I'm waiting." He lifts his chin, cocky and confident.

"It's not even that big a deal."

"So do it, then."

I falter, thinking way too hard about how to execute this.

"Go on," he says.

"Shut up."

I turn my body to face him. Then I lift my hand out of the water and rest it on the side of his jaw, trickling water down his skin. His eyes look amused and expectant, but also a little nervous. "It's not that big a deal."

"If it's not a big deal, then why are you stalling?" he whispers.

"Shut up," I say again, but quieter. I lean closer. So close that I can smell the Cîroc on his breath. So close that I can feel his breath beat against my lips.

"You're still stalling."

My lips part slightly, and my eyes draw down to his mouth. "I'm not stalling."

"You are."

We're saying words, but they don't mean anything. Our lips are moving and we're leaning closer and our voices are getting quieter. When I say "I'm not" again, my bottom lip brushes his top lip, and a shock wave bursts through the bottom of my abdomen, spreading lower, all the way to my pruney toes.

As I gently take his top lip between mine, his hands take hold of my hips. I can't recall how many times I've imagined something like this happening, but wow, I got it all wrong. I thought when we finally kissed, it'd be hungry and *desperate*. But kissing Mal is no different than talking to him. We meld and caress each other gently, alternating between leading and following.

Then there's a click behind us. We pull away with heavy breaths just in time to see a security guard step outside. "Roof is closing for the night, guys." It's only me and Mal left out here.

When I look at him again, my cheeks burn hot. "So . . . there, I did it."

"Yep," he says, looking at my lips like he really wants to lean in again.

My head is spinning with how much I want to as well. Hell, I want to stay in Cactus, just to be able to kiss him like that all the time.

NOTE TO SELF: Seriously stop.

11:17 p.m.

He lets me take a shower first, and while he showers, I get distracted by a missed text from Daryl: **I need you to know that we can fix this. Please come home.**

Heat spreads across my forehead, and my temples thump mercilessly. He says we can fix it, like it's our job to fix it. He shouldn't have to step in every time that woman forgets how to be human.

I don't blame Daryl, though. He's not responsible for any of this. And at least he's trying.

My real dad ran when he found out I was swimming in my mama's tummy, and she met Daryl soon after. He took care of me like I was his own, up until I was four (and Vae was two). The only thing I really remember about that part of my life was how gentle he was, how he'd save me from Mama's rampages, and I guess, yeah, that was the hardest part about their divorce—I no longer had anyone to save me from her.

But as Vae and I grew older, he continued to call me his daughter. During his court-ordered visitations with Vae, he'd always insist I come along. I was never fond of the family reunions, though, what with the fact that the only things we could eat were either barbecue or fried fish, and the fact that I didn't know anybody there but Vae and her dad.

Vae was damn near mute. The entire time, she would cling to my side, as if I was her mother. She's always done that, ever since she was little. I've never felt less than like a whole sister to her . . . not until yesterday.

The bathroom door swings open. I see the steam before I see him and the water beading in his hair. He's shirtless, wearing long black pajama pants, and he hasn't met my eyes yet.

"Cozy?" he asks, stuffing his duffel bag full of his dirty clothes, then zipping it back. "Try and get some sleep, okay? We've got a big day ahead of us—skiing, snowboarding, maybe hiking if you're up for it. We can really get a good view of the mountains once daylight—" Then he stands up and sees my face. "What's wrong? Are you okay?"

I nod, but my weary expression doesn't change.

He walks over and sits on the edge of the bed. His eyes inspect mine, trying to find the reason for my sudden mood change.

After I got out of the shower, I passed him in my short pajama shorts and thin tank top with the flirtiest of smiles, and said, "Sorry if I used all the hot water." Then he checked me out blatantly, and said, "It's all good." It was so obvious, the energy between us.

But now, I look like somebody died.

"Is it about your mom?"

I roll my eyes away. "It's more about Vae."

"Okay," he says, nodding, hoping I'll continue on my own. But when I don't, he asks, "Do you wanna talk about it?"

I don't answer him. I don't even meet his eyes.

During my silence, he pulls both of his feet on top of the covers, wrapping his arms around his legs and pressing his bare chest against his thighs. "I'm gonna tell you something, Nikki—something I've never told anyone."

I raise my gaze and my eyebrows curiously.

"It's something that happened before we met in eighth grade. . . ." Then he turns and looks at me. "It's the reason I moved here."

He looks so uncharacteristically uncomfortable.

So I lift the covers, offering him a cozy spot in the king-sized bed, and with a smidge of a smile, he scoots in.

11:39 p.m.

There's at least two feet of mattress between us. I'm lying on my side, facing him. He's lying on his back, staring up at the ceiling, like that's the only way he can get this story out.

"You don't have to tell me, Mal."

"No, I want to. Honestly, I can't believe I waited this long. I know, of all people, I can trust you. Especially with something like this."

"Something like what?" I can see the apprehension in his dark eyes. His hair is dripping on the white hotel pillow as he searches above our heads for the words.

"My parents and I moved here to escape a dangerous situation. Back in Houston . . . Well, I guess I should start by saying that . . . I'm adopted."

My eyes bulge. I try to rein in my surprise, but it's written all over my face. *Adopted?* Melanie and Hutch aren't his birth parents?

"My birth mom was a drug addict, and she would make a lot of promises. You know? About getting clean. But before I knew it, I'd be stranded at the supermarket again, while she was off getting high."

"Oh, fuck," I say. It just slips out.

He nods for a while. "I ended up in the system when I was ten. Floated between a few *terrible* foster families, until I finally ended up with my . . ." He struggles to say it: "My mom and dad."

I wonder how long it took him to start calling them that.

"They accepted me and treated me with so much love. After about a year with them, they wanted to adopt me, but my mom wasn't very cooperative. She tried kidnapping me twice."

"Seriously?"

"The first time, I was so dumb. She came to my school and said that my foster parents had asked her to pick me up. Back then, I was so—*God*—" He sighs heavily. "I just wanted us to be a normal family. I hated having to live with strangers. She was the only thing I knew in the world, so I went with her willingly, the first time."

My eyebrows crinkle. "But not the second time?"

"The second time she threatened to hurt herself if I didn't come with her. Me and my parents moved after that. And my birth mom lost all chances of ever getting me back."

It feels like someone is stomping on my heart and throwing every complaint I've ever had about my mama in my face.

"I'm so sorry, Mal." I scooch closer to him, eat up a foot of mattress, and rest my hand on his arm. "I'm sorry if I ever made you feel like your life was easier than mine."

"No, I get it." He grabs my hand from his arm. "My life *is* easier now. I love my parents. And they love me. And they take care of everything I need." He licks his lips and furrows his brow. "I wish you could have that too. You deserve it as much as I do."

He squeezes my hand, then turns on his side to face me, too. There's a lonesome streak of tears on his left cheek. He's so free to cry. He doesn't care what other people think or how they'll react. He cries if he feels like crying. I wish I could do that.

"There's that face again," he says.

I stare down at the white sheet between us, then back up into his watery eyes. I can't cry in front of him. I just can't. I didn't even cry when Mama kicked me out.

But he doesn't push me. He just scoots closer, squeezing my hand and rubbing his thumb across the tops of my fingers. "I hope I didn't make it weird by talking about my past."

"No!" I shake my head, sitting up on my forearm. "I'm so glad you told me. I feel . . ."

His hand continues up past my elbow, then all the way back down to my fingers on the mattress. He covers my nails with the soft tips of his fingers. "You feel what?"

"Like . . . closer to you."

There's only enough space between us on the mattress for my hand to rest between his abdomen and mine. His head is on his pillow, facing me. I lie back down, mirroring him, staring into his teary eyes.

"Truth or dare, Nikki?"

I sigh. "I thought we were done playing. It's so late."

"Just this last round."

The bathroom light is still on, and so is the lamp on my bedside table, but otherwise our room is dark.

"Fine. Truth *and* dare." Might as well use another safety, since this is our last round.

He sighs lightly. "Okay, here are your options: Truth, did you enjoy kissing me? Or dare . . . kiss me again."

My bones turn to stone, while the rest of me turns to mush. If I answer truthfully, of course I liked kissing him. But why tell him that when I can show him?

He leans in at the same time I do. And when our lips meet, the force between us is strong. Too strong to overthink. Too strong to deny.

I push on his shoulder, push his back against the mattress. He pulls on my hips, pulls me on top of him. And after our lips get reacquainted, our tongues meet for the first time. His hands slide over my shorts. My hands press against his pecs, then slide up and around the back of his neck.

"Can I sleep in here with you tonight?" he asks between kisses.

I say, "I don't think we'll be doing much sleeping. But sure."

He smiles, lips curling up against mine, then his voice rumbles up his throat. "Perfect. 'Cause I'm not in the mood to sleep."

So we don't. We stay up. We kiss and laugh and kiss some more. And at some point, in the early morning, we pass out.

@AntTheProdigy: Okay . . . The second audition is fine, just don't bail on me. I've been bragging about you to Derek. He's expecting greatness.

Sunday

(Daylight Saving Time begins)

5:45 a.m.
(after the best night of my life)

I wake up from a deep sleep to the sound of Mal's phone ringing. The second my eyes open, I remember where I am. I see his bare chest because my forehead is pressed against his collarbone. And I feel his slow breath on top of my hair.

When did we get tangled up like this? Our legs are squished-squashed together. My hands are pressed against his low abdomen, while his arm is swung across my waist and wrapped around my back.

I hope he doesn't freak out when he wakes up, because I have no intention of moving.

His phone stops ringing. I pull my forehead away from his chest and look up. For a second I get to see his shut eyes and his slightly parted lips, and just how incredibly sweet he looks when he's sleeping, but then his eyes open.

"Hi," I whisper.

"Hey," he says, voice raspy. My worries instantly melt

when I see him smile.

His phone starts ringing again, but he doesn't move. He presses his hand against my back, bringing me even closer.

"Your phone's ringing," I say as a distraction from the crackling tension between our bodies.

"Yeah." And that's all he says. His lips are getting closer to mine.

"Aren't you gonna answer it?"

"I'll call 'em back later. I've got something more important going on right now."

A cold wave flows through the whole of my body, leaving my middle parts warm and tingly. The phone stops ringing and immediately starts back up again. "Someone is *really* trying to get ahold of you," I say.

He licks his lips "Well, I'm really trying to get ahold of *you*." Then his hand cinches tighter around my back. I laugh at how corny of a line that was.

He sits up then, and starts tickling my stomach. I squeal. "Stop!" I'm laughing, falling onto my back. And he's falling on top of me, his legs between mine.

He looks down at me like I changed overnight. As if I morphed into a beautiful butterfly, and he can't help but inspect every inch of my wings. "I'm sorry. Is this okay?" he says, smile slipping from his face. "I feel so incredibly close to you right now."

My smile widens. "Yeah, it's fine . . . I do too." And my hands find their way to his waist.

His phone is ringing *again*, but it's like we can't hear it. He bends his elbows, lowering himself slowly. "Can I kiss you?"

That warm tingly feeling in my middle intensifies. I nod, then close my eyes. His thick lips press soft against my jaw—not where I was expecting to feel him, but somehow, it's even better. He trails soft kisses along my jawline, then he mumbles against my chin, "Can I kiss your neck?"

He can kiss me *anywhere* at this point.

I nod again. He moves a few of my locs away from my neck. I raise my chin higher, waiting to feel his lips on my excited skin. But when it doesn't happen, I open my eyes. He's looking at the nightstand with a confused expression. "What?" I say, breathless, hoping he doesn't want to stop.

"This is like the sixth time they've called."

He snaps me out of the moment. I can hear the ringing again. It is pretty worrisome. Whoever's on the other end is clearly desperate.

"Be right back," he says. "Don't move. Okay?" He raises himself off of me and runs to the dark living room. "It's probably my mom," he says distantly.

"Yeah, probably." I pull the covers up to my chin.

But then he comes back, with that confused expression contorting his features again. "Actually, it's your mom."

5:52 a.m.

Why is Mama calling Mal? I didn't even know they had each other's phone numbers. Is she calling about me? Is she actually worried? It's not like I've ever been gone this long. Any time I ran away to Mal's house, it was only for one night.

He sits on the bed with his back to me. "Hello?"

"Malachai." Her voice doesn't know how to be quiet. No matter what the situation, she always sounds alarmed, so I can hear every word of their conversation.

"Yes, ma'am?"

"Is Shaniqua with you?"

My stomach drops. Wait, so she actually *is* worried about me? I can almost feel myself about to smile, but I force my lips to remain in a straight line. Mal looks over his shoulder and raises his eyebrows in question. I shake my head.

"No, ma'am," he says, staring at me while we both listen for her response.

"Okay, well, have you heard from Vae recently?"

Mal and I both furrow our brows at the same time. "No, ma'am," Mal says, more like a question.

"I found her bed empty this morning."

My body breaks out into a sweat.

"Vae's gone?" Mal asks in disbelief.

"She ain't been answering my calls."

Vae—the girl who's never gotten written up in school, never gets in trouble at home, and *never runs away* is missing? It can't be by choice. She's too scared, too innocent, too obedient. Someone must have abducted her, and now they're about to murder her.

I roll out of bed and grab my own phone off the bedside table.

"Yes, ma'am, of course. I'll call her right now."

"Let me know if you hear from her," Mama says before they hang up.

As I put in my code, I ask Mal, "What's going on?" even though I just heard the whole thing.

"Your mom says Vae ran away last night." He's looking down at his phone, searching for Vae's contact.

"How does she know she ran away? How does she know she wasn't abducted?"

Mal puts the phone to his ear and searches my eyes. "I'm not sure."

I look back down to my and Vae's text thread while he calls her. She texted me a few times last night: **I know that after what**

I did, I don't deserve to know if you're safe. I don't deserve to have you in my life.

Twenty minutes later she sent: **You're the only person in my life worth fighting for.**

Ten minutes later: **I'm gonna make it up to you. Promise. I'm gonna find you.**

My throat constricts. *I'm gonna find you.* She chose this.

And then her last text: **Unless you find me first.**

My brows scrunch together. What is this? Some kind of game to her? Mal hangs up after getting her voice mail. I desperately text her, while Mal tries calling again. **Vae. Where are you?**

I feel so heavy. I should have texted her back sooner. I didn't even have to say anything, it could have just been three dots, just so she knew I was still alive. *God, Vae, answer me!*

After he gets her voice mail again, Mal looks up at me. "Nikki, she's not answering. . . . I should call your mom back, right?"

I give him my watery eyes. His face instantly falls, and at the same time he stands up, closes the space between us. "Can we just go home? Please?"

He nods hurriedly. "Yeah, of course, Nik. Let's go."

NOTE TO SELF: Mama still hasn't cut my phone service.

Why hasn't she?

7:26 a.m.

Mal drives with one hand on the wheel, and at some point, he takes a call from his dad, but is otherwise silent. We coast around mountain peaks, all covered in brush that I guess is technically brown but looks purple and red and blue. I would never think to color a mountain purple, but in Colorado they can be.

We pass through peaks capped in beautiful white snow. Pass by signs warning of bears and moose. Pass through cities that look unnaturally pasted at the bottoms of mountains. You would think with all these other worldly sights that I could stop thinking about Vae—that I could concentrate on something besides my guilt and worry, as if that's helping anything.

I stare out of my window, vibrating with anticipation to get back to Texas, hoping she's not all alone on the side of the road somewhere. How far could she really have gotten? She doesn't have a car. Did Mama even *try* looking for her? Or did she see an empty bed and immediately call Mal to do all the looking for her? Wouldn't surprise me one bit. She's got a history of abandoning her girls. Or at least of abandoning *me*.

Back in eighth grade, back when I played basketball, I had a home game one night. We won, and I was really proud of myself for putting up half the points on the board. Coach was really proud of me too, but my mama . . . I mean, I hadn't expected her to show up and watch. I knew she wouldn't. She was too tired to be around all those people—too tired to have to act human for that long. But she was supposed to pick me up after.

I told her I would be done around six thirty. When the game ended, it was five after seven. I hurried to get my stuff out of the locker room and ran through a cloud of pats on the back to the front of the junior high. I knew she hated it when I kept her waiting. And you know what I saw? Her car turning onto the highway, leaving me. I watched with parted lips, fear making my hair stand on end. And I didn't have a phone at the time.

The sun was going down. I had my gym bag on my shoulder. I was a thirteen-year-old girl alone on the sidewalk. A group of high school boys passed me by. I felt exposed. And it was like, all at once, I realized that I couldn't rely on my mother to keep me safe. It sank in from the top of my head to the bottom of my feet as I slid down a pole and sat on the curb, just watching the highway, waiting for her to turn back for me.

Until my coach exited the gym and found me. "Nikki, you're still here?" She was aghast. It had been an hour since the end of our game. "Where's your ride?"

"My mom . . . um, she was . . ." Tears sparkled in my eyes, because I knew I could have gone back inside to use someone's phone, called Mama and told her to come back, but I was curious, and maybe a little masochistic. I wanted to see if she'd turn around on her own, if she cared enough to wonder why I was so late, or why I hadn't called. I wanted her to worry about where I was . . . but she didn't.

I didn't know I had put so much hope into her turning around until I started crying uncontrollably. Coach was taken aback. She called Mama. And Mama showed up fifteen minutes later, pissed, because I had made her look bad in front of the nice white lady. I had *cried* in front of the nice white lady. Last time I ever cried in front of anyone.

I just know that, had it been Coach's daughter, Coach would have been scouring the streets looking for her. And if Mama won't do that for Vae, *I* will.

9:40 a.m.

We're in New Mexico, and Mal and I haven't said a word to each other since we left the hotel. It's not awkward or anything. We've always been comfortable with silence. I'm just so caught up in my thoughts . . .

"Nikki," he says suddenly. "What do you wanna eat?" We're passing a Jack in the Box on the right, and there's a McDonald's up ahead.

"I'm not really hungry."

"Hmm," he says, then swiftly turns into the McDonald's. "Well, I'm starving. You sure you don't want anything? Like, just a hash brown or something?"

I shake my head.

"All right," he says. "Don't try and stick your greedy little hands in my food, either."

I smile over at him. I know he's trying to lighten the mood, make me laugh, but I just don't have it in me.

We're quietly listening to Kendrick Lamar. He turns it down more when he pulls up to the order box and orders his usual—sausage, egg, and cheese biscuit with two hash browns, no drink. But then he says, "Can you actually double that? Give me two biscuits and four hash browns, please."

I look at him like he's lost his mind. "You must be *really* starving."

Once he pulls up behind the car in front of us, he turns to me. "The other one is for you."

"Mal," I groan.

"You can eat it once you get hungry. And if you never get hungry, whatever. It's not a problem."

I sigh, staring out of my window. The McDonald's here is on the side of a joint gas station and convenience store, so there is a lot of activity. A lot of people coming and going in this tiny pass-through town. Mal's is definitely the newest car here, *and* the loudest. People can't help but look our way every time he presses on the gas.

Once he gets his food, he swings around to park in front of the convenience store. "Is it okay if I eat this real quick? I know you're in a hurry to get home. I can eat on the way, if—"

"No, no, it's fine. You should eat," I say.

Still haven't looked him in the eye.

"Hey." He reaches over and grabs my chin. I raise my eyes to his close inspection. "You're really worried about Vae, huh?"

At the mention of her name, my eyes fall to the console. I nod, while the truth burns at the back of my throat.

"It's gonna be okay. We're gonna find her."

I swear, all of her unanswered texts are weighing my phone down. It's burning a hole in my thigh, so I toss it in one of his empty cup holders. "Yeah, I know. Everything is fine," I say, and as I say it, my eyes start to water.

When I look at him, he's watching me even closer. "Nikki, do I even have to say it?"

"I'm not making the face. I'm fine. I'm just worried about her." I turn back to my window, watching as a chubby white man with a really red face climbs out of a teeny-tiny truck. I watch him go inside while Mal eats one of his hash browns in damn near one bite.

He doesn't push me on the issue. And because I stop fighting it, the guilt climbs farther and farther up my throat. I turn to him suddenly. "It's my fault she's gone, Mal."

He's mid-bite of his biscuit. "How?"

"She's been texting me nonstop since Friday night, and I haven't answered her. She thinks I'm in California right now."

He slowly chews and swallows his food. "You feel guilty for not answering her texts?"

I nod.

"Well, that was some toxic shit Vae did to you. She can't just *treat* people like that. Especially not the people she loves." Here he goes like usual, validating me—just as pissed off at Vae as I am. "This isn't your fault." Then he says it again. "It's not your fault."

"Okay." My face softens, because I actually believe him to a degree.

He looks at me closely, mirroring my lightweight, sunny smile with doe eyes and slightly parted lips. And we just stare for a few seconds, until his phone starts ringing.

We both look at his car's central touch screen. *Dexter.* Mal doesn't make the mistake of answering while connected to his car—not with Dex. There's no telling what's about to come out of that boy's mouth.

"Hello?" Mal says. Dex, unlike my mother, talks like a normal human being, so I can't hear anything he says. Mal kisses his teeth. "Aww, bro, I didn't know she'd actually call you. What'd you say?"

I try to stop listening to their conversation, but then Mal says, "Nah, Nikki isn't with me." My head swivels in his direction. "Just because I went to Colorado doesn't mean I went because of Nikki." I watch his face turn frustrated. "*Hell* no! Cynthia and I broke up, remember? I'm on my way back to Texas anyway. You can stop trying to be messy." After a few more teases and eye rolls, he hangs up and looks at me.

"How does Dex know we were in Colorado?"

"I told my mom that he was with me, and she actually called him to check."

"Did he snitch?"

Mal shakes his head, finishing off his biscuit. "Dex would never. But he thinks I was going after you." Mal wipes his mouth and throws his empty food wrappers in the bag, then tosses the bag in the back seat. "But don't worry. I got your back, Nikki."

"I know you do, Mal."

He looks up then, because it's something he'd say. *I know you do. I know you.*

My arm falls gently against the console. And he rests his elbow on the console next to my arm. His hand snakes up my bicep and pulls gently until my lips find their way to his. My mouth tingles and so do my head and my thighs.

Slowly I fall back into my seat, fall back into his doe eyes, feeling a lot more hopeful and much less guilty.

1:11 p.m.
(back to Central Time)

Texas is just how we left it—big and empty. We're nearly to Dumas when my phone rings.

"Who is it?" Mal asks, slowing down.

"Vae's dad."

He wears the same expression as me. "You gonna answer?"

I don't know if I should. I came back to Texas to find Vae. I'm sure that's what Daryl wants to talk about, but should I admit that I've been ignoring her texts? Should I admit to being with Mal this whole time?

I answer the call, "Hello?"

"Nikki? Oh, thank God. I'm at your mama's house. Vae is missing."

"I know," I say calmly.

"You know? Have you heard from her?"

"No, and she's not answering my texts."

"Well, where are you right now? You need to come home."

I blink, staring out the window. Home? I almost tell him that I don't have a home. But I know this isn't about me. "I'm with Mal right now. We'll be there in a few minutes."

He thinks that over, but he doesn't linger on the subject long—there's no time. "Okay, Nikki. See you soon."

1:23 p.m.

Mal parks his car behind Daryl's truck. I look out my window at the white gravel, at the closed blinds to my bedroom and the rickety porch steps, and remember the last moments I was standing there.

I wasn't wearing any shoes, because Mama had ripped hers off my feet. She was gazing at me from the other side of the locked screen door, while Vae was hiding in her room, maybe laughing to herself, pleased to have seen her plan work so well. Now, being back after all of that, I feel terrified to go inside. Daryl doesn't know how serious she was that night. She's gonna throw me out the second I walk in, for sure.

When I turn to Mal, he looks like he's waiting for directions, like he's waiting to hear what I need from him.

"Do you mind coming inside with me?"

His eyebrows jump into his hairline. "Wait, are you sure?"

Mal has never been inside my house. Not ever. When he

would come over to "hang out," I'd make him sit with me on the porch—because a part of me thought he was too big for my house. Like his body wouldn't fit through the door, and his head would perpetually brush the ceiling, and his wealth wouldn't let him get comfortable.

If my car was out of commission, as it so often was, he'd park in our driveway before school, and if Vae and I weren't waiting for him outside, he'd jog up our porch steps and knock on the door—he's always said it was because it's the polite thing to do, but I'm pretty sure it was so he could get a peek inside our house.

One time, when he knocked, I opened the door and said, "Vae's having a meltdown about her outfit. She'll be out in a sec."

He said, "I can turn off my car and come inside with you."

I gave him a look, letting him know he wasn't slick. "No, we can just wait in the car."

He looked disappointed, but I couldn't concern myself with that. I had seen the inside of his house at that point. I had seen what I *thought* he grew up having, and I was embarrassed to show him all the shit I didn't have.

I was embarrassed of the fact that my house didn't smell like air fresheners or anything inviting, and that our decor was mis-matched and lacked a theme. I was embarrassed of the furniture that technically belonged outside, and the patio sofa that Vae and I weren't even allowed to sit on.

But after last night, I'm so grateful that he was brave enough to show me exactly who he is, and something about that trust pushes me forward.

"I don't want to go alone," I say. He smiles and turns off his car.

Vae used to be my relief in this house. Like milk on a hot tongue. She acted human toward me when it seemed no one else remembered how. Without her, I have no shield, no saving grace, no reason to keep myself from acting just as unreasonable and explosive as *that woman*. I need Mal with me. I need a buffer, a hand to hold, a body standing on *my* fucking side.

I finally get out and lead him up the porch steps. I've never knocked on my own front door before, much less any of the ones inside, but looking at it now, I don't feel welcome to just walk in. So I knock, like a stranger. Mal's standing on the bottom step. And when he sees my hesitation, he reaches up to twist a piece of my hair around his finger. No words, but it's enough to comfort me.

The door opens then, and my blood freezes solid in my veins. "Nikki, there you are," I hear before I see Daryl's short and chubby stature through the mesh of the screen door. "Come on in here," he says when I don't move a muscle.

I check over my shoulder as Mal lets go of my hair, then I open the screen door and step inside. "Hey, baby girl," Daryl says, pulling me into his arms as the familiar smell of *home* hits me. I can see everything over his shoulder—daytime television on the TV, crystal angel figurines, baby pictures of Vae and me—but I don't see her. That woman.

When Daryl lets me go, my eyes fall to my shoes, because I don't *want* to see her. I don't know how to look at her without overflowing with emotions. Mal steps in after me, and just feeling his body standing tall behind me makes me highly aware of how low our ceilings are. I try to erase the panic. I know he was this scared or maybe even more when he told me about being adopted. I can trust him with this part of me.

"Malachai," Daryl says, voice booming like a football coach in a crowded hallway. He's always talked like that, as if he grew up wanting to be a coach but just didn't have the stuff.

Mal shakes Daryl's hand. Then I lift my head and glance through my hair at my mother. She's sitting in her recliner on my left, staring at the TV like daytime television is abundantly more interesting than her runaway daughter and the boy she's always thought was too good for me.

Daryl shuts the front door behind us. "Now tell me again, Yolanda. Was Vae acting different last night?"

Mama releases her tucked lips, but doesn't move her eyes away from the television. "I already told you she wasn't acting no different."

As if *she* would know what's different for Vae. When Vae is plotting, Vae gets silent, and she's already a quiet girl, so it's really hard to know what she's thinking. When Vae is plotting, she holds her intent in her eyes. This woman wouldn't know shit about that, though.

Daryl walks across the living room carpet, over to the couch that I was never allowed to sit on. He moves some of the pillows like he owns the place. What does he think he's doing? Mama is going to freak out if her pillows get unorganized. But weirdly she doesn't try stopping him.

"Y'all come sit down," he says to me and Mal, still standing awkwardly in the doorway. "You're making me nervous."

Sit on the forbidden couch? Surely, Mama will growl if I take a step closer, but no. Her eyes are still glued to the television.

I walk past her, leading Mal over to the beige patio love seat. He sits next to me, thigh pressed against thigh. I smell him suddenly—his shower soap and the cologne that I didn't see him spray this morning. I look over at him, and he looks at me with a reassuring grin.

Daryl is asking Mama to describe Vae's behavior last night. Mama is getting annoyed. God, this house looks so small and crowded with four people in it. Or maybe it's all the unspoken words, and the lies, and all the bullshit clouding the air.

"I'm done with your questions, Daryl."

"I just don't understand what's going on in this house," he says, hands on his hips. "First Nikki, and now Vae is running away? What'd you do to my little girl, Yolanda?"

"Excuse me?" She finally tears her eyes away from the television. "You don't get to come in *my* house and accuse me of shit. You left, Daryl, remember? You left me to take care of these girls by myself."

"Don't act like I haven't helped you, Yolanda. And I didn't leave you. You left me."

"You stepped out on our marriage long before I stepped out of our house."

This is uncomfortable. They argue, yes. Mostly over me and Vae, but I've never seen them argue about their relationship. Not like this. I glance at Mal, uncomfortable, then I open my mouth. "Hey, um. If Vae ran away, how far could she have gone, really? She doesn't have a car."

The two of them stop and look at me. Mama's gaze burns through mine, so I focus on Daryl's. "That's true," he says. "Unless she caught a ride with someone. Who were her friends at school?" Daryl asks me and Mal.

We look at each other. Vae didn't have a whole lot of friends.

"She always used to hang around that Megan girl—lives down the street from us," Mama says with a grimace. Mama never liked Megan. Honestly, neither did I, but I'm pretty sure Vae hasn't talked to Megan in *years.* Whatever, though. I'm not about to correct her.

"Maybe that's where we should start?" Daryl says.

"Has anyone tried using Find My Phone?" Mal asks.

Daryl nods. "First thing I did when I got here. Last place it shows was right here in this house."

Mal sucks the back of his teeth.

"Have you looked in her room?" I ask. "Maybe she left, like, a note or something?"

Unless you find me first.

Daryl shakes his head. "Already looked, but you can go see. Maybe you know something I don't."

I look at Mal, not wanting to leave him with my mama and her ex-husband, but also not confident that I'm allowed to take him with me.

Thankfully, Daryl spares me the aneurysm. "Mal, you can go with her."

I stand up first, avoiding my mother's gaze. Mal follows me past Daryl, past the front door, down the dark hallway. As soon as we're swallowed up by the darkness, I reach back for Mal's hand, and instantly calm once I feel him.

I turn into Vae's room and flip on the light. People probably assume that Vae's room is immaculate. She's smart, she's quiet, she's "sweet," but the girl is messier than me.

"Damn," Mal hisses in my ear as we both trip over a pile of clothes. "Vae is a total slob."

"And yet, I'm the one always getting in trouble for not cleaning my room." I walk past her unmade bed, over to her nightstand. I don't really know what I'm looking for—just anything abnormal. A clue or something. I come in here enough to know when something is out of place, but everything looks up to code.

What the fuck did she mean, *unless you find me first*?

"Wow, so she was serious when she said she collects rocks?"

I turn just in time to see Mal reaching for Vae's favorite gemstone on her bookshelf. "Don't," I hiss. "She'll know if you move something."

Mal looks at the mess on her floor pointedly. "Are you sure?"

"Trust me," I say. "Even if you put it right back where you

think it was, you're wrong and she will know."

He smiles, crossing his arms and leaning against the wall. "Doesn't it make you wonder what she might be hiding in here?"

"I'm too scared to snoop," I say with a grin. My fingers land on her nightstand and brush across the Fujifilm picture of us that she always keeps close. She took it one day when we walked down to the Cactus Park in hundred-degree weather, just to get out of the house and away from Mama. The heat brings out the absolute worst in that woman, I swear.

Vae and I have walked to the park so often in our lives that we beat a path through the thicket—our own little shortcut. On the day she took this picture, we found a mostly decomposed duck on the trail. We both squealed in disgust, but like the big sister I am, I pushed Vae toward the flattened carcass.

She screeched and ran directly to the park. I ran after her, laughing and singing a nonsensical song: "You stepped in *duck*! You stepped in *duck*!"

This picture of us always makes me think of that song. In it we're both sitting on the swings, leaning in toward each other, cheesing.

"Wait," I say, looking around her nightstand. "Where's her camera?"

Mal comes to stand close beside me, enough that our arms are brushing. "You mean that big Polaroid thing she's always lugging around?"

"Yeah. She grabs that thing before she even grabs her—"

Then I see it on her floor, sitting powered off and plugged in. "Her phone." I pick it up and make a face.

"So she took the camera but not her phone," Mal says with a hopeful smile.

I smile too. "The girl is a mess."

"But at least we know that maybe, wherever she's going, she's planning . . . to make memories?"

I nod, laughing lightly. "I guess."

Then Daryl steps in. "Find anything?" I hold up the phone, and he immediately shakes his head. "That girl, I swear."

"But she did manage to take her camera," Mal says, taking a slight step away from me, putting an appropriate amount of space between us.

"Yeah, so I'm thinking we should look around town. Go to her little friends' houses to see if they've heard from her, starting with this Megan girl." Daryl jingles his keys, and my chest constricts.

Wait. All of us go? In the same vehicle?

Not only does this house feel crowded with four people, but this grouping is less than ideal. A mom and her estranged daughter and the boy her estranged daughter has supposedly been doing sexual favors for. And the mom's ex-husband, who isn't her estranged daughter's real dad. It's just . . . messy, and I can't imagine enclosing all this mess in an even smaller space.

But here we go, I guess.

1:41 p.m.

Mal and I are buckled up in the back seat of Daryl's truck as he creeps through our neighborhood, like he might pass the house if he goes over five mph.

"Which side of the street is it on?" he asks.

Mama sighs from the passenger seat. "I done told you, I'm pretty sure it's on the left."

"But you ain't all the way sure. Don't have me pulling up in some white man's driveway—he might get his gun and try to kill me dead."

"Hush, boy," Mama says, trying not to laugh.

This is about the only thing I remember of their marriage—the car rides. Their country accents teasing and laughing in the front seat, while toddler Vae and four-year-old me were buckled in the back seat. The car rides really made it seem like they got along.

"Oh, here it is," Mama says, pointing to a weathered, beige

trailer that looks like it was planted there long before I was born. The front porch is obstructed by wind chimes and dollar store ornaments. And the yard is decorated by rusty cars and old lawn mowers. I always wondered if her parents were hoarders, but then I considered that if I had a lawn mower stop working, I wouldn't know what to do with it either.

Daryl pulls into the thin, rocky driveway, pushing his face into the windshield to get a better view. "Oooh-weee, this looks like *the* spot to get shot dead."

Mal snickers beside me.

Mama says, "Knowing how that girl was, wouldn't surprise me if her parents were racist."

Then we all just kind of sit in silence, staring out of the windshield. "Welp. Somebody needs to go knock on the door," Daryl says, looking at Mama in the passenger seat.

"I ain't going. She can go." Then she points her thumb back at me.

It immediately pisses me off, because we've come this far—I was in her house, sitting on her couch—and this is the first time she's had the heart to (barely) acknowledge me. "I have a name," I say.

Her head turns around slowly. She can finally see me through those narrowed eyes of hers. "Yeah, your name is whatever I decide to call you."

"My name is what I decide to answer to, and *she* is not it."

Mama adjusts the strap of her seat belt so she can really look at me. "You know what? You can walk—"

"Okay," Daryl interrupts, raising his voice. "That's the

problem with you girls—you can't show each other respect."

Mama turns on him. "I don't know who you think you're calling a girl. I'm a grown-ass woman, which means that li'l girl back there better stop talking to me any kind of way—"

"Yolanda, just stop."

"No, *you* stop."

Mal turns to me, reaches out his hand, and it lands on my arm. "I'll go with you. How about that? Yeah?"

Then he opens his door while I nod, desperate to get away from this argument. So much for car rides being a safe space.

I slam the door behind me, so that their voices are muffled behind the tinted windows. Mal meets me at the front of the truck, then falls in beside me, placing his hand on my lower back. "You okay?"

My breath is still blowing hot through my nostrils. "I'm just . . ." I shake my head, starting on the brick path that leads to the disheveled porch.

"Frustrated?" he asks.

I turn to him at the bottom of the steps, eyes wide. "Yes."

"No, yeah. This has been really tense." His hand slides from around my back to my wrist.

"It's just like, she gives me no reason to wanna come back here. She doesn't even care that I was gone, Mal." I furrow my brow to block up the muscles in my tear ducts, because I think I'm just now admitting this to myself. I've been gone for *days* and the first time she calls, frantic, it's not even about me.

His hand clenches tighter around my wrist. "No, she's just . . ." He pauses, because he wants to assure me that of course she cares, but he can't. He knows better than anyone that moms don't *have* to love their children unconditionally.

"She may not care, but I do. And my parents do. And Vae does—I mean, she's out there trying to find you right now." He moves his hand down to clench my fingers. A jolt shoots up through my toes. "Just because your mom doesn't recognize how awesome you are doesn't mean you aren't."

But mothers are supposed to think impossible things about their kids.

Mothers think their round potato babies are beautiful, despite the fact that they look like aliens. Mothers think their kids are God's gift to humanity, even when their kid is only average. My mother has never believed in me like that. She's never called me beautiful, capable, or *more than* capable. It can be confusing growing up hearing exactly the opposite from the person who made you. Warps your brain.

So, I don't know, it feels monumental, realizing that Mal may be onto something. Just because my mother fails to see my beauty doesn't mean she's right . . . about *anything.*

We're standing, facing each other, at the bottom of the porch, when we hear two quick taps of Daryl's horn, and the whirring down of a window. "Hurry it up!" Mama shouts.

And just like that, my blood pressure rises again. No other person on this planet pisses me off as efficiently as she does. Mal rolls his eyes with a comforting smile, then leads me up the rotted steps. But before we can get to the top, the front door creaks open, and out steps a barefooted, freckle-faced, redheaded Megan Meadows.

NOTE TO SELF: Vae dropped this girl for a reason.

She ain't loyal for shit.

1:58 p.m.

She's the kind of girl whose father would be pissed to find out she was dating a Black boy. She's the kind of girl who runs through Black guys for that reason alone.

When she sees us on the steps, her eyes immediately fall to Mal's triceps. She glances at me, says, "Nikki?" then trains her eyes back on Mal. "What are y'all doing here?" She swishes her hair to one shoulder, bites on the nail of her index finger, and unbuttons one of the buttons on her already low-cut tank top. "God, it's hot out here."

This is a primary reason me and my family can't stand Megan Meadows. She be on some *Get Out* shit, I swear.

I deliberately step in front of Mal. "Sorry for just showing up like this, but we're wondering if you've heard from Vae recently."

She's forced to look at me, and her eyes look much less patient. "Um, Vae and I haven't spoken in years."

I nod, glancing at Daryl's truck, idling in her driveway. "Yeah, I figured."

"What's going on? Did she run away or something?" I nod again. "Weird," she says, with a lift of her eyebrows. "I always thought that was *your* schtick."

I press my lips tight, because she's giving my mama a run for her money on the whole *pissing me off* front. "Anyway, thanks," I say, turning away before I can get into it with this little girl. Hands on Mal's waist, I start rushing him down the steps.

"She's been hanging out with the band kids at lunch. Maybe try interrogating them." Then she opens her creaky front door.

"Wait. Which band kids?"

She's got a hand on her narrow hip. "I don't know. I don't keep tabs on her anymore, but I'd start with Asher, if I were you. They clearly have a thing for each other."

I look at Mal with scrunched eyebrows. He nods. "Yeah, I know him."

Megan says, "Good luck," unfeelingly, then shuts the front door behind her.

NOTE TO SELF: Figure out who Vae's friends are.

It's been so long since I've seen her hang out with anyone, but I guess it's also been a long time since we've *talked*. Like, really talked. It sucks that Megan Meadows knows more about my little sister than I do.

2:14 p.m.

Daryl is driving aimlessly around our neighborhood, as if Vae will just pop out of nowhere. Mama is complaining about how all of this is a waste of time, and I can't help but think that she doesn't sound like a concerned mother.

Mal is messaging Asher Weaton to see if he's with Vae, but Asher isn't answering. I'm stalking his Instagram page, because Megan seems to think that Asher and Vae have something going on. He's a Black kid, a sophomore like her, who plays trumpet in the marching band. The last day I ever saw Vae, she was tongue-wrestling with Sarge. Where has this Asher kid been in the mix?

"So, what exactly did that girl say?" Mama asks, turning in her seat to look at me. She actually looks at me, eyes calm and not completely full of hatred.

"She said to ask the band kids."

"What band kids?"

I sigh, readying myself to catch my mother up on the social happenings of her favorite daughter. "Vae and Megan haven't been friends in years. Vae's been hanging out with the band kids lately, particularly some boy named Asher."

"Vae is hanging out with a *boy*?"

"Yep." I hand her my phone.

She takes it and looks through Asher's Instagram profile. "Oh, he's pretty cute. You think she's with him right now?" She still seems surprised that Vae would be within ten feet of a cute boy, much less running away with one. I shrug, unsure myself.

Mal says, "I'm about to post on the community Facebook page, asking if anyone knows where either of them are. If Asher is still in town, maybe he's talked to Vae since she left."

Mama hands back my phone, and suddenly I remember that she'd had plans to cut off my service. She still hasn't yet. I wonder if she changed the locks like she said she would. I wonder if she'll still have the heart to completely disown me after we find Vae, especially if it means she might lose Vae in the process.

Or is she so self-centered that she'd rather be completely alone than concede for her favorite (formerly perfect) daughter?

After a while of driving around Cactus, we end up at Juanita's—me and Vae's favorite taco place. As much as it's our favorite, though, we don't come here a lot, because eating out is a luxury for our family. And Mama has never been a huge fan of Mexican food. So, the only time we really get to come here is with Mal.

Daryl, who I'm guessing has had enough of the tension in his truck, volunteers to go inside—ask the people if Vae has stopped by recently, which, again, I'm guessing she hasn't. But the grown-ups don't like to listen to me.

So it's just me and Mama and Mal, all staring at our phones. After a few minutes of this, Mal looks at me with a halfway smile. "Remember that time we came here and Vae dropped her whole taco on the floor?"

I instantly smile. "She was being a little brat the whole drive here."

"What was it she kept saying about us?"

"She kept threatening to tell on us about that time in study hall."

"Oh yeah! The time we were supposed to be getting interviewed for the yearbook . . ." He trails off, because it's probably not smart to snitch on ourselves in front of my mother.

I lean closer to him, letting myself sink into the memory of our little crew—me in his passenger seat, Vae in the back seat, without her seat belt on, hanging on to the sides of both our chairs. "I bet the yearbook people were looking for y'all!" she shouted. "That's not cool."

"You're just jealous." I smirked at her over my shoulder. "You wish you were as badass as us."

"No, I'm sorry, I value my education. I have never skipped class, and I never will."

"Never say never," Mal said, smiling at her through the rear-view. "As soon as you fall in love with one of these stupid boys, you'll see—you're gonna be doing a lot of things you said you'd never do."

"And you know this from experience?" I asked. "Which stupid boy did you fall in love with, Mal?"

Vae giggled.

Mal laughed, appalled. "Shut up, Nikki—you know what I mean."

"No, I don't."

He glanced at me, then back at the road. "So, you're saying you never did something stupid for a boy?"

"Nope." I turned my nose up, leaning over the console.

"She's lying," Vae said. "She did something stupid for a boy today—that's what this whole conversation is about."

"Mal is Mal. He isn't . . . a boy."

His eyebrows shot up. "That's news to me."

"You know what I mean! You're not, like, a boy that I'm involved with romantically. It doesn't count."

"I don't count?"

I pushed his shoulder, turning to the windshield. "I didn't skip class for a stupid boy. I skipped class for myself. School has been *hell* today."

I stared at the flashing lines on the road, listening to the AC blast through his air vents.

Vae leaned forward then and said, "I mean, it was a good idea—I just think that since I caught you, you should accept the consequences of not being stealthy enough."

"The only reason you know about it is because I texted you a picture of us!"

"In hindsight," Mal said, "that was pretty stupid of us. How could we not have predicted this? Vae has always been a savage."

"And you best not forget it," she said.

Mal was right, though. Vae *has* always been a savage. She's always been clever and strategic. If Mama should worry about anyone turning on her in the end, she should worry about Vae. That girl has always been a big-picture, long-game kind of opponent.

"That taco was karma," Mal says, laughing.

I smile, remembering the look on Vae's face when it fell splat on the floor.

But then Mama looks at me over her shoulder. That repugnance is back in her eyes. "And when did this happen? Another one of the times you lied about staying at Riley's?"

The energy between me and Mal dies as tension fills the car again.

"Actually, no," I say. Mal immediately reaches over and places his hand atop mine, because he can feel me getting heated. "That was the week you refused to give me gas money, so Mal had to pick me and Vae up for school every day. He even waited after school for Vae to be done with band rehearsal."

She flicks her eyebrows up and turns back around in her seat. "Good for him."

"Good for him?" I scoot forward and Mal starts shaking his head. "You should be thanking him for chauffeuring your daughter around."

Then she faces me again, venom in her expression, venom on her tongue. "I'm betting you already thanked him more than enough." She looks pointedly at his hand covering mine.

My eyebrows knit together. I'm about to fire off words that I won't be able to take back when Daryl returns with a huff. "They ain't seen her, either."

Mama huffs too, turning back around to face the front—argument over.

I wasn't holding my breath, though. I *figured* Vae wouldn't come here. Still I huff, too, because I have no idea where to look next.

4:04 p.m.

The four of us spend half of our afternoon driving around town, looking for Vae and bickering.

After we've asked around at Cactus Park, Mal suddenly runs up to me, holding his phone for me to see. "Hey, I got something!"

It's a comment on his post, by some white lady—a Carol Stromberg. Mal pulls the phone back with an excited grin. "She says that multiple marching band kids ran off last night, and it seems they stole her minivan to do it."

"Wait, *stole*?" My jaw drops. "Vae stole something?"

"Mrs. Stromberg is the mother of one of the kids. Apparently, these band kids steal her van pretty often to do pranks and stuff—it's primarily the brass section. She doesn't seem all that concerned. More annoyed than anything."

"Wow . . ." My heart rate slows. "So is she Asher's mom?"

"No. But she confirmed that Asher is one of the kids who ran away last night."

"This is huge." I smile at him. "Thanks, Mal."

He smiles back. "Vae's like a little sister to me, too, you know."

I've always thought so, just by the way they act around each other, but I've never heard him say it. And I didn't realize how much I wanted to hear him say it, until now.

After we tell Mama and Daryl, we find ourselves back in Mama's driveway. Daryl tracked down Mrs. Stromberg's phone number and is chatting with her about next steps, and whether or not she has any idea where the kids might be going. She doesn't. And I know that she doesn't because her voice is just as loud and annoying as my mama's when she's on the phone.

Daryl suggests we pick this back up tomorrow, after he gets off work. Mrs. Stromberg has invited all the parents of the missing band kids to her house for dinner tomorrow. Mama doesn't want to go, though, because Mama hates fraternizing with white folks unnecessarily. Daryl is trying to convince her that this *is* necessary.

Mal and I are standing next to his car—him leaning against the door, while I'm standing in front of him. "Thank you for staying with me today."

"I had to," he says, searching my eyes with the cutest smile.

"Thank you for making that Facebook post."

He nods, eager to move past all of my thanks.

"I'm serious, though, Mal. I don't know if I've ever told you thank you without a stank attitude and an eye roll, but thank you. Seriously. For always being so kind."

He grins sheepishly. "You're welcome, Nikki. Always." Then he reaches his hand out for mine.

My heart stops, and after a few seconds of not beating, it restarts with a vengeance. Suddenly I remember what we were doing before this Vae situation interrupted us. He'd already kissed my jaw and my chin, and he was about to move down to my neck. If only that moment had never ended.

"So, uh," he says, smiling down to his shoes nervously. "I hope this isn't outta pocket or, like, a bad time . . ."

I raise my eyebrows, taking note of the fact that for once he's avoiding eye contact.

But then he looks up. "I just hope it's clear, from all of last night and today, that I'm very much into you."

My face freezes.

He smirks at me. "There's that face again."

I laugh an exhale, moving warmth through my facial muscles, stretching them out. I've gotta stop doing that. "No, yeah, I . . ." I look down at his shoes, too. "And I hope it's clear to you . . . how I feel."

"Honestly?" he says. I look up expectantly. "I wasn't completely sure until now." He pulls on my fingers, pulling me just one step closer. "But I've been hoping."

I stare into his dark eyes until Daryl barrels over to us. "Nik-Nik! Your mama and I agree that you should stay here tonight."

My head swiftly turns, eyes shifting between Daryl and Mama. "But . . ." I trail off. She's standing on the porch, not looking at anyone.

"I know what happened Friday night, and I really wish you would have called me." Daryl frowns. "But we talked about it, and you know how your mama is." He says that last part really quiet, so that only Mal and I can hear him. "We think it's best to keep you near, while we're looking for Vae. Too much craziness going on. I need to know you're safe."

This is not at all what I had planned.

What I had planned involved disappearing forever, never seeing that woman again. Definitely never moving back in with her. The whole "she's calmed down" shit doesn't make me feel better. I don't give a fuck if she's calmed down. She doesn't want me. That's it. The truth is *she doesn't want me*. And I don't wanna be anywhere I'm not wanted.

It's his eyes, though. It's the plea in Daryl's eyes that keeps me contained. Makes me nod and say, "Okay. Fine."

"All right, good. I'll drop by tomorrow evening, and if your mama don't wanna go, you and I will go to Mrs. Stromberg's house. Okay?"

Mama goes inside the house, leaving the front door open, closing the screen.

Daryl is opening the door of his truck, parked behind Mal's car. "Go on inside, Nikki. Call me if you need me." Before shutting his door, he says, "See ya, Malachai."

"Bye, Mr. Williams."

And as Daryl is backing out of the rocky driveway, all of my calm is being sucked out of my body. Because somehow, I'm supposed to follow my mama inside, and I know for sure that I can't bring Mal with me.

NOTE TO SELF: Before you leave, say a real goodbye to Daryl.

He deserves it, despite everything.

Yes, sometimes he can be a lot. And sometimes it feels like he just doesn't *get it*. But I don't know . . . maybe he does. He was married to the woman for three years.

Every time I've ever run away, he's come to pick me up at Mal's house. Typically, I'm still asleep in the guest room at seven a.m. when Mal will come in and say, "Mr. Daryl is here," but I remember one time I was already awake. I was coming out of the bathroom when I heard the doorbell.

I crept to the top of the stairs and hid behind the wall as Mr. B opened the door.

"Hey, how you doing? I'm here to pick up Nikki," I heard Daryl say in that booming coach's voice of his. Such a big voice for such a small man.

"Oh, okay, yeah. Come on in. She's upstairs." But after shutting the door, Mr. B didn't come get me. He started asking questions.

Then a pair of hands closed around my shoulders. "Whatcha doing?"

I jumped and shushed Mal at the same time. Then we were both pressed against the wall, eavesdropping.

Mr. B was trying to keep his voice down, but the conversation still carried up the stairs. "You're Nevaeh's dad, right? But you don't live with them?"

"Nah, but I've been in Nikki's life since she was a baby."

"Right, right, so I guess I'm just wondering . . . what the deal is at home. She's come to stay with us several times over the years. And of course, my wife and I love Nikki. We don't mind one bit. I'm just"—then he sighed—"should we be worried?"

I could tell that the question caught Daryl off guard. "You know, it's just, teenage girls and their mothers—"

Mr. B didn't let him go far down that line of thinking. "Yeah, I get it. I mean, sometimes my son likes to backtalk and every kid threatens to run away, but I've never seen a kid do it *so many times.* I mean, is there . . . physical abuse?"

"Nah, nah, nah," Daryl said. "They're both just hardheaded."

"I've spent a good amount of time with Nikki to know that, sure, she can be stubborn, but she tends to listen to reason."

"Well, that's the thing, her mom's not always reasonable. She can be proud and all that . . . but she's not *abusive.*"

"Yeah, no, of course. I'm not trying to accuse her of anything. Just worried."

"Yep, yep. So, is Nikki upstairs?"

"Yes. Right. Let me go get her."

Mr. B found us standing at the top of the stairs—we didn't even bother to pretend like we weren't listening. Like I said, there's no fear in the Brown household.

"You hear all that?" he asked.

We nodded.

"Dad, you were grilling him pretty hard, don't you think?" Mal whispered.

Mr. B kept his eyes on me. "I don't want you to think I have a problem with you coming over. I don't—not in the least. Just trying to hear an adult explain the situation."

"He didn't really do very well," I said.

"Not too great." Mr. B gave me a sympathetic look. "But you'll let us know, right? If it's too much to handle at home? Or if she physically abuses you?"

I nodded, barely meeting his eye. "Let me go get my stuff."

In the truck, Daryl and I were mostly silent. Per usual, he took me to get breakfast at an old diner in Dumas. He ordered himself grits, eggs, and bacon, and I got my usual stack of pancakes. He always used this place to talk me down after a run-in with my mama.

The thing about Daryl is, he knows what's up. He knows how she can be. But he also knows that if I decide I can't stay with her anymore, he can't exactly take me in. His house is already overcrowded with him and his wife's children. I wouldn't want to stay there in a million years, anyway—there's no privacy.

Daryl's whole strategy has always been to keep my head down, graduate, and get out—and he holds tight to it like it was his strategy in their marriage. *Do what you have to do.* Because every other option is worse. Especially knowing what Mal went through in foster care. Sure, he lucked out in the end, but he had to kiss a lot of frogs to finally find loving parents.

Nikki . . . Just do what you have to do and get out.

4:48 p.m.

My room has always been the safest place for me in the house, because staying out of sight has always been the most effective strategy for not getting bitched at.

The second I walk inside, I go straight down the hall. I don't know if she's in the living room, the kitchen, or her bedroom, and I sure as hell don't go looking for her. I hurry down the dark hallway to my room and shut the door.

It looks the same as when I left it Friday morning. I genuinely was holding my breath, expecting to see my bed and my dresser gone, sold back to the thrift store from where they came. I expected to see all of the song lyrics I had tacked along my walls shredded and scattered on the floor. I thought I had lost everything.

But seeing all my stuff, right where I left it, I suddenly feel . . . comfortable, like I can take my bra off and my socks off just to scrape my feet against the hard parts in the carpet—from whatever I spilled and didn't clean up all those years ago.

The first thing I touch is my keyboard.

Don't get me wrong. Staying with Mal was nice and luxurious, but the second I touch my keyboard, I breathe differently—*better.*

First, I practice my audition songs. Then I lay down some new lyrics that have been floating in my head since yesterday in Colorado. And then I play through a couple old songs, just to make sure I still remember the keys and the presets, ending with "Yesterday."

While I'm holding the keys on the last note, my door opens. Mama walks in, pointing to her ears. "It's too loud." I let off the keys, my throat getting ready to fire off a healthy dose of attitude, when I notice the pain on her face. Like my playing isn't just annoying her, but it's actually hurting her ears.

I turn the volume down on my keyboard, then slowly roll my eyes back to her figure in my doorway. She's staring with her eyelids low, and her body is slumped against the wall, exhausted. "What's that song called?" she asks out of the blue.

My stony expression cracks down the middle. "W-what?"

"What's the name of that song you were just playing? Sounded really pretty. Just wanna know what it's called."

"'Yesterday,'" I say, confused.

She nods slowly, never dropping eye contact. "What's it about?" she asks. The way she says it, I can tell she already knows what it's about. But she won't come out and say it. She wants *me* to.

"It's about a girl who had a really good time with a boy who wasn't actually into her—someone who was leading her on."

Mama blinks a few times. "Hmmm. Okay . . . ," she says, sounding like she doesn't believe me. "Dinner's ready. Betta come eat." Then she spins around and stomps her heavy feet back down the hallway.

That's when the smell hits me. Red sauce and meatballs—*spaghetti*. My stomach growls, and my mouth starts to water. Did she make my favorite on purpose?

NOTE TO SELF: "Yesterday" is a reminder to not get sucked in.

I wrote it the summer I turned fourteen.

Not about a boy, but about my mama. After a really nice day grocery shopping with her, I thought we were both on the same page. Turns out she couldn't have cared less that I was there.

Such a stupid way to get your heart broken, but that shit cut deep.

6:16 p.m.

I get up from my bed and follow her footsteps down the hall. When I enter the living room, she's sitting in her recliner with a bowl of spaghetti in her lap. I get a quick glance at her face before dropping my eyes. She looks serene. She looks as excited to eat as I am.

But I also notice her refusal to make eye contact. I can feel the uncomfortable tension wafting off of her, so I hurry past.

Her black Dutch oven is sitting atop the stove, heavy ceramic lid sitting facedown on the eye next to it. I quietly pull a bowl from the cabinet, a fork from the silverware drawer, and noodles from the pot. And as I'm filling my bowl, I recognize the host's voice from one of my favorite TV shows: *What Would You Do?*

John Quinones calls my eyes to the screen immediately. It doesn't matter the scenario, I'm always hyped to see how people react to things. So instead of skittering back to my room, bowl of spaghetti in hand, I sit at the kitchen table. She turns up the television, because I guess she can't hear it as well as she'd like. But maybe it's because she wants *me* to be able to hear it.

What is this warmth, huh? Am I reading things wrong? Do I actually have some kind of dormant hope that she'll act like a real mom?

Dumb. That's dumb. I need to get rid of it.

She laughs at a man who decides to run instead of helping. I chuckle too. She slurps her noodles messily and noisily—I do too. She makes predictions about what a person will do based on their appearance, and I add on to her predictions. For those forty-five minutes, we are symbiotic. Like nothing ever happened between us.

But then the show goes off—and she stands up, empty bowl in hand. She says, on her way past me, "And I bet not see a single dirty bowl in this sink when I get up in the morning."

I say nothing. I *want* to. But there's no point. Just when I think we're doing good, laughing like a family, she always shuts me down. *Always.*

After washing my dishes, I make it to my room. Just as I sit down on my bed, turning my keyboard back on, my phone buzzes on the mattress beside me.

Mal: **Hey, are you doing okay?**

I smile and pick up my phone: **You missed it—my mom and I just had a civil-ass dinner.**

A civil-ass dinner you say?

Yes. It was civil AF.

I watch his reply bubbles dance with the girliest, stupidest smile on my face. He texts back: **Lol . . . can I FaceTime you?**

My fingers automatically start primping my hair and wiping around my lips. **Sure.**

"Hey," I say as soon as I answer.

He comes on my screen wearing a loose black tank top. And he's leaning forward, so none of the cloth is touching his chest. My eyes are drawn to the new muscles he's been building since last summer. "Hey," he says, giving me one of those overtly sexy side smiles.

I try to control the smile on my lips and the giggle working its way up my throat.

"What are you doing?" His eyes dip quickly, then come right back up. "What's that on your shirt?"

I look down at the gray T-shirt I'm wearing and frown at the red sauce soaking into the middle of my chest. "Spaghetti," I say regretfully.

"Your mom made you spaghetti?" he asks, as shocked as I was.

"I don't know if it was *for* me. But it was good. And we watched some TV. And it was weirdly civil."

"I'm really happy to hear that, Nikki. I was worried that you'd be fighting with her all day. I really didn't want to leave you there by yourself."

"Yeah, I know. Surprisingly, it hasn't been so bad."

He nods slowly, shifting his gaze. "Do you think things are good enough for you to, you know, live there?"

"Mal, I don't know."

"I just think you shouldn't let her stop you from doing your best—because then she wins."

He looks like he's begging me to hear him. Begging me to make the two months I have left of high school a priority. But I've never really taken school seriously. Several people have told me that school just isn't my thing, and I've believed them for a long time. It's a little too late for change.

"Don't worry, Mal, she can't stop me from doing anything." I glance over my shoulder at the shut door, hoping she's not on the other side of it, listening. "But anyway," I say, changing the subject and lowering my voice, "I wanted to show you something."

"Show me what?" he asks, eyes zooming in on that stain on my shirt.

"Not that!" I bite my lip, glancing toward my door again. "I was working on a song, and I wanted to play it for you." Then I turn my keyboard on.

I glance at the phone screen, at his face, with my fingers on all the right keys. "It's kind of inspired by my experience in Colorado."

He's studying me carefully. "Oh yeah?"

"Yeah. About how I felt, or whatever."

My heart is racing right now—just like it was in that bar in New Mexico. But I figure if I'm serious about going to Cali, I better get used to this feeling.

I play him the song, sing my lyrics, full of truth and feeling, and avoid looking at my phone screen the entire time. This, I realize, is the only way I ever express my raw emotions. It's how I say all the things I could never really say to someone's face. Like I hate you and I love you and I need you.

Only ever through song.

When I finish playing for him, I hold my fingers on the keys for as long as possible, holding myself within the safety of my song, until Mal finally says, "Wow," breathlessly, and then I let go.

@nik_nik_nikki23: Don't worry, I'm bringing my A game. There's no way I'm messing up this opportunity. I need this.

Monday

6:52 a.m.

Grandma Bobbie used to live in Cactus, too—apparently down the street from us. But after Grandpa died, she moved back to Dallas.

I have very little knowledge of the situation, but it's my understanding that she was happy when Grandpa died. I mean, this all happened before I was born, so I've never experienced her living in Cactus, nor did I get to meet Grandpa, but I think she finally felt free when he died. I think he was a monster to her.

Mama never talks about him, and when Bobbie did, she would always call him *He*, or *Williams* (our last name), or "That Man." I only ever learned that his name was Charles by looking at the backs of old photos yellowing in Bobbie's back rooms. *Charles, 1966.*

I've heard here and there about how controlling he was. About how Bobbie wanted to go to college, but he wouldn't let her. About how she wanted to get a *job*, but he wanted her to stay in the home. She was a homemaker for much of their marriage, until he couldn't work anymore. Bobbie had to step in and work at the meat factory. The fact that she was going to college when I was starting elementary school had always been weird to me, but now with context, I think I get it.

Every time we went to Bobbie's, she'd ask me and Vae what our dreams were. Like, she assumed we had revised them since the last time she saw us. Vae's dreams always changed. Doctor, lawyer—typical high-dollar shit. Mine was always to be a singer.

And every year, Bobbie would insist that I perform a set for her. Bobbie and Vae would sit on the couch as my audience. Mama always found something to do outside—pick greens out of the garden, wash a load of clothes, clean out the junk house, prune the overgrown bamboo stalks lining the left side of Bobbie's yard. Once I finished singing, she'd find her way back inside, always sour. "I don't know why you encourage this impossible dream of hers."

And Bobbie would say, "Don't you *dare* stifle this baby's dreams."

I would smile. I would feel safe, because Mama couldn't do shit to me with Bobbie around. I could dream at Bobbie's house. I could sing and dance and hope. . . .

Guess that's why I found myself driving to Dallas instead of California after I left Mal's party Friday night.

Wait . . . *Unless you find me first.*

Suddenly, I sit up in bed, in the dark of my room. "*Vae.*"

8:07 a.m.

Mal is backing out of our driveway, with me buckled in the back seat and Mama up front. It's awkward, and I told Mal it would be, but he insisted on driving us to Dallas—saying his car was the most fit to make the trip, especially since we're only going on a hunch and there's a big chance Vae may *not* be there. Neither my mama nor me can afford to waste that much gas.

"Nikki," Mal says to me once we're on the road, "there's a bunch of food from the doughnut shop in that bag beside you. Help yourself, then pass it up here."

"Mal," I groan, giving him the attitude I always give him when he buys me shit. "You're already doing too much by driving us—"

"Girl, if you don't want none, just say that. But hurry up and pass the bag up here," Mama says, holding her hand over her shoulder, not even wasting her time to look back at me. "I ain't eat before we left."

I hand the bag to my mother, holding in all the words on my tongue because I know better than to talk back to her. If I wanna have anything resembling a good day, I know better than to talk back to her.

She takes the bag and starts rifling through it, pulls out a sausage, egg, and cheese croissant sandwich. "Want something?" she asks, holding the bag up to Mal. It's weird. My bones are rigid, and my head is filling up with embarrassment and confusion and something else I can't identify.

"Yes, please. Can I have the other croissant that's in there?" he says.

God, it smells good. My stomach growls.

She gives him the croissant, and he immediately thrusts his hand back at me. "Here, Nikki. I know this is your favorite."

I sigh and sit back against the seat, defiant.

"Take the sandwich, girl," Mama chastises me with her mouth full. "Don't turn down free shit. Take it."

"Yeah, Nikki. Please take it," Mal says, glancing at me through his rearview.

I snatch the food out of his hand, but I don't put it anywhere near my mouth. Not immediately. I watch my mother closely as she rips her teeth through her croissant, and start to identify that feeling I couldn't put a name to earlier: disapproval.

Seeing her rip her teeth through that breakfast croissant turns my stomach.

"Sooo, what about all that stuff you said about Mal and his family only giving me free shit because they feel sorry for me?

You told me not to accept their help."

I can feel Mal's eyes on me in the rearview, but I don't meet them. This is between me and my mother.

She whips her head around and gives me her eyes—eyes that I'm only just now noticing are red and swollen. "You watch your mouth, Shaniqua Lenae. I don't know who you think you talking to like that."

I lick my lips, letting the familiar fear of her gaze wash over me. "I just think it's hypocritical."

Mal is driving through our neighborhood slowly, like any faster and all hell might break loose. He looks worried. Daryl had a way to stop me and Mama when we'd get to arguing, but Mal has absolutely no voice in this.

She studies me over her shoulder, slowly chewing. She kind of looks regretful. "Well, I said all that before I knew him." She glances at Mal then.

When did she get to know him?

"Nevaeh had a lot to say about you," she says to Mal.

His brows shoot up, just as surprised as I am that she actually addresses him directly. He gives her a polite smile. "She did?"

"Yeah, she went on and on—Mal *this* and Mal *that*—"

Okay, wait, when did Vae go *on and on* with Mama? She barely goes on and on with *me*.

"She's definitely a fan," Mama says. "Seems to think you're a good influence on Nikki."

"Ew, what?" I say, frowning. "Vae said that?"

"Uh-huh." Mama nods, not meeting my eye. "It was the night you . . . that night."

She wants to say *the night you left*, but she knows that's not exactly what happened. I didn't just leave. She kicked me out.

"Mal is *not* a good influence on me. If anything, it's the other way around."

"What?" Mal laughs, confused. "Everyone on *Earth* would say the exact opposite, Nikki. You're a bad influence on me."

"I am *not*." I screw up my face. "I've done nothing but good for you."

Mama laughs. She actually *laughs*.

"You've done good? Remember that time you told me to put tea bags in my shoes to help with the smell?"

"Now, wait a minute—I taught *her* that," Mama says, pointing at me.

"Well, it was . . . not as effective as she claimed it would be."

"You were supposed to take them out before you wore them, Malachai!"

He smiles, because we've had this argument several times over the years. "That wasn't *clear*, Nikki. I thought the tea bag would soak up my sweat or something."

"That's just . . . stupid, Mal." I shake my head, playing my part.

And Mama is laughing. She's actually *laughing*.

8:34 a.m.

As soon as we get to Dumas, Mama starts navigating. "You're gonna wanna take 287 when you get to Amarillo."

"Will do," Mal says. "Is the air okay? Too high? Too low?"

"Too high," Mama says, taking the liberty to turn Mal's AC down. Really unexpectedly *comfortable*. I thought this was going to be much more awkward and tense. I guess it started out that way, but then Mama laughed . . .

"You good back there, Nik?" Mal asks.

"Yep."

"You got a CD player in here or something?" Mama asks. "We got six hours ahead of us."

"Oh, yeah, sure," Mal says, fiddling with the touch screen between them. He opens his Apple Music and says, "You can put on anything you want."

She stares at it, not moving. "I don't know how to do all that."

"Here," I say, holding my hand over Mal's seat. He hands me his phone. I type in his passcode, then search her favorite artists on Apple Music—put together a quick playlist titled "Gospel" and press play.

The first song that plays is a Mary Mary song from their old days singing together. It's been so long since I've listened to this kind of music. We'd always turn over gospel CD after gospel CD on the drive to Bobbie's. On the drive anywhere, really. But ever since Aunt Mari gifted me her old car and its endless problems, I haven't ridden much with Mama. This music clogs my throat instantly.

"Hmmm," Mama says, nodding, seemingly satisfied with my song choice and settling in for the ride. I can hear her humming along under her breath. Mal can too. He glances in his rearview at me and smiles. Something in me wants to smile too. The sound of her voice makes me soft, makes me tense, makes me wish everything could be as perfect as her singing.

Mama's voice is the reason I ever wanted to sing in the first place. I hated singing in church, hated singing those ancient Negro spirituals, but I loved watching Mama. When she'd get to sing lead, everyone automatically knew they were in for a treat, because her voice could overtake you. She made singing look so easy.

When it was Mama's turn to sing, no one had to tell me and Vae to pay attention. I always got this feeling watching her sing. I didn't know what it was back then, but now I know it was pride. It made my eyes water, and my skin prickle, and my stomach flip.

She's staring out of her window, and her humming is turning into words. She's full-blown singing now and my eyes are starting to water. I mouth along with her, like I used to do in church. "I just can't give up now. Come too far from where I started from . . ."

And then I sing, confidently, like I did in that bar. I sing as loud as her, harmonizing perfectly. The sound of our voices eclipses the rumble of Mal's tires. It sounds so full.

NOTE TO SELF: Mama gave lead-singer energy with everything she did.

I need to give lead-singer energy with everything *I* do.

Mama's genre was contemporary gospel. She studied the popular gospel artists closely and created her own style of singing. She would get up in front of a church full of people and sing proudly, with her heart and her soul.

I need my own version of that. *Heart and Soul.*

Then I need to make myself known. Convince everyone in my area that I'm really talented. Because that's what my mama did. She sang around Moore County and at Bobbie's church in Dallas, every time we'd visit. We were those church members who only showed up once a year—typically for New Year's. And getting to hear Mama sing was seen as a *treat* for those people. They *treasured* her.

Yolanda Williams was said to be the next Yolanda Adams. She was that good.

One time I asked her what she wanted to be when she was a kid. I had been wanting to ask her, but I knew the timing was crucial. It was a Sunday. She was watching church on television, singing along with all the songs. She was as happy as she could be. So, during a commercial, I said, "Mama, did you ever think about being a singer? What'd you want to be when you were a kid?"

Her eyelids fluttered, but her face didn't fall. I thought she might start frowning, yell at me to leave her alone, but she just shrugged. "I thought about being a physical therapist, or . . ." She smiled. "A court stenographer."

I didn't know what that was. The word surprised me coming from her mouth. "What's that? A sten—"

"The person who types up everything going on in the court."

That's it. A physical therapist or a stenographer. That's all she wanted to be. Not a famous singer or a doctor or anything too big. Mama didn't go to college. She got pregnant with me young. And then she got tangled up with Vae's dad and with becoming a single mother of two.

It was hard to hate her in that moment. Especially when she said, "You know the Anointed Praise Warriors invited me to audition for their group when Deidra left."

"The gospel group? What happened?" I asked eagerly.

She twisted her mouth. "Couldn't find a sitter for you and Vae."

12:11 p.m.

We stop at the halfway point: McDonald's.

Mama tells me to order her a burger the way she likes it, with a Coke, then she hustles to the restroom, leaving me and Mal alone, standing in line at the counter. As soon as she's out of our eyeline, he turns and looks at me with an eager smile.

"What?" I ask.

"Nothing." And yet, he continues to stare at me like he has a secret. "I just haven't gotten a chance to really look at you today."

I haven't had much of a chance to look at *myself.*

This morning, by the time I told Mal that I thought I knew where Vae might be, he said he was on his way. And then I had to explain to Mama why I thought Vae was in Dallas. *That* was a whole thing.

So getting dressed happened mostly in the background of it all.

Instead of overthinking, though, I get distracted by how good *he* looks. He's not wearing his diamond studs or his gold chain or his favorite Jays. He's wearing a blue plaid collared shirt, tucked into tan business-casual shorts. He looks like he's on his way to play golf with his dad, or to a job interview or something. It's not his usual fit, but it still looks really good on him.

"Know what you want?" he asks, reaching for one of my locs.

I nod, not even looking at the menu or the line that's moving up without us. I hold his gaze, then peek down at the shine on his bottom lip. Yesterday morning, waking up in his arms, feels like ages ago. Our night on the rooftop feels even longer. I don't remember how it felt to kiss him.

I think he knows what I'm thinking about, because he grins, glancing down at my lips. He gives the bathroom hall a quick check, then he leans down and pecks my cheek. "I've missed you."

My hand finds his jaw and his prickly stubble, and just as I'm about to pull his lips to mine, the cashier calls, "Next in line, please."

We wait for our order in an empty booth. I stare out the window at Mal's car in the parking lot, kinda wishing this trip could have been just me and him.

"Wichita Falls is so close to the border that we might as well be in Oklahoma right now."

I grin. "Wait, so I'm looking at Oklahoma right now?"

"Yes," he says matter-of-factly. "Practically. That's exactly how it looks. Just more . . . Texas."

While I'm laughing, eyes twinkling, Mama walks up with wet hands, wiping her backs and fronts against a stack of brown napkins. "Bathroom only had the air dryer," she says, sliding into the seat across from us. "Saw a news report talk about how those things just coat your hands with bacteria."

"Yeah, I've heard about that."

I jerk my head back, looking at Mal, confused. Here I was, thinking that Mom was about to go on her daily tirade about some crazy conspiracy she saw on the local news. "You have?" I ask him.

"Yeah." He looks at me, pinched eyebrows. "Everyone has. It was the first thing my mom taught me about public restrooms. Never use the dryer."

"I never knew that," I say, shrugging at him. "I use those things all the time."

"And you haven't died yet?"

"Nope. Not yet." I smile. "My immune system is probably stronger than yours."

"Probably."

And then we're doing that thing we do. Voices lowering as we slowly lean into each other, eyes slowly lowering to each other's lips. Like magnets, eager to crash together again.

"All those summer allergies you get—they're probably just gas station measles," he says.

I laugh, leaning in closer. "Gas station measles? What's gas station measles, Mal?"

"You know what it is," he says, looking at me up from my chin and back down. "You know exactly what that is."

"No, I don't."

"Yes, you *do*."

My mom coughs, and we jump apart, suddenly realizing where we are and who we're sitting across from.

Mal stands up, clutching his receipt. "Maybe I should see if they've called our number yet?" If his cheeks weren't so dark, the beet red would be visible. *I* can see it, because I know what he looks like when he's blushing.

"I don't think they've called it," I say.

"Just gonna make sure." Then he bustles back over to the counter, leaving me stranded with my mama.

And I used to think he was a hero. Wow.

"That boy is pretty funny, ain't he?" Mama says before he's even out of earshot.

"He tries to be," I say. I answer as if this is normal. As if we always act so civil with each other. I don't know what's going on, but it's trying to mess with my head.

I watch as Mal grabs a large bag sitting on the counter. Then he brings it back and sits down beside me, listing off orders and handing out food. "Wait, they didn't give you your barbecue sauce," he says, handing me nuggets and fries. Then he's back on his feet, rushing to the counter before I can argue.

"He's definitely got a thing for you," Mama says, unwrapping her burger. "He'll do *anything* for Shaniqua Lenae." Her head wags, elbows propped up on the table. "I don't know what kind of charm you put on that boy, but it's definitely working."

"I didn't put a charm on him."

"Well, *something* you're doing has him hooked. That boy looks at you like you put the sun in the sky."

She always says that when she thinks two people are in love. She and Bobbie used to talk like that. They'd say all kinds of things about the sun.

"I don't do anything for him. I really don't."

"I guess you're just being yourself." She looks over my shoulder as Mal comes back with my barbecue sauce. "Sometimes that's all it takes."

NOTE TO SELF: What will your stage name be?

My mother says my name in a particular way. She emphasizes the "nee" part. Not just when she's mad, but even when she says my name gently. "*Sha-NEE-quah.*"

When I hear it, I always think that it must be the official way of saying it. Who but my mother would know the precise way of saying my name? She was saying my name while I was still a part of her.

She yells my name when she's angry. Screams it when she needs something. It triggers me, hearing that name. Sha-nee-quah. So, I changed it. Started going by Nikki when I was thirteen. Everyone—Vae, Daryl, even Bobbie—would call me Nikki. Only my mama still calls me Shaniqua.

I don't think I'd ever want a stadium full of people screaming that name.

I'll leave that name in Cactus with my mama.

2:34 p.m.

"So, Malachai," Mama says as we get closer to Dallas. "You're going to school out here next year?"

"Yes, ma'am. UT Dallas."

She nods. "That's good. That's real good. You gonna run track?"

Mal takes an audible breath. "Coach thinks I should, and my dad does too, but I kinda want to be done with trying to balance sports and academics."

"Then quit." She shrugs. "Get your education. You've earned yourself some peace."

"Yes, ma'am," he says, nodding. "That's how I feel."

"I know your parents probably want you to go all the way, but it won't do you no good if it costs you your education. College is supposed to be fun anyway. All the parties, and the new people, and being on your own for the first time. Just don't go crazy out there."

He chuckles politely. "No, ma'am. I won't. I'm not about all that partying. At least not every weekend."

"Yeah," she says. "That's good. Have fun, but be safe."

It's weird to see them chatting like this. It's like she's a completely different person. She's never been this nice to Mal. She's always saying how he's spoiled and uppity, even though she's never said more than two words to him (until now).

"Be careful with them fast girls, though. I know a lot of people find their wives in college, but they also find VD."

"Oh," Mal says, surprised. Then I catch his eye in the rearview. "I was actually hoping I'd still be dating Nikki through college."

My eyes widen. Stomach drops. Heart stops. All the shit.

Mama turns to look at me. She could say some really mean things to me right now. I'm bracing myself for it, but instead she says, "Maybe you can convince her to go to school in Dallas with you."

Mal smiles at me in the rearview. "That would be awesome."

But I'm still stuck on the dating part. We're dating? A spring meadow blooms in the cavity of my chest. We're *dating*?!

Mama instructs Mal on how to get to Bobbie's old neighborhood. I stare out the window at the cracked streets, the leafless, dead trees in every brown yard we pass, and the run-down houses the size of a single room in Mal's house.

Passing all of these homes, *recognizing* them, brings back so many memories. Me and Vae playing in the dirt in our church clothes and immediately getting yelled at by both Mama *and*

Bobbie. Pretending that the out-of-control bamboo stalks bordering the property were like our passage to Narnia—getting yelled at about snakes.

And the pecan tree in the back.

The pecan tree was always base when Vae and I would play hide-and-seek. And when it would start dropping its seeds, Bobbie would send us out with brown paper bags. We weren't to come back inside until they were full. Then she'd turn around and sell them to her neighbors.

The pecan tree sat at the center of her yard. It wasn't just base in our games, it was base in our lives. Under the pecan tree we were safe, we were home, we were whole.

Unless you find me first.

It's the first thing I see when we pull up along the curb, towering over the back of Bobbie's tiny blue house. The second thing I see is a gray minivan parked in her driveway, with the doors open and a bunch of teenage boys spilling out of it.

Found you.

3:10 p.m.

Mama doesn't wait for Mal to turn off the car. She's already storming up the driveway.

"Hey!" she shouts at the boys.

"Uh-oh," Mal says. We both hurry to take off our seat belts and rush after her. Panic crosses every single one of the boys' faces. There's at least six of them—a pretty diverse group—except I don't see Vae anywhere.

"Excuse me," Mama says, "what are you all doing on my mama's property?"

"Oh, umm." A tall, thin Black boy steps out, points his thumb behind him. I recognize him from his Instagram photos—Asher. "We were just—"

"Are y'all the ones who stole a minivan and kidnapped my daughter?" Mama accuses them. And Mal chimes in, "Where's Vae?"

But I tune out the conversation, walking away from the

group of them, staring at the mess of bamboo taking over even more of Bobbie's yard. I make my way around the house, noting the weathered picnic table, the old propane tank sinking into the overgrown grass and the dirt Vae and I used to scrape together to make leaf tacos.

I make it around to the back porch and spot the trunk of the pecan tree. Then I spot my little sister sitting against it, with her hair pulled together in a puff ball, wearing a shirt too big for her and an old pair of jeans. She's looking up into its leaves. Pecan season will be this fall, but there's no telling if this thing still drops seeds. Everything around here is pretty dead, ever since Bobbie stopped taking care of it.

I walk up to her, and she doesn't even drop her chin to look at me. She just says, "I knew you'd come for me eventually."

3:23 p.m.

The boys are spread out along the dilapidated porch, with Asher and Vae sitting together on the steps. Megan said the two of them had something going on, and now I can see it. In the way they sit so close together, and the way Asher leans forward, like he's ready to take the brunt of Mama's scolding for Vae.

"I want all of you to call your parents, right now. Tell them where you are."

The boys all exchange glances. "None of us brought our phones," a tan-skinned blond boy says.

A kid who looks like he belongs in junior high says, "We didn't want our parents to track us until we found Nikki."

"Shut up, Tiny!" a rotund Black boy hisses. Then he fixes his face and winks at me. "Hey, Nikki. Looking good—I mean, it's good to see you. Really good to see you."

I crinkle my brows and nod at him, confused. Is he hitting on me right now? What is he, a sophomore?

Mal says, completely unfazed, "I'll alert the parents on Facebook."

Mama nods at him, then narrows her eyes at Vae's little crew. "What were y'all thinking?"

"Nikki was gone, and it was *my* fault. I had to do something," Vae murmurs, looking down at her shoes.

Mama opens her mouth to retort, hands on her hips, but then she looks at me and pauses. During our conversation this morning, she had the same look in her eyes.

"Why would Vae be at Bobbie's house?" she asked, after I told her my hunch.

"She texted me the night before she ran away that she was going to try and find me."

"Find you?"

"I hadn't been answering any of her texts after . . . that night. She was worried, so she's out there looking for me. And I think she's waiting for me to come find her. I think she's at Bobbie's—"

"Okay, let's go," she said, agreeing so fast I was surprised. I just knew that she was going to rip me a new one for being the reason Vae ran away. But she didn't.

Mal comes back, looking down at his phone. "Timothy, your mother has been notified, and she's notifying everyone else's parents as we speak."

"Aww man," they all groan.

"Get packed up. Let's go," Mama says, spinning on her heel. "It'll be dark before we get back to town."

Asher leans into Vae's ear to whisper something.

"And Vae, you're riding back with us. Let's go!" Mama shouts over her shoulder.

Vae and Asher look at each other, sitting shoulder to shoulder. They both look worried, exchanging thoughts between each other without using words. They look like they wanna kiss. Asher covers Vae's hand with his own and says something under his breath. She nods at him.

The boys all hustle down the steps. Vae hurries to my side, eyes never leaving Asher's, and we walk together to the back seat of Mal's car, readying ourselves for this long drive home.

3:37 p.m.

"Got me running all over the world, looking for you. Why wouldn't you take your phone, Vae?" Mama doesn't give her a chance to answer. "Can't even imagine how much money it would have cost me to get to Dallas, had Malachai not driven us."

She goes on, not pausing long enough for Vae to respond. Vae stares out of her window, silently watching the world flash past, as she likes to do anytime she gets in the car. Mama's gospel music is still playing, albeit quietly, but that and the blasting AC is enough to cover my hiss. "Hey!"

Vae turns to me, apprehension in her gaze.

"Why'd you do that?"

Do what? she mouths to me.

"Run away like that."

She shifts her eyes, like she's already answered this question. "You were missing. And you weren't answering my messages."

"I wasn't missing. I was mad at you."

"Well . . ." She looks ashamed, but too proud to show her shame. "You were missing to *me*."

"I told you the night you got me *kicked out* that I never wanted to hear from you—"

"I know," she says, raising her voice too loud, cutting me off.

The whole car stiffens.

"You know what?" Mama says, whipping her head around. "If you know all this, Nevaeh, then why would you do something so careless?"

But Vae doesn't answer Mama. Instead, she turns to me.

"You don't get to just leave me like that, Nikki. . . . You're the one person I need."

Her eyes shift in the silence of the car. She's so uncomfortable baring her heart. But if Vae was going to bare her heart to anyone, I know it would be me.

6:07 p.m.

Mal turns into the same McDonald's that we stopped at ear-lier today. "I kinda want to go through the drive-through this time," he says, creeping toward the long line.

"Y'all can go through the drive-through. I'll be inside," Mama says, grabbing her purse and opening her door once he comes to a stop.

"Oh," Mal says. "Okay, we'll—"

She slams the door shut and hustles around the front bumper.

"Okayyy," Mal says, watching her go.

"Thank God." Then I take a deep breath and let my body slouch, immediately snapping my eyes over to Vae. "Because this little girl has got some explaining to do."

"What?" she groans. "I already told you why I ran."

"Yeah, but you never told me how you could sell me out like that."

When she looks at my face, guilt drowns out her features.

Then I watch her try to wrangle in her pride. "I, um—" She glances over the edge of Mal's seat.

"What do y'all want?" Mal asks. He's letting his window down, slowly driving up to the order box.

"Nuggets," I say.

"Same," Vae says.

"Drinks?"

"Sprite," we say at the same time. We look at each other, no doubt thinking the same thing: *Jinx, you owe me a Coke.*

He's going back and forth with the person over the order box. They keep misunderstanding everything he says.

Vae turns back to me with those same regretful eyes. "There really isn't an excuse, Nikki. What I did was really, really bad."

"Vae, you've always been selfish. Just never *this* selfish. I mean, you knew what Mama would do to me. You knew how much she hates me. And you still did this."

"I know," she says, still not making eye contact. "I knew that she'd flip out, but I didn't think she'd kick you out." Then she looks at me, the bewilderment clear in her eyes. "She's never done that before. I didn't think she'd go that far."

"How could you not see that she's been *waiting* for an excuse to kick me out?" I shake my head. "Things just aren't as bad for you."

The whole car goes silent. Mal is inching up toward the first window. Both me and Vae are staring at our shoes, not quite capable of looking at each other.

Then, once Mal rolls his window back down to pay, she gets

the courage to say, "I was just really, really mad. You know? About the whole Sarge thing."

I laugh, frustrated. "The Sarge thing justifies what you did?"

"No!" She begs me to understand with her glossy eyes. "Not at all. I just liked him for a really long time, and he was the first guy who never mentioned you before talking to me."

I scrunch my face. "What do you mean? Never mentioned me?"

"Nikki, you're like this icon at our school—and you don't even know it. Boys in my grade are always like, *Whoa, you're Nikki's sister? I don't see it.* You don't know how hard that is. To feel like I don't exist, and that no one can see me behind your shadow."

My face is still, but my brows are pinched. "I had no idea that's been happening to you, Vae. . . . But I do have an idea how it feels to be invisible. That's exactly how I feel at home. You are *so smart*, and you have a promising future—at least Mama is proud of you."

She looks uncomfortable for a second. Vae has never liked talking about how Mama favors her. She always gets a little defensive, because sometimes I forget that she has to deal with Mama just as much as I do, if not more. Mama's always parading her around like a trophy. And that's something about their relationship that I will never be able to fully understand.

After she swallows her discomfort, though, she grins, ever so slightly. I know that all this grinding and late-night studying she does is just to feel loved by our mother. And I can't blame her for that. I can't.

"I had another question for you," I say.

She raises her eyebrows cautiously, while her brown eyes radiate in the evening light.

"Who was that boy?" I ask with a teasing smile.

Her eyes go round. "Who? What?"

"The one who was whispering in your ear. The one sitting really, really close to you on the porch."

"He wasn't sitting that close."

Mal peeks in the rearview as he finds a spot close to the door for when Mama decides to join us. "He was sitting pretty close," he says.

"Shut up, Mal," Vae hisses.

I poke her side, and she squeals. "Is he your boyfriend?"

"No!" She scratches the back of her neck. "I mean maybe? Maybe he's my boyfriend." Then she starts smiling, all girly like.

She looks a lot more relaxed now. She actually looks really different. . . . Different than she did the night I left. Her hair was straightened that night, tips to her shoulders. Now her hair is kinky again, and she's not wearing any makeup. And she looks almost happy.

"Listen, I don't mean to bring up the past," I say, cocking up an eyebrow, "but weren't you *just* making out with Sarge? Since when do you move through boys like that?"

She sighs, rolling her eyes to the window. "It's not like that. Asher and I have . . ." She huffs, while Mal passes out our food. "We have history."

"I've seen them flirting at my football games," Mal says, ripping his teeth through his burger. "Just laughing it up, passing their instruments between each other—nasty, vile shit like that."

"Shut *up*, Mal! That never happened!"

He laughs. "I saw y'all—not even listening to your band director—you were so busy flirting."

"We were not *flirting*." She blushes. When did this little girl grow up on me?

"You had to've been doing *something* if you went and made this man your boyfriend in less than three days."

She smirks at me. "Like I said, we have history."

6:23 p.m.

While we eat, Vae talks nonstop about Asher and "the brass boys." She talks more than I'm used to her talking, and I don't mind one bit. I should already know this stuff about her. I shouldn't have had to learn about Asher from Megan Meadows.

"We didn't steal a random van. We took the brass van—the brass van belongs to brass."

I shift my eyes, confused. "I'm sorry, what?"

"It's a band thing. Even though I'm a woodwind, Asher initiated me into brass."

I blink at her. "Oh, I get it now. Asher is a cult leader."

She laughs, pushing my shoulder. "Asher is not a cult leader. He's . . . too caring and selfless."

"Uh-huh," I say. "Tell me more."

"He has a little brother, who he takes care of." She smiles at me. "Kind of like how you take care of me."

I blush back at her, completely taken off guard, as I'm not

exactly *ready* to forgive her. I force my smile down. "Okay, so what else?"

She obliges excitedly, filling me and Mal in on all the great things about Asher—even the stuff that I don't want to know, like how soft his lips are and how he has a cute mole on his abdomen. I'm so caught up in her excitement, I forget to ask how she knows what his abdomen looks like. Mal keeps cutting in to tease her about being in love, and she keeps denying it.

But then I peer through the big glass windows of the McDonald's and I see my mother sitting alone at a table. She's got her phone beside her food, but she's not looking at it. Mama's never been a huge social media user, even though she doesn't have any IRL friends, or a man, or hardly any family checking in with her. She looks so alone. So small. So human.

Vae goes quiet as her eyes follow my line of sight. Mal sees her too. I mean, I know that only a few days ago she kicked me out of her house, but . . . she's still my mama. There's still some part of my heart that splinters for her.

"I'm gonna go in," Vae says.

I look at her, surprised, and my overprotective big-sister instincts kick in. "You want me to go with you?"

She shakes her head with an unexpectedly mature smile. "The two of us need to talk. It's safer for me to go than you anyway. She won't dare throw me out. You know?"

"But she'll probably still chew you out."

"I can take it." She opens her door. "I'll be back."

Mal and I watch in silence as she goes inside and sits across from our mother. Mama looks up. She doesn't look happy, but also doesn't look angry.

After watching them for a while, Mal turns in his seat to look at me. As soon as our eyes meet, I realize we're completely alone for the first time all day, and that realization instantly makes my body ache to get closer.

"Hey," he says, and smiles, checking me out real quick. His eyes twinkle. His teeth are incredibly white and straight. He goes to the dentist way more often than I ever have. The dentist has always been something of an emergency-only type thing in my house.

At some point he unbuttoned one of the buttons on his shirt, skin on his chest poking out. My eyes stay there for longer than they should.

"You should come up here with me."

"Oh yeah?"

"Yeah. Come sit beside me for a second."

"Why, though?"

He kisses his teeth. "*Nikki.*"

"Okay, okay." I get out. Then as I'm walking around to the passenger seat, I concentrate really hard on not walking too fast. Don't wanna seem too eager or anything—even though I am.

Eager as fuck.

The sun is getting ready to turn everything gold when I open the door and slide into the seat next to him. The inside of his car is so much darker than the white light outside.

His twinkling eyes take me in slowly, smile widening. "I've missed you."

I smile back, turning into squeeze butter.

He leans closer to me, with his eyes on my lips. I lean closer too. It's like magnets pulling us closer, pushing our lips together, quite brazenly—our noses bumping. I pull away slowly, and the sound of our lips parting fills the car. Really sweetens the kiss. So much so that Mal grabs my chin and plants one, two, three more kisses. Then his eyes lift to mine.

Breath heavy, beating against my mouth, he asks, "Did you miss me?"

"Yes," I answer quickly. I know there isn't much time before Vae and Mama come back.

I reach across the console and place my hand on his chest, right below his collarbone, moving in to kiss him again. And as our lips meet, my hand slides down his chest and rests against his abs.

There's not a lot of time between now and Friday.

"Wait . . ." He whispers, then kisses me one more time before he says, "Wait, baby."

My eyes open, and I pull away. "What is it?"

He takes a slow, deep breath, laughing on his exhale. "I wanted to tell you something when you came up here."

"Oh?" I remove my hand from his abs and lean against the console instead. "Okay?"

He settles his smile and falls into my eyes. "I wanted you to know that I'm proud of you."

I raise an eyebrow. "For what?"

"Like, I mean, how you handled today. With your mom. Y'all were civil as fuck. It was actually kinda nice?"

I smile and nod. "No, actually, *yeah*. It has never been this easy dealing with her. What do you think that's about, Mal?"

"I think you made your point." He shrugs, sliding his hand up my arm. "I think she missed you, and she finally realized that she was being irrational."

I screw up my face. "Do you really think it's possible for her to miss me? I don't think you know her well enough."

"Maybe not. But what I *do* know is, things are going to be better after this. I feel like the tide is really turning, Nikki. Maybe you guys will even repair your relationship." He's smiling at me with so much hope. *God*, it's cracking me wide open.

He wags his head. "Seriously, Nikki, I know what it's like to have an absent mom. And I also know what it's like to *love* an absent mom."

"I don't love—" I stop myself, because I know it's not something I'm ever supposed to say out loud. *I don't love my mother.*

"Yes, you do," he says, looking very sure of himself. "It's fine. That's just natural." He turns to the windshield then, and casually places his hands on the wheel. "I mean, I dreamed about having a moment like this with my mom. Just a nice, un-crazy day." When his eyes return to me, they're slowly lifting again, and so are his lips. "You *deserve* this, Nikki. Just a nice, un-crazy day with your mom. You deserve this all the time."

NOTE TO SELF: How are you going to leave now, Nikki, when you have this boy going around saying that you're dating?

10:05 p.m.

Of course I want him to want me to stay.

Of course I want him to beg me, cry about me—care that much for me.

But I never expected him to make me want to stay too. For me to hope for the impossible, like I try to never let myself do anymore.

The whole ride home, Mama acts extremely human, and I can't help but think that maybe Mal was right. Maybe things *will* be different after this.

She sleeps for much of the way home, after complaining about how she has to work early tomorrow morning. Mal puts on his soft R & B playlist—my favorite playlist. Vae stares out of her window, even when it gets too dark to see anything.

I stare out of my window, too, thinking of how to reply to Mal's text—sent while he was sitting at the last stoplight. **Truth or dare.**

It takes an hour for me to text him back: **Truth and dare.**

He doesn't reply at the next stoplight or the next. He keeps me on edge all the way until he pulls into our driveway.

"Mom," Vae says, shaking Mama's shoulder.

Mama lifts her head, stares at the empty, dark trailer house for a few seconds, then turns to Mal. "Thanks for helping us today."

"It's no problem," he says, his voice way too jolly.

"Welp," she croaks, opening her door and lifting her tired bones out of the car. "I'm going to bed."

"All right, good night," he says to her. She nods, not saying it back. We don't say that in our house.

Vae gets out, thanking him too. "Be good," he says as she shuts her door.

I open mine slowly, staring at his face in the rearview mirror. "You not gonna reply to me?" I ask, in the brief second that we're alone.

"Check your phone," he says.

At some point he must have snuck and texted me. I get out of his car, and he rolls his window down as I'm passing by. **Is it true that you're free to spend the day with me tomorrow . . . ? I dare you to spend the day with me.**

I smirk, reading it. "Hey," he says. I turn into his twinkling eyes and that gorgeous smile. God, he's making this difficult. "Text me your answer, okay? Good night."

I hesitate at first, not used to the taste of those words in my mouth. But it's all I can do right now. I can't kiss him in front of my mama's house, even though I really want to. So I say it back to him. "Good night."

Once I get inside, and as he's backing out of my driveway, I text him: **See ya tomorrow.**

Two seconds later, he texts back: 😘

10:10 p.m.

The house is mostly dark. I look down the far hall, where the laundry room and Mama's room is, and spot the blue light of her television flashing against the floor. Down my and Vae's hall, the bathroom light is on with the door closed. So I slip out of my shoes and creep into Vae's room.

While she takes a shower, I lie facedown on her bed and listen to the water, thinking about tomorrow with Mal. She comes out after about ten minutes—trained like me to take quick showers. "If you're sleeping in here, you're gonna have to move over."

"You're tiny! What do you need that much room for?"

"To stretch my body. Just because I'm small doesn't mean I don't need as much room as you. Plus I slept in a van with a bunch of loud-ass boys last night. I would like to get some sleep tonight, please."

"Fine, fine, fine." I scoot over until my body touches the

wall. She turns off the light.

"You gonna sleep in all your clothes?" she asks, getting in bed beside me.

"I'll get up in a minute," I say, closing my eyes, head on the edge of her pillow.

"No, you won't."

I turn over on my side, facing her, pushing my feet up against her legs.

"Ew, get off me," she hisses, kicking my shins.

I squeal, "Clip your toenails, you gremlin."

"Be careful. I'll scratch you up."

"Keep them toes over there!"

And as we're giggling, pulling the covers up to our chins, I'm reminded of when we were kids. When Vae would beg to watch a horror movie, knowing it'd make her see ghosts for the next few days. I would always end up having to sleep with her those nights. And we would always end up talking about stupid shit. Just sleepy mumbles about inchworms and where they came from. But at some point during the night, those convos always led us somewhere closer to each other.

I calm my laughter and blink my eyes at her until she stops laughing too. We look at each other, and just like that, all that pain we had been pushing away *all day* comes flooding into our eyes. We're not gonna cry . . . but it sure feels like we might. Because we know exactly how much the other is hurting.

"What'd you and Mama talk about in McDonald's?"

She shrugs, blinking away the shininess in her eyes. "She

was just asking about Mal the whole time."

"Mal?"

"Yeah, like asking what I thought about him and his family and their money and stuff."

I furrow my brow. "And what'd you tell her?"

"I don't know." She shrugs again. "Something like, 'Mal's great, his family is nice' and that I think his donations to us are just his way of paying girlfriend fees for Nikki."

"Girlfriend fees?" I whisper. "What the hell are girlfriend fees?"

"*Fees*," she says, like it's obvious. "You know—boys like to show their worthiness to date you by paying *fees*." She shakes her head at me, like she can't believe I don't know what she's talking about—going into full TED Talk mode. "Movie tickets, dinner, shopping, ice cream at the mall," she lists off. "And they figure if they pay enough fees, they will pay their way into your vagin—"

"Vae," I cut her off, then cover my laughter with my hand. "What the hell are you talking about? Girlfriend fees? You told Mama that?"

"Mama understood immediately," Vae says. "You're the only one who's behind here. She was like, 'Yeah, I figured they had to be more than just friends—way that boy runs after her like a puppy.'"

"He does not *run after me like a puppy*," I say, offended.

"Nikki, be serious."

"Vae, *you* be serious. Malachai is his own . . . person.

He—I—we're not—"

"Yeah, so, I told her that y'all have been obviously in love with each other since the eighth grade and that it's pathetic, and then I told her something about you both being cowards and stupid."

"Vae!"

She tries reeling it back in. "But that you're definitely, *definitely* in love with each other."

"You told her that we're *in love*?" I ask, struggling on the L word.

"Yeah." Vae laughs. "Because you are."

"I am not in love with Mal." There's that L word again, struggling to hop off my tongue.

"Whatever, Nikki. We saw you making out in the car."

"Wait, you saw . . . ? What did Mama say?"

"It was kind of weird," Vae says, lowering her voice. "She, like, stared at y'all for a few seconds, then she said that she really hoped he would take *care* of you."

I stare at the ceiling. "That's weird."

"It was really weird. I was surprised, but I said that I was sure he would. He'd do anything for you."

I ignore that last part. I'm still caught up on her reaction to seeing us kiss. She hopes he takes *care* of me? What does that even mean?

The moon is bright, low, and full. Crickets chirp to fill the silence between me and Vae. We don't talk for a long time, and I think she must be asleep, until she turns over on her side to face me and says, "Are y'all, like, dating now?"

The question catches me off guard. "Um . . . in Mal's words, we are."

"What does that mean? You don't wanna date him?"

"Of course I wanna date him. I've wanted to date Mal since I met him." I sigh. "But Vae, I don't know if I'm coming back."

I can feel her energy drop suddenly. "Why are you still going to California? Didn't you miss the audition?"

"There's another one this weekend."

I can hear her suck in her breath. "No, but . . . you have to come back. Why wouldn't you come back?"

"If I get the spot, I won't need to. There's gonna be a crazy advance that comes with the contract—enough to get my own place out there. Why should I come back?"

"For—for school," she stammers. "Graduation, prom—"

"None of that matters to me. My grades are barely good enough to graduate. And I'm not going to prom."

"But what about me?" she asks.

Why is that everyone's question when they find out about me leaving?

"Vae, you'll be fine."

"No, I told you, I need you."

"We can still talk every day. This was going to happen eventually."

"Yeah, but I just didn't think it'd be so soon. I thought I had at least a few more months with you."

Her voice is shaking—I can hear it. And it brings heat to my face and my neck. "Vae, you'll be fine. And I promise I'll visit as soon as I can. A few weeks, tops, then I'll be right back. Or maybe I could even fly you out to LA. Wouldn't that be cool? To be on a plane for the first time?" I'm trying to cheer her up, but it's not working.

"Yeah, I guess," she says coolly.

If we were the kissing and hugging type, I'd pull her into my chest. She's so strong, and she doesn't even know it. I sincerely believe that Vae was never too "afraid" to run away—she's just been smart and strategic and ready. In no time, she'll be running away from this shithole town, just like me.

@AntTheProdigy: Make sure you bring that same energy when you get here. I believe in you, but Derek found a girl during the first audition that he swears will be the lead singer. Please, prove him wrong.

Tuesday

6:37 a.m.

Mama's already gone to work. I tiptoe across the kitchen, wearing the same thing I had on yesterday, looking down at my phone.

Mal: **Call me as soon as you wake up. Even if it's super early.**

I don't question it. I call.

"Hey, good morning."

"Hey," I say, completely under his spell, but still trying to sound surprised. "What's up?"

"Oh, nothing. I was just trying to see when you wanted to come over."

"How soon is too soon?"

He clears his throat. "It's never too soon. I will come get you this second."

"I need to take a quick shower and tell Vae where I'll be, but that's cool."

"Be there in twenty."

I smile. "See you in a sec."

Then we hang up. And I'm entirely too smitten for my own good. Like, he has *no right* being so sexy—*sounding* so sexy—this early in the morning.

I bite the corner of my lip and scurry across the living room on my tiptoes when a voice emerges from within the shadows—

"Can Mal take me to Asher's when he comes to pick you up?"

I stop and lose my shit, almost *peeing* myself. "What the fuck, Vae?"

"I thought you knew I was standing here," she claims. "I could have sworn you looked right at me."

I stomp away, rolling my eyes. "We need to get you a bell before you give somebody a heart attack."

"Is that a yes?" she calls after me.

I groan, "Yes."

7:04 a.m.

Vae is the first one out the door. "Hey, Mal," she says, running past him down the steps.

"Wait, Vae, I'm here for Nikki."

I step through the door right behind her. "Is it okay if we drop her at Asher's house first?" I lock the front door, then spin around to face him.

He's *dressed* dressed, but not like yesterday. He's back to his favorite Jordans, gold-linked wristband on his Apple Watch, chain around his neck. I'm wearing my lowest cut T-shirt, my pushy-uppiest bra, and my best pair of jeans—the ones with the holes in the knees and the slashes across the thighs. The ones I was never allowed to wear to school.

"Yeah, that's cool," he says, after he's done drinking me in. He laces his fingers between mine loosely, like he's *comfortable* holding my hand. And he walks me around to the passenger side of his Charger.

When he opens the door, we find Vae looking up at us, perturbed. "Um, hi?" she says.

"Move," I say. "Get in back."

"I already have my seat belt on, Nikki. Asher's house is right up the road. Just—" She lifts a hand like she's already tired of my shit. It's way too early for all this attitude.

Mal merely smirks at me and proceeds to walk me to the back seat. "I'm a little scared of your sister. See you in a sec, though, baby?"

"Yep. Can't wait, baby," I say, sarcastically, ducking my head inside. But I have a much harder time saying *baby* than he seems to. He enjoys saying it, I can tell.

Baby. That's another one of those words that struggles to make it up my throat. It's something mothers call their children. Something aunts call their nephews, even after they grow up. Something lovers call each other. . . .

Baby is one of those words that I wanted to hear, all my life, more than anything, from my mother. Words like *love, sorry, good night.*

Vae and I taught each other the word *sorry*. It takes a while for us to say it to each other. But we say it. And Mal just taught me good night last night. So. I mean, I'm learning. I'm working on it.

Hmnm. Baby . . .

In Asher's driveway, which I notice is only about two houses down from Megan's yellow trailer, I get out at the same time Vae does. "Hey," I say, before she can run up his steps, "are his parents here?"

"No, he's watching his little brother while his dad is at work."

"Do his parents know *you're* here?"

She gives me an awkward shift of her eyes, then stuffs her hands into her pockets. "His dad doesn't really care that I'm here. He doesn't care about much, really."

I nod, pocketing my questions about Asher's family for later. I get a good look at her before I let her out of my sight. "Get home before Mama does."

"I will. And you should too," she says, giving me a hard look.

"Yeah, okay."

"Nikki, I'm serious."

"I *know.* Text me if you need me. Okay? See ya later!" Then I slide into the front seat of Mal's car and watch her roll her eyes at me through the tint.

"Where to next?" I ask, putting on a smile for Mal.

"Have you eaten breakfast yet?"

7:34 a.m.

I can smell the fry grease from here—makes me want to get everything on the menu, and I'm not even that hungry. Mal lets his window down, allowing the heat and the car exhaust outside to beat against our faces. Then he reaches for the red order button.

"Wait! I don't know what I want yet."

He falls back against his seat, impatient, as I lean over the console to peer out of his open window. I bargain between getting mozzarella sticks, Tater Tots, or onion rings, while he stares at my profile. "You always end up getting the same exact thing every single time—a small order of *everything*, so long as it's fried."

I squish my face to the side, thinking. I mean, he's right. I want to taste *everything* that touches that fry grease. "I might change it up this time, since it's technically breakfast time."

As I stare at the burger and then the hot dog choices, he

doesn't refrain from staring at my face. After all, I'm kind of leaning all up in his personal space—all up in his body heat. "Do you really need to look at the menu that hard? You ain't got it memorized by now?"

"Why?" I say, rolling my neck so that I'm looking directly in his eyes. "Do you want me out of your space, Malachai?"

"Nah." He combs his teeth over his bottom lip as his eyes linger on my mouth. When he smiles, my throat catches on fire. Then my chest, my *thighs* catch on fire, as I imagine what it'd be like to sit in his lap right now. "You can stay in my space for however long you want."

"So this is okay with you?" I lean farther over the console, playfully leaning closer to his face while I stare at the bottom of the Sonic menu panel.

"Is *this* okay?" he answers, then he slides a hand around my elbow, leans his face in, and brushes his nose across my cheek. I don't say anything. It's taking all of my concentration to remember how to breathe. *In through your nose, Nikki. Close your damn mouth.*

But then he starts kissing the edge of my jaw, soft and slow. I can feel my muscles about to give out, I'm so weak. My head turns, and our mouths meet instantly.

"Seriously, Nikki," he says against my lips. "What do you want?"

One, two, three more kisses . . . and we can't stop.

7:55 a.m.

Back at his house, the living room sofa is still pushed against the far wall, as it was for his party. Neither of us feels like moving it back—especially not with hot food in our hands. So, we run upstairs and spread everything out on his bed. Turn on his PC and pick up where we left off in that indie horror game.

I'm lying on my stomach, tossing Tater Tots into my mouth. "*Mal*"—I roll my eyes—"you've already searched that room. Just go upstairs." He searches the room anyway, and I groan, biting down on a mozzarella stick dipped in marinara.

"You know what, Nikki? You do a lot of shit-talking for somebody who ain't playing."

"Just admit that you're scared, Mal."

"No. The only reason I got a crowbar right now is because I searched all the rooms. If it was *you*, you'd be walking 'round here weaponless."

"No, I'd be walking around killing mofos."

He turns to me, unconvinced. "Yeah? You think so?" He slides his controller over to me. "Prove it."

I look at him like he's out of his mind.

"Go on. Show me how it's done." He smiles, like he's already proven his point.

I grab the controller with a smug expression, then immediately leave the dark room he's searched at least twice. "Some ugly clown boy ain't about to scare me out of my own house."

"All right." Mal laughs. "But make sure you time your attack precisely. Sometimes he dodges and goes for the kill—he's really good at that shit."

"Yeah, yeah," I murmur, climbing the creaky stairs.

"You can't run up the stairs like that! He'll hear you."

"You think I care? Let him come at me! I'm ready for—"

I take one step onto the top floor, and out of nowhere that ugly-ass clown boy slices me with a chainsaw. I barely see it coming. Any time that he gives me to fight back I use to scream and throw the controller across the bed.

The room goes black, then a bloody "Game Over" drips down the screen. We are silent.

Mal looks at me, blinking. I blink back at him, my blood running hot from embarrassment. "Um," I say. "That was . . . unexpected."

He stares at me, calmly, still silent. Laughter is building up inside both of us at the same time, and then all at once, we burst. I fall back on his bed, holding my abs. He rolls onto his side, eyes closed. "You can't say another word to me,

Nikki! You died in *five seconds*. You will never live this down!" And while I'm laughing, he's poking at my sides, making me laugh even harder. "You lost my crowbar, and everything else I found!"

"A crowbar ain't gon' do shit against a chainsaw."

Then he's hovering over me, hands pressed into the mattress on either side of my body. "It would if you knew what you were doing."

His thin-linked chain is hanging down from around his neck. I reach up and tug on it lightly. "Okay, fine. Sorry I lost your crowbar."

"You really should be."

I take the liberty of letting my hands slide down his T-shirt. He leans down to kiss me. We are completely alone, in this big ole house, in the dark of his room. This is what I've been daydreaming about for days. He shifts his body on top of me, and I try to wrap my legs around him, but my jeans are too tight. . . .

I'm getting ready to take them off when he lifts himself up and lies on his back next to me. "Nikki, I need to tell you something." My mind conjures up at least ten worst-case scenarios before he finally comes out and says, "I'm supposed to go to the high school and train with Coach in a little bit."

"Oh," I say. "Oh, sure. Okay." I fix my tank top and my bra straps. "So . . . should I go home?"

"No," he rushes to say, placing a warm hand on my thigh. "I want you to stay here. If you want."

"Yeah, sure. It beats staying in my hot-ass room at home."

He smiles and steals a quick kiss. "I'm supposed to be there at nine. Then stay until noonish."

"Okay, that's not too bad."

He gets out of bed and starts taking off his jewelry. "But *then*, I'm supposed to go help Mr. Dawson around his house."

I groan.

"I know," he says. "But I gotta get my volunteer hours in for Beta Club."

"It's spring break," I say as he crawls over to hook his gold chain around my neck. "Aren't you supposed to take a break?"

"I won't be gone that long, I promise. Then when I get back," he says with a cute smile, "we're gonna have fun. Trust me."

"And what am I supposed to do until then?"

"Whatever you want. You're welcome to hang out in my dad's den—play his keyboard and his drums and shit. *Or* watch a movie. I know you love that surround sound."

"I can't just hang out in your dad's den."

"What are you talking about? We hang out in there all the time."

"Yeah, *we*. Not just me."

He rolls his eyes. "Well, I trust you. My dad trusts you. It's fine." He walks to the door and turns on the bedroom light, nearly blinding me. When I can finally see again, he's staring at me, biting his bottom lip.

"What?" I ask.

"Nothing. I just like seeing you in my chain. It's sexy on you."

"Get out of here," I say, blushing.

"All right, all right." He turns and heads out of the bedroom, snatching his phone and keys. "I'll see you in a bit."

"Can't wait," I say, playing with his chain around my neck.

9:41 a.m.

After Mal leaves, all I really want to do is swim in his bed. In his scent. In whatever heat is left over from his body. But I don't have much time. The audition is this Saturday.

I sang through my songs at home, but my delivery wasn't perfect. It was *fine*, but I have to be better than fine. I have to prove to Derek Atkins that I have what it takes to lead his girl band.

I've been in Mal's home gym since the second he pulled out of his driveway, warming up my voice. I should have brought my keyboard with me this morning, but I knew it'd raise questions with Mal—or at least a conversation about my future that I'm not interested in having.

I sit on Mal's bench press and sing the acoustic version of my song "Sidewalks." I take my time, giving life to every note and every run. The sound is crystal clear. Makes me remember how scared I was of going inside Mama's house yesterday—the nerves must have shown in my voice, because now that I'm in this big house, all alone, I sound as good as my heroes.

After singing a cappella, I perform "Bow Down" to the performance track, and I lose myself for hours in my performance, singing the lyrics like I mean them: "So bow down and give me everything I ask for." When the drill hi-hats come in and my dance turns from sexy to hip-hop, my back suddenly crashes into someone. "What the—" I jump and spin around to find an apologetic Mal, holding his hands up in surrender.

I rush to turn off my music, my heart in my throat. "What the hell are you doing, sneaking around like that? Did *Vae* put you up to this?" I ask, hands on my hips.

"I didn't mean to scare you. I just got back, and I heard you jumping around up here, so I thought I'd make sure you were okay." Then he glances around the room, smiling cautiously. "Turns out you're just rehearsing."

I nod, trying to slow my breath. "Second audition is Saturday. I wanna be ready."

"And how do you feel now? Are you scared?"

"Nope. I'm pretty confident." Even though I'm shaking in my boots, I can't give him any kind of in to try and change my mind about going.

He nods at me, seemingly impressed. "All right, great. That's good to hear." Then he inspects my gaze for a while. "I actually got something for you." He backs into the hallway and picks up a shoebox he had set on the floor.

I stare at the box like it's diseased. "What did you do?"

He opens the lid, revealing a pair of black stilettos covered in glitter. And my eyes pop out of my head. *They're gorgeous.* And no doubt expensive.

"Mal?" I say, waiting for him to explain.

"They're shoes."

"Yeah, no shit. But . . . are they for *me*?"

"Yeah," he says, with a knowing smirk. I can tell he's gearing up to reveal something. Something I'm not going to approve of.

He says, "I figured you would need some shoes for your performance in Lubbock tonight." He thrusts the shoes into my hands, then crosses the room to start my music over.

12:11 p.m.

"What did you *do*, Mal?!" I chase after him, one arm out in front, trying to catch him by the shirt.

"I lied to you, Nikki." His voice is jiggling because he's running down the stairs—running away from me.

"I didn't actually have to train with Coach today." He gets to the bottom, spins around with his hands up. "Don't kill me, don't kill me."

"What. Did. You. Do?" I stop right in front of him.

"You know how my dad represented that rap group from California? When they had that lawsuit against a bar in Dallas—"

"What does that have to do with anything?"

"My dad had to meet with a club promoter for the case, and they actually, like, hit it off. They hang out occasionally—"

"Malachai," I snap, urging him to get to the point.

"Anyway, the promoter works for clubs across Texas—even one in Lubbock . . . which is where you're going to be performing tonight."

I slowly process what he's saying. After a few blinks, I ask, "So you got your dad's friend to get me a gig tonight?"

"Yes, that's what I was out doing today."

Nerves switch on in my gut, bringing with them a wave of nausea. "So, I'm performing at a club tonight?" I look down at my feet, filling up with a slow panic.

"Yes, and you're gonna kill it! You said you're feeling confident, right?"

"No!" I say, appalled. "Now that this is actually *happening*, hell no, I'm not confident. I've never—"

"I know," he cuts me off. "Never done a talent show or anything. But I know you're talented live," he says, grabbing hold of my arms, "because I've seen you live. But how will you do in front of Ant, or Derek, or your competition?"

I swallow hard, looking up into his calming gaze. "So you did this for me, to give me practice?" I ask. "For my audition in *California*?"

He looks slightly confused, like he doesn't understand why I'm so surprised. "Yeah, Nikki. I'm not against you going to California. I'm against you *staying* in California. Go! But just come back afterward—that's all I'm asking."

"So, you think the audition is a good idea?"

He slowly releases my arms. This is it. These are the feelings we never talked about. The fight that led us to go mute for weeks.

"Because I specifically remember you saying the audition would be a mistake. That it could ruin my career before it even got started."

My disappointment in him comes flooding back. How could

he not *congratulate* me? After all the years he's watched me write song after song, and teach myself how to play keyboard, teach myself how to use a DAW, watched me burn my meager savings on a microphone. How could he not immediately jump for joy when he heard me say, "Ohmygod, Mal, Ant—that producer I was telling you about—DM'd me on Instagram!"?

I thought he would scream louder than I had. But instead, he stared at me in silence. "Audition for what?"

"Derek Atkins is putting together a girl group!"

"A *girl group*?" The disgust in his tone was unwarranted, but not totally surprising. We'd been silently fighting for *weeks*. Harboring unsaid feelings for each other.

He gives me an exasperated sigh even now. He really doesn't want to talk about this, but we need to.

"I couldn't believe that's how you reacted. I came to you with good news and you . . . *shat* on it."

"I've thought about how I handled that moment literally every night since." He reaches out for my shoulders. "I shouldn't have been so cruel. I knew how important it was to you—I'm sorry. And I am really happy for you, Nikki. I am. I should have told you how proud I was. Those weeks of not talking to each other were *hell* for me."

After a few seconds of silence, I say, "Yeah, it was hell for me too."

NOTE TO SELF: He's on board with me going—just not on board with me staying.

But like I told Vae, I'll visit as soon as possible. And maybe I can fly him out too. There's no reason this week has to be the last time I see him. . . .

2:34 p.m.

Okay, so, despite everything, Mal's right. I've never per-formed in front of a crowd. Yes, I'm good on video, and I'm superb when I'm alone with my own reflection, but in front of someone like *Derek Atkins*?

Fuck.

Okay, it's fine. I got this.

"I don't know, Nikki," Mal says, straddling his weight bench, "it looked perfect to me."

I stare at myself in the wall-length mirror across the room. I gave up on my jeans a long time ago, opting for an old pair of shorts Mal found for me in his dresser.

"One more time," I say.

He takes a deep breath, glancing at his watch, then starts the track over.

I turn on my performance persona. She's confident and sexy and irresistible when I, myself, feel like a pile of dog shit. Being a musical artist is about more than just singing and music production. Becoming a *famous* artist requires an image, a brand, something that fans come to expect from you. So I built a whole new person—I built myself up, like a sculpture in a garden, and when I become her, everything I do is art.

I move my body fluidly and purposely, getting into my routine, when the gym door opens and I jump out of my skin. "Who the—" I spin around. I'm just about tired of people scaring me today, but then my eyes show me the culprit, and I barely believe it. "Riley?"

"Hey," she says, a guilty look on her face. Mal hurries to turn the music off. "I tried knocking downstairs, but clearly y'all couldn't hear me."

Mal gives her a *duh* expression. "You could have just texted me."

"Wait, you knew she was coming?" I narrow my eyes and switch my head between them. "What's happening? What are you doing here?" *She's not even supposed to know I'm in town.*

Mal smiles mischievously. Then Riley strikes a pose, holding up a bulging purple bag. "Hi, I'm Riley. I'll be your stylist and makeup artist today."

3:18 p.m.

I'm sitting on Mal's toilet seat in his guest bathroom. Riley's playing Beyoncé on her phone, standing over me with a brand-new tube of eyeliner.

"I knew it, I knew it, I knew it," she keeps saying. "I knew you were in love with each other." Thank God the door is closed, or Mal would definitely be laughing at how much she's gushing over us. My cheeks are burning up as it is.

"We haven't used those words, Riley."

"Not yet, but you *will*. I know it. Watching you two has been like watching four years of foreplay."

"Ew."

"Don't *ew* me. I know you've been all over each other since Saturday."

I open my eyes, and she frowns, so close to poking my eye out with black eyeliner. "How much did Mal tell you?" I ask, horrified.

"*Everything*." Then she laughs, motioning for me to close my eyes. "Ultimately, he told me that he wanted to surprise you with a performance tonight. And the way he said it—*God*, I could hear the heart-eyes emoji all up in his voice."

"Whatever." I smile.

"I'm serious. He's got it bad for you. I knew you'd come back for him."

My stomach sinks, and I sink with it. "Riley." I say her name quietly. "I'm still going to California," I admit.

There's a moment of silence between us. "But you're coming back, right?" she says, and I can hear the hurt in her voice. "I thought your mom let you come back home."

I open my eyes. "I mean, she did, but—"

"But what, Nikki? Mal broke up with Cynthia for you. He's supporting your decision to go to the audition. Your mom let you come back home. What's the problem? Why can't you come back and graduate, go to *prom*, and have a normal fucking relationship with the guy you love?"

These days, I don't have a clear answer. For why I absolutely must *never come back to this sinkhole of a town.* I was angry at Mama. And hurt. I wanted to make a point. But then yesterday happened. *Yesterday.* I just don't wanna get sucked in again. I don't want another crack in my heart.

"Nikki, at this point, I feel like you're self-sabotaging."

"I'm not," I argue. "Nothing is certain, Riley. Absolutely nothing about my life is certain."

"Except how much Malachai Brown loves you," she says immediately.

I resist shaking my head, especially when she has pointy shit so close to my eyes. "I can't live off of Mal's love."

She snorts. "Have you seen his house? His car?"

"Riley," I snap.

"I know, I know. And I'm not asking for you to give up your future. Just come back after the audition and finish high school. Get your diploma. Go to prom. Be Malachai Brown's girlfriend—do you know how much status you'll have? People will bend over backward for you."

She goes on and on about how great my future could be. And I only half listen. Nobody understands that the most uncertain thing about my life is where I'll live if I do come back.

4:09 p.m.

Riley left as soon as she finished laying my edges. Mal and I are sorta running late. The slot is at seven, and it will take more than three hours to get there, if we stop for food.

I step out of the bathroom, wearing Riley's black Fashion Nova dress and the shoes that Mal just bought me—probably under Riley's direction. Put together, they look incredible—Riley's vision completed. *My* vision completed. This is exactly what I imagined I'd be wearing for the video of "Bow Down," if I ever had enough money to hire a professional videographer.

I walk down the hallway, glancing through the crack in Mal's bedroom—it's dark. He must already be downstairs. Hell, I know he is by the fog of cologne I walk through. The smell hits my nostrils and I swoon. It reminds my lips how his lips feel against them. The whole top of my chest burns red under the skin. Then I round the corner, and he's standing at the bottom of the stairs, waiting for me.

He looks up at the sound of my footsteps, wearing a whole-ass suit.

Holy fucking shit, he looks good, with that sleek gold chain around his neck, that crisp white shirt and fitted black suit. And when he sees me, his eyes light up at my face, then slowly they make their way down my body. He's smiling the whole time and I don't have a choice but to smile too.

By the time I hit the first floor, his eyes have made their way down to my shoes, where they linger. His smile widens. "Fuuuck," he hisses, bringing his eyes back up the length of me. "I didn't get the chance to say that to you at my party." Then he meets my eye. "*That* would have been my first reaction, but—"

"Cynthia was sitting in your lap," I say.

"Right. But I've wised up since then." He sashays forward, hands landing on my hips. "And I lucked out by getting with Nikki—the girl I've been choked up about since eighth grade." He looks down into my eyes, and I'm surprised to find his gaze so intense. He's studying me closely, looking for something. "Nikki, you look absolutely beautiful," he says, laying all jokes aside.

"I, um—thank you."

He grabs my hand. "Ready?"

I nod. *Now* I am.

NOTE TO SELF: The words

Beautiful

Sorry

Love

Good night

Baby

5:15 p.m.

We're heading out of Amarillo now—'bout a forty-five-minute drive from Dumas—after having stopped for food. Mal got Cane's chicken, while my stomach churned with nerves. He begged me to eat something, but I was sure anything but water would fuck up my voice.

I'm staring at the outskirts of Amarillo flashing past my window. Mal's speeding up as we get closer to no-man's-land, and the music is kinda soft. I'm mumbling the lyrics under my breath.

"You wanna piss on my name, then turn around and say hey," Mal says, a notch louder than me. Then he turns up the volume, and the twelves in the trunk rumble through my chest. Without hesitation, we both shout the chorus. "You got a problem—with how I make art—so fuck everything that you say!"

I close my eyes on that line and keep them closed for the

next line. "Who the fuck are you?"

I'm not the biggest Vontae fan, but even *I* gotta admit this is a good song for pregaming. I recite the lyrics and try to internalize his confidence. *Who the fuck are you?*

I'm trying to forget about that DM from Ant, but I can't stop worrying. Derek found a girl he loves already. How am I supposed to sway his opinion? I mean, I'm no Beyoncé looking for my Kelly and Michelle. But I keep telling myself that *Ant* approached *me*. He saw my music video and loved it. There's no reason to think that I don't have what it takes.

This performance tonight is my chance to prove to *myself* that I have what it takes.

6:57 p.m.

Closer to Lubbock, I feel drunk on his cologne and his smiles and the sound of his laughter.

Not to mention that suit, clinging to his arms and legs.

The music has been off since we left Abernathy, but the car hasn't felt empty or awkward at all. It's actually been pretty loud—the static between us.

He drives with his left hand on the wheel. Right elbow resting on the console, hand open and up for the taking. I stare at the way he's holding his fingers—like an invitation to grab hold. I run one of my locs behind my ear and subtly rest my elbow on the console, beside his. He subtly moves his elbow close enough to bump mine, tipping my hand forward and down into his grasp. Our fingers naturally lock, and my body tenses and loosens at the same time.

We hold hands all the way to the bar, but once we park at the club, he lets me go. We run across the parking lot, me a few steps behind him, until we get inside. Immediately, Mal is swarmed by a white man with a potbelly and a teeny woman with a clipboard. "Malachai, this is bad business."

"I know, I know, Kirk, but you owe my dad anyway. I know about that game of poker y'all played." Mal motions to me. "*This* is Nikki."

"Well," Kirk says with a sleazy kind of greasy smile and a hand that I guess I should shake.

"Hi," I say.

"I saw your video on YouTube—you're a really talented performer."

"Oh," I say, surprised. "Thank you."

"You think you're ready to perform on that stage?" he asks, pointing his thumb over a significantly large crowd, toward a big empty stage.

NOTE TO SELF: Remember Sabrina.

I've only been to one music show in my whole life: Sabrina Claudio in Houston with Mal last year.

It was a birthday present I didn't think I should accept. The perfect birthday present.

The show was so sexy, so sensual. Mal was standing next to me, but the whole time I wanted his arms around me. It was the music that tempted me. Her voice. The chords. The smooth ride. Made it feel like I was melting into him.

That's what I want to be able to do. Turn people into liquid with my sound.

7:11 p.m.

The stage isn't huge, but I've never performed on a stage—it looks *ginormous* to me. The lights aren't anything to write home about, but then again, they make me realize that I never had to think about lights before. Especially not while I was coming up with songs in my bedroom.

Then the DJ introduces me as Nikki Williams. My heartbeat is deafening.

I walk out slowly to scattered applause, and then the spotlight finds its way to me. I stop at the microphone parked in the middle of the stage. The crowd murmurs curiously.

My heart is racing, and then my eyes find him standing at the very front, his phone pointed at me. My biggest fan. I instantly calm down. And then decide that my whole performance will be just for him.

My track starts playing over the speakers. My heart leaps out of my chest for him. Then I lean into the microphone and sing.

7:37 p.m.

I'm frozen in my last pose, my chest rising and falling, and my hair is all over the place.

Then the whole club fills with chaotic applause. I smile ear to ear, and start laughing and bowing as the room goes wild. This is the best feeling in the world, I swear.

After my performance, I run to join Mal on the dance floor, but before I can reach him, I'm stopped by fan after fan, praising my performance and asking for my social media. Mal swoops in past the crowd and scoops me up in his arms. I laugh, slinging my arms around his neck. "You were incredible!" he says, setting my feet back down.

"Mal! *You're* incredible." My eyes are as wide as saucers. "I mean, the gig, the shoes, Riley. How long have you been planning this?"

He slides his arms around my waist. "You haven't even seen all the shit I got up my sleeve, Nikki Williams."

My eyebrows shoot up.

Then the DJ tells everyone to give me another round of applause. The people around me clap and smile, including Mal. I watch him closely. He's backing away from me, a sly smile taking over his lips. "Where are you going?" I call to him, but he disappears into the crowd.

Everybody is still clapping and smiling in my direction when the DJ calls them to settle down. "All right, y'all. I wanna introduce everybody to a friend of mine. Come on, give it up for Mr. *Malachai Brown*!"

My eyes go wide, as the house lights dim. Mal walks onstage and the spotlight follows him. He's got his hands behind his back, then he steps up to the microphone. "How y'all doing tonight?"

People whoop and applaud in response.

What is he doing?

He squints his eyes into the crowd, and then he finds me. His lips curl up. "That was a hell of a performance, wasn't it?" And as they applaud me again, he says, "That Nikki is something else. Look out for her, y'all. She's on her way to the top."

"Hell yeah she is," somebody says in the crowd.

My heart burns bright.

"I've watched her music grow over the years. And I'm so proud of her, y'all."

People murmur and say *awwwww*, looking from me to Mal and back again.

My face wants to freeze up—wants to hide my emotions—but I can't stop the heat spreading across my cheeks or the smile spreading across my lips.

"Nikki, you did that shit, baby. But I just got one question . . ."

The entire club goes silent. He smiles at me, and I immediately know what the question will be.

"Truth or dare?"

7:40 p.m.

I look at Mal, speechless. "Choose dare," he says into the microphone.

Then the audience, random people all around me, start shouting, "Truth! No, dare! Choose dare!"

This is obviously a gesture. A *huge* gesture. If I choose dare, what will be on the other side of that? Mal could very well dare me to stay in Cactus. And if I refuse, not only do I ultimately lose the game, but that would be the end of our date. Both of us would be publicly humiliated. It's a strong move on his part, but I'm not taking this shit lying down. "Truth *and* dare," I say with a cocky lift of my eyebrows.

He smiles and rolls his eyes. "I thought you might say that." Then he brings his hands from around his back and presents a clear box cased around a bloodred corsage. "Nikki Williams, I dare you to go to prom with me."

My eyes grow wet. Everyone is smiling at us. Cooing,

"Awww, how sweet."

"Or," he says with a shrug, "is it true that you wrote 'Bow Down' about me?"

My wet eyes instantly dry as I think of the very sexy, very suggestive dance moves I just did, and the matching lyrics I just sang before this very crowd.

"Okay, fine. I'll go to prom with you."

He smirks at me knowingly.

And the club fills with applause.

NOTE TO SELF: Make a playlist of all the songs I ever wrote about Mal, starting with "Bow Down."

It'll be like compiling a diary, because my songs read like secrets. *Feel* like secrets.

Mal has always been pretty good about not reading too far into my lyrics, but maybe all these years, he's just been sparing me the embarrassment, because "Bow Down" definitely isn't the first song I've written about him. It's just the first song that wasn't so much about my heart and the butterflies and all the sweet things as it was about my . . . sexual attraction to him.

10:23 p.m.

First, he tried to take me to the Burger.

I immediately protested. "Nooo, Braum's burgers are a shit ton better. But the Burger has some good-ass curly fries, I'll give you that."

"The only acceptable thing about Braum's is their fries," Mal said. "I like the crinkle ones better than the curly ones."

I shrugged. "So, let's do it."

He shifted his eyes this way and that. "Do what?"

"Get your li'l burger or whatever, and then give me your curly fries. Swing around to Braum's, get *me* a burger, and I'll give you my crinkle fries. Burger Swap."

He smiled and nodded. "Burger Swap."

Now we're parked in the very back of the spacious and mostly empty Braum's parking lot, eating burgers and fries from two different restaurants.

Mal asks "They give you any ketchup?" with his mouth full.

"Here." I hand over the cup of ketchup I had been using for my fries. He takes it happily, while I devour my burger—without any concerns about what I look like. And when I'm done, I sit back and close my eyes.

"Full?" he asks.

"Yes," I whisper. "Thanks, Mal."

"Yeah, bae," he says casually.

I squeeze my closed eyes, trying to let it run past me, but I can't. I grab it and hold on tight. *Bae.*

When I open my eyes, he sees something on my face. "You got ketchup." I reach up, but he says, "Wait, I got it." Grabs a napkin and wipes my face.

I can't stop staring at him.

"You still cold?" he asks. "I gotta turn this AC back up. I'm burning up." He reaches over and turns the AC to the highest setting, and instantly the air draws out the hair on my arms.

"Damn, Mal." I rub my hands over my arms.

"My blood runs hot—you know that." He reaches into his back seat. "Here. Put this on."

He hands me the gray hoodie he wore to all his track meets during February. The same hoodie he wears to all of his classes in the infamously cold B hall. Over the months, it's been soaking up his cologne and his sweat and his mom's sports laundry detergent. It's clearly his favorite hoodie.

I don't hesitate. I put it on with gluttony, and even pull on the strings to tighten the hood around my face. He watches me, swallowing his food—like the sight of me wearing his hoodie is monumental in some way.

It *feels* monumental.

"Is that better?" he asks, not looking away.

"Yeah," I say, blushing. "It's really warm." I snuggle into it, subtly taking a sniff at the sleeve. "So what's next?"

He glances at the clock. "I guess we should get going."

I make a face, disappointed, even though I know he's right.

"What?" he asks, mirroring my pout. "You wanted ice cream or something?"

"No—"

"You wanted to stay the night with me?" he asks, looking at me with those intense eyes.

I rest my temple against the seat. "I mean . . . I really should get home. Right?"

He smiles, nodding. "Yeah. Don't wanna mess anything up at home."

Mal speeds all the way back to Cactus. And the whole way, we talk about the performance.

After the promposal, Kirk had walked up, beaming. "All right, Malachai, you might be onto something here. Nikki, I know for a fact that this club hasn't seen talent like that since the seventies. If you're looking to do more shows around here, or in the Dallas area—honestly, I could get you a spot anywhere in Texas—just let me know. And they'll be paid gigs, too," he'd said. "You deserve money for talent like that."

My eyes had bulged when he'd handed me his business card. "Wait, seriously?"

"I know you're about to graduate, but let's talk after. Yeah? I think it's time to get your career off the ground."

Mal had shaken hands with Kirk, thanked him, and said goodbye as I'd dreamed about the possibilities. Performing as a solo artist around Texas around *Dallas*—with Mal?

"Nikki, this is huge," Mal says, turning in to my neighborhood. Then he starts talking of the future, how when he goes to UT Dallas, I could move in with him. "Dallas actually has a pretty dope music scene, if you didn't know. Kaash Paige came out of Dallas."

He grabs my hands, pulling into my driveway.

"Forget college. I could buy my own equipment to create a bedroom studio. Hire a producer to professionally mix and master my tracks—"

"Or, *shit*, maybe you can go to school and learn how to mix and master your tracks *yourself*," he says.

I pause, thinking about that. "Wait, you think I could actually . . . do that?"

He breathes an easy laugh. "Why not? Nikki, you taught yourself how to *produce*. You taught yourself how to write songs and play keyboard because you love music so much. Do you know how good you would do in a class about music? And then, once you get that formal training, think about how good you'll be. You're already unstoppable. I can't even imagine . . ."

I gotta admit, that does sound pretty good—working and supporting myself, and having the rest of my time to devote to music (and loving him). I bite my lip, really letting myself believe in his fantasy. Why does that sound better than going to California? I'm so close to getting a record deal, to working with Ant and Derek Atkins, but I'm tripping over this little fantasy of going to college and learning how to engineer, of being with Mal.

"Maybe I'll come to class with you, distract you from the professor," Mal says.

"If I actually decide to go to college, you definitely won't be distracting me."

"You know I'll come over and distract you from your books every day," he says, pulling me closer.

Mal's V8 engine doesn't know how to be quiet, so I know Vae and Mama hear us idling out here. We keep the kiss short, since someone could be watching us from inside. "See you tomorrow?" I nod and he says, "Good night, baby."

"Good night, Mal."

I open my door, waving at him once more as his headlights hit my body. I've changed out of Riley's dress and the shoes he bought me. I know Mama would never be okay with seeing me in that outfit. Now I'm back to wearing Mal's old gym shorts and my tank top, under his hoodie. I feel so taken care of, wearing Mal's hoodie. I feel wanted and pampered and cared for. This whole night has been absolutely amazing.

When I start up the porch steps, I hear Mal's tires slowly backing out. I open the screen door, then twist the knob on the front door, but it's locked. I have my phone in hand. I would call Vae to come open it, but it died a long time ago, so I start knocking. My eyes look at Mal's headlights. He's sitting with his foot on the brake, at the bottom of my driveway, waiting for me to get inside.

But it's quiet. And dark.

I keep knocking.

After a full minute of me standing outside, Mal opens his car door, one foot out on the driveway. "Want me to call Vae?"

I nod. And keep knocking. It's happening again.

"Straight to voice mail," he says. Both his feet are planted in my driveway now. "Want me to try calling your mom?"

This porch has seen so much of my pain. People shouldn't come home this scared. Home is supposed to be safe. Home is supposed to always *be* there—it's in the definition. Why do I always show up here and experience the worst pain of my life?

"No, don't call her." My keys are hooked to my phone case. I pick up my house key. My heart is racing.

The knob looks exactly the same as it always has, but my key doesn't fit in the hole.

Even though I thought I'd made my mind up a long time ago to leave this godforsaken shithole town, apparently I still had a bit of hope that I wouldn't *have* to.

11:12 p.m.

I'm doubled over, lying in the middle of Mal's bed, crying my eyes out.

NOTE TO SELF: Wash your face.

Don't get all that makeup and sweat and tears on Mal's pillow tonight. I'm already feeling sorry that he's had to watch me cry for the past hour.

11:22 p.m.

I've tried stopping. I'm able to quiet myself for a few minutes, but then it starts right back up again. I can't seem to stop. I have never in my life cried this much.

11:32 p.m.

He's been wrapped around my back like a blanket this whole time. Both of his bedside lamps are on. There's a pile of my tissues growing on the corner of his bed. The taller it gets, the more I realize how much this fucking hurts.

God, why does it *hurt* so much?

I already knew what was up. The whole reason I dared to even get home so late was because I had no intention of staying in this shithole town in the first place. As if I could just go back home and act like everything was normal. Go to prom, graduate, then start a life with Mal in Dallas. God, it sounded good. . . .

But nope. I'm still homeless.

I open my eyes and blink a couple of times, pushing my way through the muck in my eyelashes. I look around his room. It's so massive compared to my room. The bed is so comfortable. Carpet recently cleaned. He's got trophies on his bookshelf, knickknacks on his desk, but for the most part, he doesn't like clutter. Mal warms this place up—both figuratively and literally. When he's gone, to the bathroom or wherever, this room gets noticeably colder. And it almost seems like the lights get dimmer too.

This place is functional, like a hotel, but it's not "home." His mom and dad are not my parents. If Mal suddenly has to pick up and move again, it's not like they're going to take me with them. Let's be serious. Because this is not my *home* and they aren't my *family*.

At this point, I'd be stupid to deny myself the golden ticket that fell into my lap. I'm *going* to get a spot in that girl group. I'm confident of that. So long as I go and do what I did tonight, I'm going to be taken care of by Derek Atkins.

11:46 p.m.

The hiccups are gone. The sniffles have slowed. It's quiet.

Mal coos to me, "Is it okay if I turn this off?" He reaches his arm over my body to the lamp.

"Wait, I need to wash up real quick." I climb out of bed, untangling myself from him, then I jog to his bathroom.

My makeup held up pretty well after all I put it through today—all except my eyeliner and eye shadow. There's something to be said about that setting spray and whatever else Riley used on my face.

As I lather Mal's face wash between my hands, I try to not think about anything. I try to not worry anymore. I've made up my mind. Now all I have to do is stop feeling.

11:56 p.m.

I come out of his bathroom to find him sleeping. It's been such a long day. We've felt so many new feelings together. I stare at his peaceful face for a while, glad that he's resting. Then I turn out the light.

NOTE TO SELF: Apologize to him in the morning.

We were having such a good time together that he even asked me to spend the night with him. But I'm pretty sure he imagined us making out or having sex or something—not watching me cry my eyes out for an hour.

Mama would be so pissed if she knew. Crying in front of her was one thing, but crying in front of people *outside* our house was forbidden. It made her look bad.

That's what she said to me long ago, that time in the car, when she finally came to pick me up after my basketball game. Coach watched us drive away and Mama waved out of the window, smiling, while I was trying my best to fix my face.

"Did you see the way that nosy white woman looked at me? What were you *crying* for?"

Because I was scared.

"Acting like a three-year-old, like I wasn't gonna come back. I had shit to do, Shaniqua. Food to cook. Clothes to wash. Instead of sitting in my car, waiting on you for half an hour. You coulda took yo' ass back in that gym and watched the boys play while you waited for me. 'Stead of sitting on the curb, crying. You *knew* I was coming back."

I wasn't sure.

"But no. You wanted to try and make me look bad. You coulda borrowed somebody's phone and called me. But you decided to make a scene."

I just wanted to see that you cared about me.

@nik_nik_nikki23: If I do get the lead-singer spot . . . are there any real benefits to that? Would I have any kind of creative control in this deal?

Wednesday

7:11 a.m.

The first thing I do when I get up is find my charger, then I squat next to Mal's bedside table to plug my phone into the outlet. The light, as it powers on, burns my swollen eyes.

I need to talk to Vae. I need to know what's going on. Is it over? Did Mama really mean to lock me out last night?

Of course she did. No reason to get your hopes up.

But still. I need to talk to Vae.

Once my home screen comes up, I wait for it to find a signal. After three minutes of staring, nothing happens. No notifications flooding in. No missed calls from Vae. I try opening Instagram. All I get is an error message.

She cut my service.

She changed the locks and cut my service, just like she promised she would.

I drop my phone on the floor. I knew this would happen—don't know why my body is so surprised, threatening to shut down all over again.

I grab it off the floor and stumble back to bed. "You good?" Mal asks as I get back under the covers.

"Uh-huh." I can feel the powerlessness pulling down my walls again. The hopelessness wetting my eyes. Nope. I'm not crying again. Nope. Nope. Nope.

It's still really dark in his room. His blackout curtains are closed, so only tiny streaks of morning light peek through the sides. It's enough that I can see the shape of him. We're lying facing each other. His hand is traveling slowly from my knee up to my hip and back again.

I wrap myself in his body heat. Then I quietly apologize to him for my display last night.

He whispers back, "You don't need to apologize."

"I just couldn't stop."

"I know."

"That's probably not what you meant when you asked me to spend the night with you."

"No, but it is," he says, scooting closer. "I've never seen you cry before. I'm honored you felt comfortable enough to do it in front of me."

I've never felt pain like that before, or the instant fear that washed over me when I realized I was locked out.

"Thanks for comforting me," I say. "I don't think I've ever been . . . comforted while I cried."

"Really?" he asks, sounding surprised. "Not even Vae?"

"Vae turns into a statue when she sees other people cry. Mama acts like she's offended."

"What do you mean?"

"She's always gotten pissed at me for crying—told me to go to my room and stuff. It was like breaking a rule."

"Nikki, that's really fucked."

"Is it?" I say with a hopeless laugh. "I mean, crying is showing weakness."

"Crying is a natural reaction to pain. Your mother, of all people, should *hold you* when you're crying—not force you to hide away in your room. That's not normal."

"My mother has never exactly been normal, though."

He takes a deep breath. "Yeah . . . neither was mine." He leans closer to kiss me on the forehead. "Feel free to cry in front of me, any time. I will never push you away." He leaves his lips pressed against my forehead until I close my eyes.

8:45 a.m.

"Where are you going?" I croak, opening my eyes just in time to watch him tug a gray T-shirt over his head. He's already wearing black joggers with white stripes down the sides.

"Know how I lied about training yesterday, so I could get the surprise set up? Well, I actually do have to train today."

"God, Mal. Don't you ever take a break?"

He smirks at me, reaching down for one of his running shoes. "I'll be right back. Then we can have a chill day together. Okay?" He places a knee on the mattress beside me, bends down and kisses me.

He grabs his keys off the nightstand. "There's some frozen breakfast sandwiches in the freezer. Plenty of cereal in the pantry. Help yourself."

"Okay," I say with a sigh.

He smiles. "Don't pout like that. I seriously can't take it."

"I'm not pouting."

"Yes, you are," he says, looking down at me, amused. Then he drops his keys back on the bedside table. His amused expression turns into a dreamy smirk. Then he finds his way back to bed, finds his way back to my lips. My arms ring around his back, and he lets his body settle on top of me, shoes on the bed and everything. And astonishingly, I'm not self-conscious of my morning breath, even though I can taste that he's already brushed his teeth.

I slip his T-shirt up and press my hands into his bare back. His kisses fall soft and slow to my chin, to my neck, to my collarbone. Then he mumbles against my skin, "God, I love you."

My eyes pop open.

He stops. And he looks just as surprised as me.

"I—" I say nothing else. I'm mute. Completely stunned.

Instead of awkwardly climbing off me and running away forever, though, he smiles. Then he closes his eyes and kisses me again. "I'll be back soon, okay?"

I nod, eyes wide open.

"Go back to sleep, and I'll be back before you wake up." Then he leaves.

I don't take another breath until I hear the front door close downstairs. *Go back to sleep?* After he just told me he loves me, and I said absolutely nothing? I don't think I'll ever sleep again.

NOTE TO SELF: This is bad.

9:00 a.m.

She knocks, and I'm already opening the door.

"What's going on?" Daeja asks, pushing past me, looking around the house. "Is he not here?"

"He's training at the high school right now."

I grabbed my laptop as soon as he left, connected to his Wi-Fi, and DM'd Daeja: **Come to Mal's house. SOS.** Because I needed someone who would say something different to me.

Riley and Vae look at the world through rose-tinted glasses. Daeja is a realist. She's been down for my California plan since I told her about it, because she knows how it is. We've lived in the same trailer park since we were tots at Cactus Elementary. Our very similar mothers get the same amount of food stamps and work at the same meat factory.

"I can't believe you're still here, Nikki. You came back for Mal? Riley told me about the little dates he's taken you on, and the prom thing, but dammit, don't throw away your future for this guy. He's not worth it."

I lead her into the kitchen, halfway ignoring her chiding. She takes a seat at the bar, while I lean across from her, silent—I'm still so shook.

"I mean, good for him, he finally gave you the promposal you deserve, but—"

"Mal just told me he loved me."

She pauses. I expect her to continue bad-mouthing him, but she doesn't. She can see my distress. She can see how conflicted I am. "And what did you say?"

"*Nothing.*" I bury my face in my hands and groan.

"You don't have to say anything back," Daeja says. "Just because he loves you doesn't mean you have to love him back."

"But . . ." I look up at her, clenching my teeth.

"Oh, Nikki. You love him?"

"I don't know! That's why I called you here. I said yes to prom even though I have an audition in California in three days. Oh yeah, and I'm also technically homeless."

"Riley said you slept at your mom's house the other night. She said that y'all made up or something."

I laugh. "As if I could ever make up with that woman. She changed the locks and turned off my phone, so no—we didn't make up."

"*Whoa.* Seriously? I'm so sorry, Nikki."

I settle back against the counter, getting completely real with her. "I have this awesome opportunity in California . . . but I also have this boy in Texas who apparently loves me. How am I supposed to deal with this?" I beg for an answer to just fall out of the sky. A solution—a win-win scenario.

"He loves you, but do you love *him*? Because if you don't, then none of this matters. Can't let some boy in high school stop you from achieving your dreams. This is about your future—not what Mal wants."

"Okay, but what if I do? What if . . . I do love him?"

Daeja makes a face. She really doesn't want to consider that an option. "How do you feel about him?" she demands. "Describe it."

I sigh, glancing at the clock on the stove. He'll be back at noon. "I don't know. Words are hard."

"You're sitting in class, and then Mal walks in. How do you feel?"

I imagine every time he's ever walked into one of my classes, delivering a note to my teacher, or some other random reason. My stomach sank. And the rest of me filled up with butterflies.

I smile. "Excited. Like suddenly, my day got better. Like anything could happen. Suddenly, there's so much possibility."

"Uh-huh." She thinks to herself. "Okay, but that could just be a crush. That may not be love."

"How do I know the difference? You love Riley, right? How did you know the difference?"

She takes a breath, in through her nostrils, out through her mouth, while staring up at the pots above our heads. "At first I wasn't sure. Riley said it first, and I said it back without really thinking about it. She's the first person I've ever said those words to."

"Was it hard to say?"

"No, but like I said, I wasn't sure if it was actually true. It took me a few months of saying it for me to know for sure."

"And how did you know?" I beg, leaning closer.

"It just felt right. Like, being with her felt like . . . home. We were no longer two separate people. We were a unit. You know?"

I nod slowly. "When it comes to Mal, I'm so *comfortable* with him. I'm comfortable talking to him. I'm comfortable looking like trash around him. Bringing him into my home, bringing him into my family *drama*. I even cried in front of him, and I haven't cried in front of anyone in years. Am I in love?"

Daeja gives me a conflicted shrug. "You might be."

"If I am, what does that mean? What can I do?"

"You'll have to factor him into your decision."

11:55 a.m.

His car pulls up, woofers turned up so loud, I can feel the vibrations under my toes. I can tell from here that he's listening to J. Cole.

I watch him through the window beside the front door, sneaking my head around Mrs. B's drapes. When he gets out, he looks sweaty and somehow even better than he did this morning. He takes the bottom of his T-shirt and wipes his forehead. My eyes zero in on his exposed abs and his tight brown skin.

My heart is turning flips.

Once he starts up the porch steps, he spots me in the window. I stiffen. "What are you doing?" he says. His voice sounds so far away. He smirks and continues up the steps, opening the door with a big smile. "Did you miss me?"

"I . . . yes."

He looks over his shoulder at me, curious about my soft tone and my timid steps following behind him down the hallway. I feel so fragile right now. So confused and yet *certain*, all at the same time.

"What'd you wanna do today?"

"I don't know," I say, my voice barely turning on, because I'm so enraptured in the smell of his sweat. It's not that it smells *good*. It just brings up a weirdly good feeling in me. "I'm game for whatever you want."

"Yeah? Anything?" He spins around, trading my hand from his left to his right. He walks backward toward the stairs, licking his bottom lip and checking me out.

"What are you in the mood for?" I ask. "Horror games? Maybe some pool time?"

"Or maybe some Netflix and chill . . . with a little extra chill on the side."

I laugh and sweat profusely. "Stop it!"

"I'm just kidding." He laughs. "Well, not really. But whatever we do, I gotta take a shower first."

So, he does. He showers, while I'm left in his bedroom with my rampant thoughts. Then we go out to eat at a steak house down the road. Just about everyone in the restaurant greets Mal, and we even get our drinks for free—perks of dating the most popular boy in Moore County, I suppose.

We get back to his house, and it's like we both feel too full for comfort—and not from food. We're spilling over with a need to get closer.

It starts in the kitchen.

He puts our leftover food in the fridge, while I watch,

leaning against the bar. I can hear Daeja in my ear saying, *You might be in love.*

Dammit, I might be.

He notices me watching him. After closing the fridge door, he slowly swaggers over to me. “What now?”

“I’m kinda tired,” I say. “We could take a nap together.”

His gaze turns up the fire. “Sounds good to me.”

1:38 p.m.

He leads me by the hand, up the stairs and into his cold, dark room. As soon as the door shuts, he's got my back pressed against it.

We don't sleep.

1:49 p.m.

Mal is eager, steering my body to his bed. I'm eager too, pull-ing him down on top of me and wrapping my legs around his waist.

I try to say it—try to whisper it in his ear, but it won't come out.

3:23 p.m.

He's lying on his stomach, watching his stories (rewatching *My Hero Academia*)—and I'm lying beside him, tracing the tattoo on his back. "Why a crown?" I ask.

I honestly can't believe I never asked before. Not even when he decided to get it.

"Oh, um . . ." Then he grins uncomfortably. Grabs his mouse from across the mattress.

"You don't need to stop your show. It's okay—"

"No, I wanna tell you." He pauses his show, then lies on his side to face me. "So you know how we had to move to get away from my birth mom?" I nod. "Well, when we moved, my parents also changed my name. My name used to be King."

I take a good look at his face, like I'm seeing him for the first time. "King," I say, trying to fit the name to the person.

I lift my finger to the tiny mole beneath his eye, and he smiles. "Been a really long time since anyone has called me that." He grabs my hand, using my palm to cup his cheek. "But you can't call me that around people—especially not my parents. No one can know."

"Okay, I won't."

"But I do like it, though, hearing you say it." He kisses my palm. "It's just one of those things that nobody knows about me."

"Do your parents ever call you King?"

He rests his head on the mattress, turning onto his back. "No, but I mean, I get it—the name and the house and the new town was supposed to be like new beginnings for our family. They look at King as my deadname. They think it'll bring up bad memories."

"Does it?"

"Makes me think of my old family. Makes me miss them a little. But mostly it just reminds me of the good parts of my childhood."

I grin. "I'm glad you told me."

"Me too." He grabs my hand and pulls me closer to his bare chest. I'm staring down into his eyes. *Now would be a great time to say it, Nikki.* I part my lips, conjuring up those big, clunky words, but I'm cut off by the doorbell.

Both of our eyes widen. "Another surprise guest?" I ask, worried. I don't know if I can handle another huge gesture right now.

He shakes his head, gently rolling from under me. "I have no idea who that is."

We tiptoe down the stairs together, then peek out of the

window by the front door. Mal instantly starts laughing. "It's just Dex." He rushes to open the door. "Aye boy!"

"Brooo," Dex howls, then they dap. "I'm bored out of my mind, man." He walks into Mal's house without an invitation and runs right into me. "Nikki," he says, surprised. "Nikki is here?" He turns to Mal, frowning. "You should be ashamed of yourself for lying to me."

"She made me," Mal says, pointing his finger at me.

"So y'all just been chilling all week and I couldn't get so much as a phone call?"

"Well—"

He cuts me off, shifting his eyes between me and Mal. "Wait, what's happening here?"

"What do you mean?" Mal asks.

"Something weird is going on. Y'all are acting strange."

"We're not doing anything." I spin on my heel, heading back into the living room. They follow me.

"You still ain't moved your couch back, my boy? Your parents gon' be pissed. What have y'all been doing all week? I'm hungry as fuck. Got anything to eat in that big ole fridge of yours? Cool if I get something? You know we ain't got food at my house." Then he passes me up, walking into the kitchen to help himself.

Mal stops beside me, and we exchange glances. "So, Dex, you hanging out today, or . . . ?" Mal calls out. I follow him into the kitchen, hoping Dex's answer will be no, or that Mal will kick him out.

"Yeah, is that cool? I've been bored as shit at home. I'm not scheduled to work today, either."

"You could still go in, though, right? Pick up an extra shift? I know you were saying you wanted to make a little extra money to take Emily on a date."

Dex is rifling through the refrigerator when he returns his gaze to me and Mal. I'm wearing a shirt that is quite obviously Mal's, while Mal isn't wearing a shirt at all. "Why do y'all want me gone so bad? Am I interrupting something?"

"No," Mal says quickly. But then he looks at me—asking with his eyes whether it's okay to tell Dex. I mean, it's not exactly a secret, but as soon as Dex knows, *everyone* will know.

"I knew it," Dex says, without waiting for our answer. He shuts the fridge door with my plate of leftovers in hand. "I knew it as soon as I walked in. Y'all were fucking, weren't you?"

"No!" Mal and I say at the same time.

"Bullshit." He laughs. "I can feel it. The vibe between y'all is different."

I roll my eyes. "We're not acting any different."

"No, for real. It's like, I can tell y'all aren't lying to each other anymore. Talkin' 'bout, *we're just friends*. Bullshit." He gets a clean plate out of the cabinet and a fork out of the silverware drawer.

"Hey, that's my food, fool."

He scowls at me. "You're Mal's girl now. He's *going* to buy you dinner. Calm down."

Mal looks at me and nods, giving up the act. "He's right, I will. Whatever you want."

"Well, at least leave me the rice!"

"Fine," Dex says.

While Dex warms up my leftovers for himself, Mal and I sit at the bar. "I know this isn't exactly what you had in mind today," he says, low enough where only I can hear him.

"It's fine. I mean, it's Dex. What are you gonna do?"

"I heard my name. What are y'all saying about me?"

"Shut up. I'm not talking to you," I say. Mal smiles, pinching my chin, and pulls my lips to his.

4:43 p.m.

Dex is playing *2K*. Mal is talking trash about Dex's skills, lovingly, and Dex is talking trash right back, while I'm sitting on the back of the sofa, moisturizing Mal's hair and trying to figure out his curl pattern. It doesn't quite look 4C like mine. The coils are too uniform and loose. I'm thinking maybe 4B.

Mal throws his arms up, shouts, "Bro, you suck!" then he falls back between my legs. His lips are level with my thighs, so he kisses the left one. "Thanks, bae. My hair really needed this."

"Aye, can I get next?" Dex asks, glancing at us.

"Next what?" Mal says.

"My hair needs some lovin' too."

"Uh-huh, and you gon' have to get your own girlfriend to do that for you. Either that or yo' mama."

Dex laughs. Then he shows me his amusement. "So this is the guy you choose, huh? This stingy bastard?"

"Shut up," Mal hisses, pushing Dex by the shoulder, while Dex continues laughing and teasing him.

I scrunch my fingers against Mal's scalp, massaging in the fragrant oil and conditioner. The mix of shea butter and vanilla makes me think of all the time I've spent in his bed, lying on his pillow or lying on his chest. *God*, I can't wait for Dex to leave.

"Know what we should do?" Dex says. "We should celebrate Nikki staying in Cactus. Call the boys over. Call up Riley and Daeja, and who else?"

"You wanna have another party?" Mal asks in disbelief. "Nikki and I were kinda spending the day together."

Dex makes a face. "It's spring break. Just spend tomorrow together."

"Nikki has a lot going on with her mom right now, and she's still planning to go to California this weekend—"

The game is paused. The house is silent, and my fingers are frozen in Mal's hair.

Dex looks at me sharply. "Wait, you're still going?"

I shift my eyes, suddenly on the spot. "There's another audition this Saturday."

"And you're going?"

"Yeah?" I say. "It's a huge opportunity."

"But you and Mal are together now. . . ."

Mal stands up too, hands on his hips, like suddenly he agrees with Dex.

"I'm *homeless*," I say. "My mother kicked me out." Like why isn't that enough for people to understand why I'm going?

"But . . . you and Mal are together now," Dex says again. "Just live here."

"No," I say, looking at the both of them like they're insane. "I can't just live with my boyfriend."

Dex shifts his eyes, confused, as if I'm speaking gibberish. "Why not?"

NOTE TO SELF: Am I being ridiculous?

Am I wasting my breath trying to refuse Mal's gifts? The guilt I feel—is it stupid?

I learned from my mama not to accept help. It's how she raised us. To always be wary and defensive and angry about being poor.

Vae refuses to eat breakfast at school, because she has this weird thing about not wanting people to know that we're on the free lunch program. Like she's afraid that people will find out we're poor.

Sometimes I want to scream at her, EVERYBODY KNOWS WE'RE POOR. WE'RE FROM CACTUS, FOR GOD'S SAKE, AND LOOK AT OUR CLOTHES. But I hold my tongue because she gets really sensitive about that kind of stuff.

And I get it. I know how Vae feels when she's standing in the school lunch line, hoping people don't notice when she doesn't pay for her food. The same way she feels standing in line at Walmart, hoping the people behind us won't notice Mama swipe her food stamps card. I was there when she learned to feel ashamed about being poor. The very same time I learned to be defensive.

Mama hadn't started working at the meat factory yet. She was still a custodian for Dumas High. We didn't have a lot of money, but her schedule was predictable. The three of us spent Saturdays garage-sale hopping in Dumas neighborhoods, and sometimes even Amarillo. Most of my and Vae's clothes and toys were from garage sales. We didn't mind back then, because it was fun, picking through dusty trash that we sometimes made our treasures.

The three of us were at Walmart after having already been garage-sale hopping. And Vae and I were still in the shopping mood, so we both asked for toys. Toys we'd seen commercials for. Toys we couldn't afford. Back then it was hard for Mama to say no to us. So she put back the light bulbs and the sandwich bags and the WD-40 so Vae and I could have our way.

There was a growing line behind us, as is always the case in Walmart, when Mama went to pay with her food stamps card. It went through. All of our food was paid for, but afterward there was a balance of $32.14. I remember the number to the penny.

Mama only had a twenty-dollar bill. We needed that laundry detergent. And we needed toilet paper. But we didn't need new toys. Mama had a hardened look in her eyes, like she refused to feel anything but strength and pride. She said, "Girls, we'll have to get your toys next time."

Vae didn't understand. "Why? No!"

"Nevaeh, stop it!" Mama pointed her finger in Vae's face.

"She's such a cutie," a white woman said behind us, her eyes shiny with pity. She started digging in her wallet.

Her husband, a white man with a baseball cap and a big fat belly, placed his hands on hers. "Honey, don't."

"Stan, she's a little girl. She should have the doll she wants."

Then he said, "You help them once, and they'll never learn how to help themselves."

Mama's jaw tightened. She turned back to the attendant. "Take the doll and the makeup off."

"They're children, Stan. Think of our kids at that age."

"They're already sucking on the government's teat."

The woman ignored her husband and pushed a twenty-dollar bill at us. Mama looked like she could have chewed that woman's head off, choked her husband out, and spit on both their graves. "I didn't ask for your money. Do I look like I'm holding a sign? Do I look like I'm begging?"

"Can we move this along?" the husband said to the attendant, completely avoiding eye contact with us, because we were beneath him, we were scum of the Earth, we were costing him tax dollars.

We got the laundry detergent, the toilet paper, and our free food, and we left. Mama hurried ahead of us, pushing the cart. "Come on, girls," she growled over her shoulder. Vae and I held hands, rushing behind her.

Vae was smart. She's always been smart. She knew that man in Walmart looked down on us. She knew we were poor and that some people valued us less because of that. She stopped her whining and cried silently.

And when Vae cries, when she's crying for real, she never makes a sound.

We helped Mama load the trunk with the groceries. Then we settled in the back seat. Mama was shuffling through her purse, mumbling to herself, "No-good racist."

"The man was nasty, but at least the woman wanted to help," I said.

Mama whipped her head around. "That woman was no better than the man. She was *worse*. You hear me?"

I nodded, eyes filling up, then I sniffled.

"Stop crying," she hissed, backing out of the parking space. "Do *not* cry because of those racist devils. Wipe your face, *now*!"

I sucked up my tears, because I was never good at crying silently, not like Vae. She kept on crying. But me? I got angry. Just like Mama.

9:00 p.m.

Before Dex came around, most of our conversations today had only involved our bodies. We made out in his bed *a lot*. But now we're back to discussing our future. And he's so full of hope.

"This week has been really good for us. Colorado, your performance, the promposal. I can't wait to take you to prom, Nikki. If you look even half as good as you did last night, you'll win best-dressed for sure."

"But Mal," I say, cutting him off, "that sounds great and all, but you saw me get kicked out yesterday."

Then it's silent, both of us caught in a held breath. "Okay, but . . . ," he says, trying to gather his words. "You're still not planning to come back?"

"Come back to what, Mal?"

"I just thought—I mean—you said yes to prom."

"How will I go to prom if I'm homeless?"

"You're *not* homeless. You're staying here," he says, like it's the obvious and only choice.

"I can't stay here."

"Why not? Tell me why not. And be serious. None of that *I'm not your parents' responsibility* bullshit."

"I'm *not* their responsibility."

He sits up on his elbow. Both the lamps on his nightstands are on. "Who *cares*, Nikki? It's a place to live."

"With my boyfriend's parents?"

"You would have your own room, and knowing my parents, they'd give you your own set of chores, too. They'd treat you just like they treat me."

"You don't know that." I sit up on my elbow too. "And what happens after we graduate? Will the clock run out? Will I get kicked out of yet another house?"

"They would *never* do that to you."

"What if I hurt you?" I say, searching his eyes. "What if we break up? What if I royally *fuck up*? Will they kick me out then?"

He looks like he's trying to imagine it. He wants to ask why I think that shit would ever happen, but instead he says confidently, "They would never fail you, Nikki. They would never let you sleep outside. They just wouldn't do that. No matter what, they'd make sure you're taken care of."

"Just because they did it for you doesn't mean they'll do it for me. I'm eighteen, Mal. You were ten. It's different."

"It's not different. Not to them."

"How do you *know* that, Mal?"

He takes an exasperated breath and looks at me like he's giving up. "Because I called them and asked."

All of the air is sucked out of the room.

"I needed to know if they'd be okay with it, so I told them what happened. They're on a flight back right now. They care about you so much—"

"You did what?" I finally spit out. "You weren't supposed to tell your parents that I'm here."

"Everybody in town knows you're here, Nikki. The charade is up."

"So they know I've been here all week? They know I got kicked out?"

"Yes," he says, reaching for me. "They want you to take the guest room. The first thing they're going to do is buy a real bed, instead of making you sleep on that air mattress."

"Your parents can't just take me in. You said they're on a flight back right now?" I'm struggling to find the right words. "What about—what about my mom?"

"What about her? You'll never have to deal with her again," he says.

"You think she'd just give me up like that?"

His eyes droop. "Nikki, she causes you so much pain and so much turmoil. It would be so much better living here—"

"But I don't *want* to live here," I say.

It slips out without my permission, but the second the words hit my ears, I realize how true they are.

I never wanted to admit it to myself, but I don't want to live in this big, echoey house, with its expensive art and luxurious furniture. I don't want to spend months in his guest room, staring up at the ceiling, thinking about how the only reason that I'm here is because my mother gave me up. I want to be out there, somewhere I consciously decided to be, shining as bright as the Californian sun. I don't want her to be able to decide another thing for me.

"You don't wanna stay with me?" Mal asks, wounded.

"Mal, it's not about my feelings for you. I feel so much for you. But I can't stay here."

Mal blinks his eyes, looking defeated. "It's not about my feelings?" he asks. "Why can't it be? Why can't our feelings for each other be . . . enough?"

"Feelings change like the wind, Mal. I can't stake everything, my whole future, on a feeling."

"But it's not just any feeling. It's love."

There's that word again.

"You said love. I never said love."

He looks at me in disbelief. "I guess that's true." Then he drops his eyes to the foot of mattress between us and stops fighting.

11:13 p.m.

"My parents will be home in twenty minutes."

"Shit," I hiss, ripping my charger out of the wall and throwing it in my runaway bag. That's it. I think I got everything.

With my bag on my shoulder, I head to the bedroom door. This would be the perfect time to kiss him goodbye. I should kiss him goodbye. But he's staring at the ceiling—everywhere but at me.

I think he can sense me staring at him, but he still refuses to look at me. "There should be enough space in the driveway for you to pull out of the garage."

"I'm so sorry, Mal."

He takes a long, deep breath. "Bye, Nikki."

He's done fighting for me. Done trying to stop me. I didn't expect his indifference to be so painful. With one last look at his stony face, I say it back: "Bye, Mal."

@AntTheProdigy: Get here first. Blow Derek's socks off. Then we can talk contract.

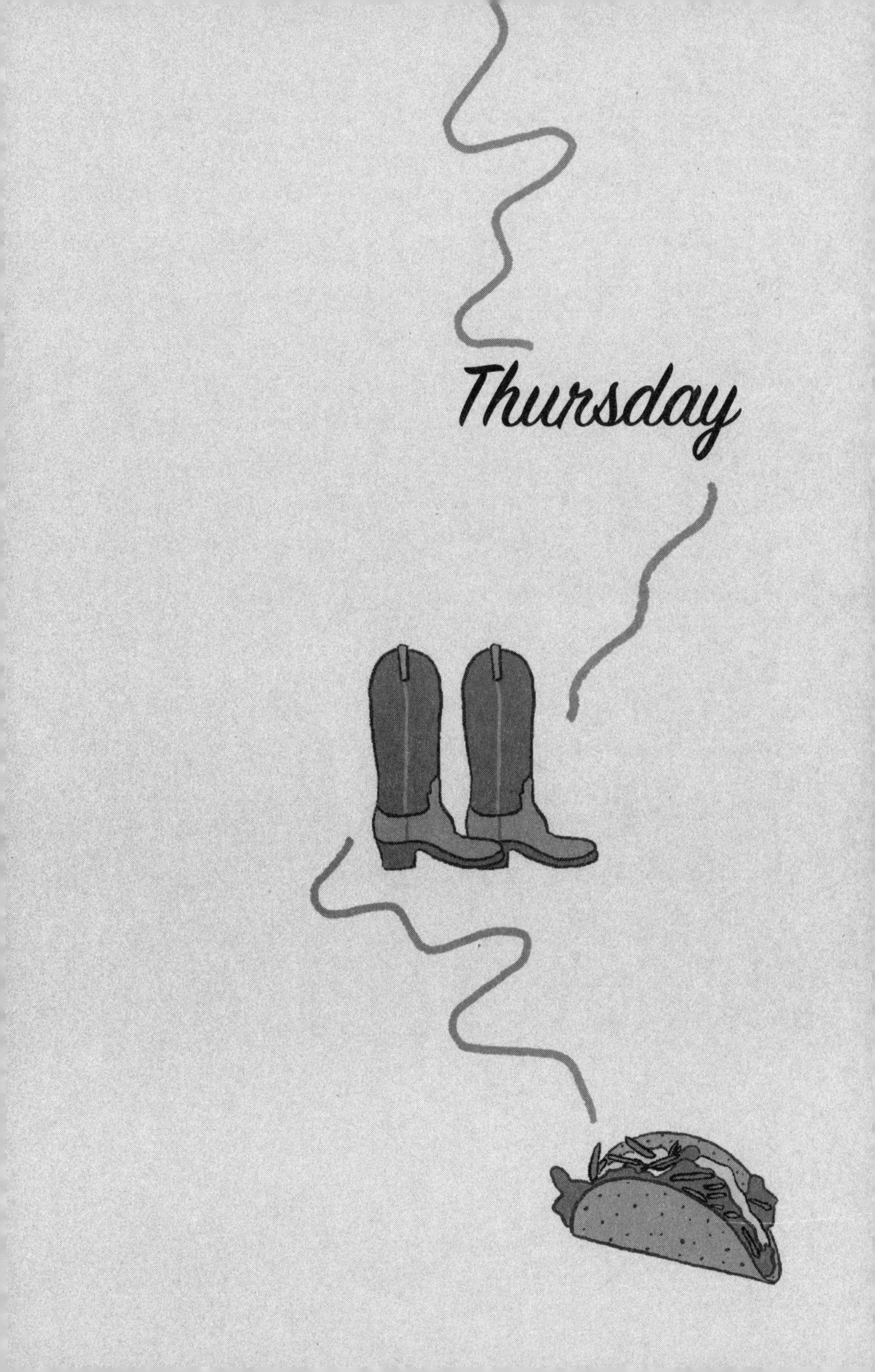
Thursday

6:48 a.m.

The sky is dark blue. It's the first thing I see when my eyes open. The shade of it is beautiful as the yellow sun slowly opens its eyes. And all I hear are birds singing and the shush of distant traffic behind me and . . . my phone ringing?

How is that possible?

I lift my head off of my duffel, eyes struggling to open. I'm sweaty and my neck hurts from lying in the same position for hours in my back seat. I didn't get very far last night. Just far enough so no one would come after me. New Mexico felt like the perfect stop—parked on the side of a dirt road, trees and brush surrounding me.

No cars have passed since I got here. It feels safe, but at the same time, if I was murdered, my body would never be recovered.

My phone stops ringing and starts right back up again.

Curious, I look for it, through all the stuff I threw in my

bag last night. When I finally find it, the light burns my eyes: Yolanda Williams.

I'm not gonna answer it.

I swear, I'm not.

That woman has broken my heart one too many times. Tuesday night I walked right into it. Never again. I toss the phone back in my bag and stare straight ahead, out the window into the skimpy woods.

The ringing stops. And starts right back up again.

I wonder what happened this time. Did Vae make a run for it? My heart is racing.

It stops and starts again.

But what if it's about me?

It's not. It couldn't be. The only way she'd ever turn my service back on and call me is if she's panicked about Vae or something else more important than me. *Don't fool yourself, Nikki.*

I climb out of my back seat and get behind the wheel. Start the engine and roll down the window. What is this—the fifth time she's called? What if Vae really *is* hurt? What if she's dead? What if it's Vae calling to tell me that *Mama's* dead? Do I . . . care?

I look at the screen. Something in my head makes me reach over and grab it. Something in my heart makes me answer. "Hello?"

Mama gasps in a shrill way that I've never heard her gasp before—I've never heard her be so genuinely surprised to hear my voice. "Shaniqua." She's . . . *crying*?

"What happened? Is Vae okay?" I ask, scared to death.

"You need to turn around."

"Why? Is Vae okay?"

"I'm not calling about Vae. I'm calling about *you*. Come home. We need to talk."

NOTE TO SELF: She can't control you anymore.

She *locked you out* of her house—*your home.*

She cut your phone service. Cut you off from the world. Cut you off from *her.* Because sure, no one else would be able to contact you, but there would have been no way for her to call you, either. She knew that, and she did it anyway.

Sounds just like . . . *God*, Mom and Vae are just alike, aren't they?

Selfish.

6:53 a.m.

I don't say anything. But I have so many words for her. So many words I've been gathering over the week. I just don't know where to start. And most of me can't believe that she has the gall to call and tell me to turn around. We need to *talk*? The nerve.

"Shaniqua?" she asks in my long silence, in that familiar way she says my name.

I don't want to say yes. She doesn't deserve peace of mind.

I'm just listening. Listening to her silence, her breath, her occasional sniffle—listening like my life depends on it.

I'm not sure how to trust when she acts human around me, because every single time, it's always eventually led to another shot to my heart. It feels like I'm slowly getting tied up by my feet, the longer I listen.

"I know you're mad. But we need to talk."

"You locked me out of the house," I say, seething. I can't help myself.

"You were out until eleven o'clock, Shaniqua. Your curfew is eight."

I laugh. "Not anymore. I'm on my way to California, so—"

"Turn around. I need you at home." She doesn't say it through gritted teeth, like an order. She says it like it's the only thing in this world that she knows to be absolutely true.

She says my name again—my birth name. "Shaniqua. I just wanna talk. I want to explain."

"Explain what?"

"Everything. Just turn around."

"Why would I come back to a house that I don't even have the key for?"

"I have your key right here. Just come back."

My finger hovers over the end call button, but I can't press it. It hovers and hovers, while the timer on our call keeps running up. It feels like she's talking me down off the ledge. But I'm not on a ledge. This audition is a sure thing. And right now, it sounds a lot better than fighting with my mother for another two months.

"Just come back," she repeats.

A car flashes past my window—the first all night. The sun cuts through a cloud in my rearview. The audition is a sure thing, so why can't I say no to her?

"I'm not in trouble?" I ask.

"No," she says. "I just wanna talk . . . about your granddad."

I blink against heavy breaths. Wait . . . *Granddad*?

7:15 p.m.

There's still so much light outside when I pull into my drive-way and park behind my mother's car. I thought it would be dark by now. But that's *right*. Daylight Saving Time. I'm not used to the days being this long.

It's been about twelve hours since our conversation this morning. I hung up without a goodbye, because I could feel myself getting swept up and forgetting about my audition Friday. I could feel myself *hoping*. But still I drove directly back to Cactus. Drove circles around my neighborhood. Drove circles around the park and the taco joint, until I ended up here.

The front door is open, but the screen door is shut. I see Vae watching me with her fingertips pressed against the screen. Her eyes widen at the sight of me. We just smile at each other, big and dumb, like we're so excited to see each other. She rushes to open the door for me.

When I step inside, I see Mama, sitting in her recliner,

looking so small and so worn-out. And I'm trusting her right now—my heart is completely exposed—but at the same time, I'm terrified.

The house smells like spaghetti. I think maybe it just hasn't faded from the night Mama and I ate it together, watching *What Would You Do?* But then Mama goes to the kitchen and hands me a plate. *Fresh* spaghetti and meatballs, with garlic bread on the side.

She allows me to eat it in the living room—on her couch, no less. Vae eats on the floor, with her eyes on the television, while listening to our conversation. "Bobbie wouldn't have us girls getting out of line—me and your aunt Marigold. We could barely hang out with friends on the weekends." Mama sits in her recliner and talks with food in her mouth—she always has. "We were never allowed at parties."

"But our brothers, your uncles Jerome and Lenny got away with so much. Me and Marigold could never dream of doing all the stuff they did."

Mama tells me about what people thought of her in high school—and I'm not sure how much of it I should believe. The only thing I know for sure about Mama is that she was prom queen. I've seen pictures in her old yearbooks. My father was prom king.

"Didn't have as many freedoms as my brothers. Didn't have as much of *anything* as Marigold."

She finishes eating and climbs out of her recliner. Takes her dirty dishes to the sink. So does Vae. Mine are still on the coffee table. I still feel like I'm only here visiting. Still haven't gotten that key yet.

Mama leans awhile against the countertop. "Marigold never got in trouble for anything. Marigold was Bobbie's favorite—we all knew it. And *I* was Bobbie's least favorite. Never been able to make Bobbie proud—not like Marigold could."

I watch her lean over the sink and stare through the kitchen window like she's watching a movie. I grab my dishes off the coffee table and walk them into the kitchen.

Mama makes eye contact with me for a longer time than usual, then she turns away. "Vae looks like her daddy, but you've always looked just like me."

7:39 p.m.

People think I'm pretty because of my mama. Mal thinks I'm a *dime* because of my mama.

She sits on the couch beside me, kinda close. And she opens a small four-by-six photo album that I've never seen before. "This was my daddy," she says, passing me the book, showing me a Black man with an Afro, a potbelly, and full-on seventies garb. "His name was Charles. People called him Charlie."

"Can I see?" Vae asks, spinning around on the floor.

I hand her the photo album.

"He was a strict man. A *mean* man. We were always scared when he'd get home. Always so scared. . . . He woke up angry. Went to bed *drunk*, just about every night. That's why I don't mess with no alcohol."

Vae passes the album back—thankfully—because I'm not sure where to rest my eyes without it in my lap. I can't look at Mama. She can't look at me.

"Anyway, he was a cheat," she says, standing and going back to her recliner. "Had about six or seven illegitimate kids—no telling how many women he slept with during his marriage to Bobbie." She shakes her head. "He'd have sex with a bunch of hussies, then come home to beat his wife and kids."

I wince, pausing on a picture of the whole family—Marigold and Mama standing hand in hand, with their twin brothers beside them. Bobbie was standing behind them, hands on Marigold's shoulders, with Granddad Charlie right beside her.

His face looks so mean and miserable. The same face Mama wears when she comes home from work.

"When I was about six or seven years old—Marigold had to be two or three—we were riding with Daddy. I don't remember where we were *supposed* to be going, but we ended up in a stranger's driveway.

"Daddy told me and Marigold to stay put—to not get out of his truck for anything—then he went inside the house without even knocking. He left the AC on high, so we wouldn't get heatstroke, but he was gone for a really long time. Marigold was starting to get fussy, and I didn't know what to do, so I got out . . ."

I look up at Mama, scared for her younger self.

"I went inside. I was only a kid—I didn't know better. There was only one light on in the house. And I heard . . . sounds." She looks up suddenly, with a frown on her face. "I called out to Daddy, and he started yelling, 'Didn't I tell you to stay in the car? Yolanda, you don't listen.' Then he came out of that room, wearing just his underwear. I could tell he had just slipped them on, the way he was pulling at the waistband.

"He told me to go back to the truck and that he'd deal with me later. But when he took us back home, he didn't say anything. Nothing. Like he'd already forgotten about the whole thing.

"Well, I ran into the house and told Bobbie exactly what happened, *exactly* what I saw, thinking she'd protect me from Daddy, and Bobbie didn't even believe me."

"She didn't believe you?"

"Or maybe she did, she just didn't want to talk about it with me." She licks her lips, avoiding eye contact. "After that, I couldn't do anything right. And Daddy always gave me the worst beatings, worse than anybody else."

I had a feeling Mama and Bobbie never quite got along. It was pretty obvious, though, when Bobbie died. Mama refused to get out of the car when Bobbie was being dropped into the ground. She said she didn't want to get her shoes muddy. The shoes—you know the ones.

I ask, "Okay, so then, what was it that I did to make you do that to *me*?"

NOTE TO SELF: I left my runaway bag in my car.

Are you leaving it outside? Or are you gonna go get it?

8:24 p.m.

Vae is sent to her room. She happily obliges, having had enough of the awkward tension spreading its way through the living room. Mama cuts the TV off, like she doesn't want anything interrupting what she's about to say. "I never hated you."

Angry tears sting my eyes, but I don't dare show them. Not to her. Never again.

"I don't hate anyone in this world."

"Okay, sure," I say. "But all that fear you were talking about, when Granddad was around, that's how I feel when you're around."

She looks down at her wrinkled hands.

"You remember how he made you feel? Why would you want to make me feel that way, unless you hated me?"

She looks at me then. She looks shaking mad. "What you don't understand is how hard it is raising two children by yourself. You wouldn't stop crying. You were colicky. And when you were a toddler you had a skin condition—you'd scratch until you bled and then you'd cry some more.

"And when you got to be four, and me and Daryl divorced, you wouldn't stop asking me all those damn questions. . . . God, I couldn't get no rest."

I scoff. "I'm sorry I was such a difficult baby, but I didn't *ask* to be here."

"I know you didn't. I'm not blaming you."

"I gave you grief when I was a baby, so you decided to punish me for the rest of my life?"

"I haven't been punishing you for no reason, Shaniqua. You're so damn hardheaded—I was the same way with Bobbie. You backtalk, you sneak out, you lie and *steal my shoes*. The shoes Amadi gave me, and you scuffed them up in five minutes. Absolutely no regard for how that would make me feel."

I shift my jaw back and forth. "Maybe because my feelings have never mattered to you. And as far as I knew, you never *had* feelings. You've never shown us any. You've never even told us that you love us. What does that mean, Mama? Why don't you say it to me and Vae?"

She swallows, blinking her eyes. "I took care of you, didn't I? Never let you go without shoes when you'd outgrow your old ones. Never let you starve, or parade you up and down the street, begging with a sign in your hand—"

"But you never hugged us. You never said you loved us."

8:37 p.m.

"I break my back to take care of y'all." She shrugs, looking into the distance again. Shutting down, just like I shut down at the sound of that word. "I ain't grow up saying all that."

NOTE TO SELF: It's important to learn how to say it.

People need to hear it.

9:00 p.m.

She has to start getting ready for bed. She has work tomor-row. But she still hasn't gotten up from her recliner. I think we're both scared to walk away from this right now, because it'd be so easy to backslide into how things used to be.

"I took a look at that video you put up on YouTube," she says, pulling her bottom lip into her mouth. "Your voice has matured. I can see why that DJ contacted you."

I smile—I can't help it. "He's actually a producer for Derek Atkins's music label."

Her eyebrows pinch as her eyes search my face. "*The* Derek Atkins?"

"Yes," I say, biting down on my excitement.

"Derek Atkins knows your name?"

"Yes! I'm pretty sure Ant has talked about me to him."

This is the reaction I was hoping to get from Mal when I told him. Mal's initial reaction is what I expected from my mother. Not *this. This* is how she reacts when Vae brings home an A-plus algebra test. I've never gotten this from her.

"Oh wow. And you have some kind of audition for them in California?"

I nod, toning down my expression, remembering how Vae was the first one who told her that. Remembering how she blew up over it.

"That's pretty major. You feel ready for it?"

I blink at her, confused. "Wait. So, you're fine with me going?"

"Shaniqua, you're eighteen. I can't really stop you. Besides, this is a big opportunity."

"And when I come back, will the locks be changed again?"

"Do I look like I got money to spend on another doorknob?"

It's not the confirmation that I want, but at this point, it's as good as I can expect from her. She hasn't told me she's sorry. She hasn't told me she loves me. Or that she won't kick me out again. But I'm exhausted from lack of sleep, and my neck is stiff. I can't sleep in my back seat for another night.

It doesn't mean I trust her. And it doesn't mean I forgive her. But I am admittedly relieved that she's allowed me to come back.

9:26 p.m.

I set up my laptop on the coffee table and press play on "Bow Down." Then I get in position as Vae comes out of her room to join Mama in the audience.

I sing with an imaginary microphone and dance my hardest, because I'm nervous. I'm more nervous than I was at the club. This is the first time I've ever performed for her by her request.

So I dance hard, because this is good practice for when I perform for Derek and Ant. This amount of pressure, anxiety, and *need* will all be working on my heart when I get in front of them. And if I had to bet, I'd say that performing for Derek and Ant won't even be half as much pressure as I'm feeling right now.

Performing for my mother.

NOTE TO SELF: You totally got this.

10:13 p.m.

Vae has retired back to her room as Mama runs through my performance, measure by measure—tightening up my vocals and my breath support. Overall, though, she praises me.

And her praise feels like a sprinkler in the summer. Now I see why Vae does so much to get it. Getting approval from this woman is insanely intoxicating.

After a while, she says she needs to get to bed. She has to work in only a few hours. I can't believe she stayed up this late, just to help me with my performance. She stayed up almost as late as she stayed up looking for Vae. I know it's kinda pathetic, but it makes me feel a type of way. Like . . . Yolanda Williams was said to be the next Yolanda Adams, right? Well, I'm Yolanda Williams's daughter. Give me your best deal, Derek Atkins.

10:23 p.m.

Before going to bed, I peek in Vae's room. Her light is off, but her bedside lamp is on, and she's lying in bed, reading a book. On spring break. Like the overachiever she is.

"Hey," she says, reading a few more sentences before slowly pulling her eyes away from the page. "I wanted to ask earlier, how far did you go?"

"Just to New Mexico."

"What's New Mexico like?"

The interest on her face reminds me of how excited I was with Mal when we finally left Texas. And it reminds me that she still hasn't done that yet. "It's so cool, Vae," I say, walking into her room and sitting on the edge of her bed. "Well, I mean, it's not *super* different from here. It's got mountains, though. Now *Colorado* is different. Like, you can *see* it from New Mexico. You can see the snowy peaks."

"Is it always snowy there?"

"I don't think so." I tell her about my and Mal's road trip and about all of my time with him—my performance, his promposal, and our fight before I left yesterday.

"You told him you don't want to stay at his house?"

"I *don't*," I say confidently. "I like spending time with him, but I would never be as comfortable there as I am here."

"Despite the fact that his parents would probably dote on you all the time and buy you a Lamborghini."

"They would never," I say, laughing. "And that's the part I'd like to avoid. They don't need to buy shit for me. I'm not their child."

"They obviously wish you *were*," Vae murmurs. "Way they were talking yesterday."

My eyes blink and blink and blink. "Excuse me, what? You talked to them yesterday?"

She sits up in bed, astounded. "They came over here last night and practically yelled at Mom."

"What did they say?"

"They begged Mom to call you and tell you to come home. Saying that they'd be happy to take you in. That they'd provide everything for you and how much they just wanted you to be safe."

"Really? Why would they do that?" I ask, as if Vae knows the answer.

She surprises me, though, when she says, "Because they love you, Nikki. It's obvious."

11:11 p.m.

The time on my phone flips to 11:11. I close my eyes and make a wish.

Please, space gods, let Mal answer my text.

Then I press send. **I know you're mad at me. I'm really sorry, Mal.**

He doesn't see it right away. After two minutes of waiting, I finally lay my head back on my pillow and stare at the glow-in-the-dark stars on my ceiling.

Then my phone chimes. I sit up so fast, I get whiplash. **Where are you?** he asks.

In my bed.

His reply bubbles dance. **You're back at home???**

Yeah, I came back this evening.

Can I FaceTime you? he asks.

Yes.

Butterflies clog my throat. No matter if he is mad at me, I

can't wait to see his face. Then there he is, filling up my screen. "Hey," he says, looking away from me, then back.

"Hey."

And that's it for a while. He won't look at me. I watch him avoid my gaze, trying to figure out what I could possibly say to make this moment less tense. Then finally he lifts his head. "Nikki, you don't have to be sorry."

My eyebrows shoot up. I don't know whether to be worried or relieved. He shifts his gaze away again. "I've run away before. Not from my mom, but from one of my foster homes. The parents were religious extremists. So, yes, I would have rather been on the streets than locked up in that house another night. I get it, Nikki. I've *been* there. I just hoped I could offer you what my parents offered me."

And now it's my turn to avoid his gaze.

"I always thought, when I was in foster care, that if I just had somewhere else to go, somewhere safe, I would have been good. I thought I could be that for you."

"I think that our situations are similar, but they're not the same. I don't think I ran because of the conditions of my place." I nod slowly. "I ran because I wanted to hurt her."

"Hmmm. Well, if that's the case, I can personally attest that your mission was accomplished."

"How do you know?"

"Nikki," he says, leveling with me, "my parents showed up right after you left. They wanted to chase after you, but I told them not to. I knew nothing would convince you to come back—nothing they could do. I knew it had to be your mom. It *had* to be."

"Vae told me about them coming over. Did they rip into my mom?" I ask, too curious for my own good. I can't imagine Mr. and Mrs. B standing in my living room, much less *yelling* at my mama. My mama is argumentative and proud. *No one* is gonna tell her what to do.

"No, no. They were very diplomatic about it. They were just . . . really hard-nosed. They were like, *She might be eighteen, but she's still a child.* And *If you aren't willing to take care of her anymore, at least allow us to.* They weren't against shaming her, either."

"Wow." I widen my eyes. "And she didn't fight back?"

"Surprisingly, no. She was too busy crying her eyes out."

"She cried when she called me, too," I say, remembering the sound of it—holding on to it for dear life. I can't ever let myself forget that one time she sounded human.

"When did she call you?" he asks. "My parents couldn't get her to do it while we were there."

"She called this morning. Really early."

He nods, licking his back teeth. "She must have been up all night, crying about it, then."

"Really? You think?" My eyes instantly get wet as I imagine it. Not sad tears. Happy tears.

Happy that my mother could actually feel sick over losing me.

"Well, um." I blink the tears away, changing the subject.

"You wouldn't believe it, but I actually just got done rehearsing with her."

"Rehearsing with who? Your *mom*?"

I nod, smiling. "She gave me breathing tips and vocal tricks. It was really helpful."

"Your mom *helped* you?" he asks, eyebrows soaring even higher.

"Yes!" I laugh. "And she was really excited about the audition, too. So that's cool."

"Nikki, that's *awesome*. I thought she'd call you. But I didn't think she'd actually try to change. You know?"

"Yeah, me either."

"Does that mean . . . you'll come back after?"

The question catches me off guard. "Um."

"Sorry, is it too soon to ask that?"

"No, no. I just haven't thought about it yet."

"Okay, so think about it now." He settles in. "I'll wait."

I smile, watching him watch me. Then he licks his lips while blinking down to *my* lips. The pause between us turns our conversation in another direction. "Will you come back?" he asks, lowering his voice. "Go to prom with me, Nikki. Graduate with me. Let me take you on another date."

I bite my bottom lip, all the while smiling.

"Spend a little more time with me before you blow up and become a superstar."

"You think after I blow up and become a superstar that I'll forget about you?"

"Will you?" He strokes his chin and raises his eyebrows at me.

"No. Never."

"Never say never."

"*Never,*" I repeat, widening my eyes. "I haven't gotten enough of you yet. I'm not going to forget about you."

"You haven't gotten enough of me?" he asks flirtatiously. "Shit, I hope you never get enough, then."

I smile. "Yeah, me either."

"Nikki, just tell me you're coming back."

"I'm coming back, Mal."

His eyes light up. "Really?"

"Yes." I roll my eyes. "I'm coming back home, right after my audition. I have too much . . . unfinished business here. I don't wanna leave like this."

"And am I part of that unfinished business?"

"Obviously."

He nods. "Cool." Then he takes a long breath, pulling away from the screen. And I notice his background is the kitchen—I see the pots above his head.

"Are your parents home?" I ask in a soft whisper.

He nods, looking to his left. "They're up in their room, though."

"Are they super mad at me?" I ask, worried.

"Nooo, not at all. They know how it is. They have always been really forgiving people. Probably because they both were in foster care at some point in their lives."

"Wait, they *were*?" I hiss.

"Yeah, they actually met in a support group."

My eyes go round. "Wow. So is that why there were so many white people at your Thanksgiving dinner?"

He laughs. "Yes, actually. Mom and Dad each have a white foster family that they're still really close with. So we see them at Thanksgiving."

"You know, I've learned so much about you, Malachai Brown. This spring break has been very eye-opening."

"One might even say life-changing."

I breathe a laugh through my nose. "Oh, life-changing for sure."

Then suddenly, he looks up from the screen, and I hear his mom's voice. "Mal, have you seen my multivitamin pills?"

"You never unpacked them," he says confidently. Then he glances back down to me with a playful roll of his eyes.

"Who are you talking to, son?" He sighs, then he mouths my name to her, as if I can't read his lips. I hear her gasp. "No, Mom," he says. "I'm talking to my girlfriend right now. No."

There's a bit of struggle, then she says, "Just tell her I love her" exasperatedly.

He looks back down at me. "My mom says she loves you."

"Thank you," she spits at him, then I hear her feet retreat.

"Um, I . . ." I trail off, wishing I could say it back to her. I wish that word didn't have so much power over me.

"Okay, she's gone, she's gone," he says, turning his charm back on. "What were we talking about before? Oh, right, you coming back after the audition. Do you still plan to drive there? Does that mean you're leaving tomorrow?"

"I mean, yeah, that's always been the plan."

"Okay, okay, cool. So answer me this, Nikki: Truth or dare?"

11:47 p.m.

"Malachai Brown," I say. "That game is over. We're done with that."

"No, we're not. You never won."

"You never won, either," I say.

"Exactly. So then we're not done playing."

A sigh escapes my nostrils. "You already know my answer, don't you? So long as we're playing this lifelong tournament."

"Oh, so that's it. You think we'll stay together for the rest of our lives. Wow, Nikki. I'm flattered. I didn't realize you were already planning our wedding."

"Truth *and* dare, Malachai. Shut up and play the game."

He smiles, amused. "Is it true that when you said you hadn't gotten enough of me, that you were talking about sex?"

My jaw drops. "Malachai!"

"*Or*," he says, laughing. "I dare you to meet up with me, early tomorrow morning, before you leave for California. I've got another surprise for you."

My open mouth slowly closes into a smirk. "How am I supposed to say no to that? You know I can't turn down a surprise."

"I know, because I *know* you, Nikki Lenae."

The sound of my middle name rolling off his tongue shoots a wave of sparks through my body. This must be how it feels when I call him *King.* I shrug, and my spaghetti strap slips off my arm. His eye follows it. "Okay, fine, I'll meet up with you. What time?"

"The second you wake up."

@nik_nik_nikki23: I know I have what it takes. Derek will have no choice but to agree.

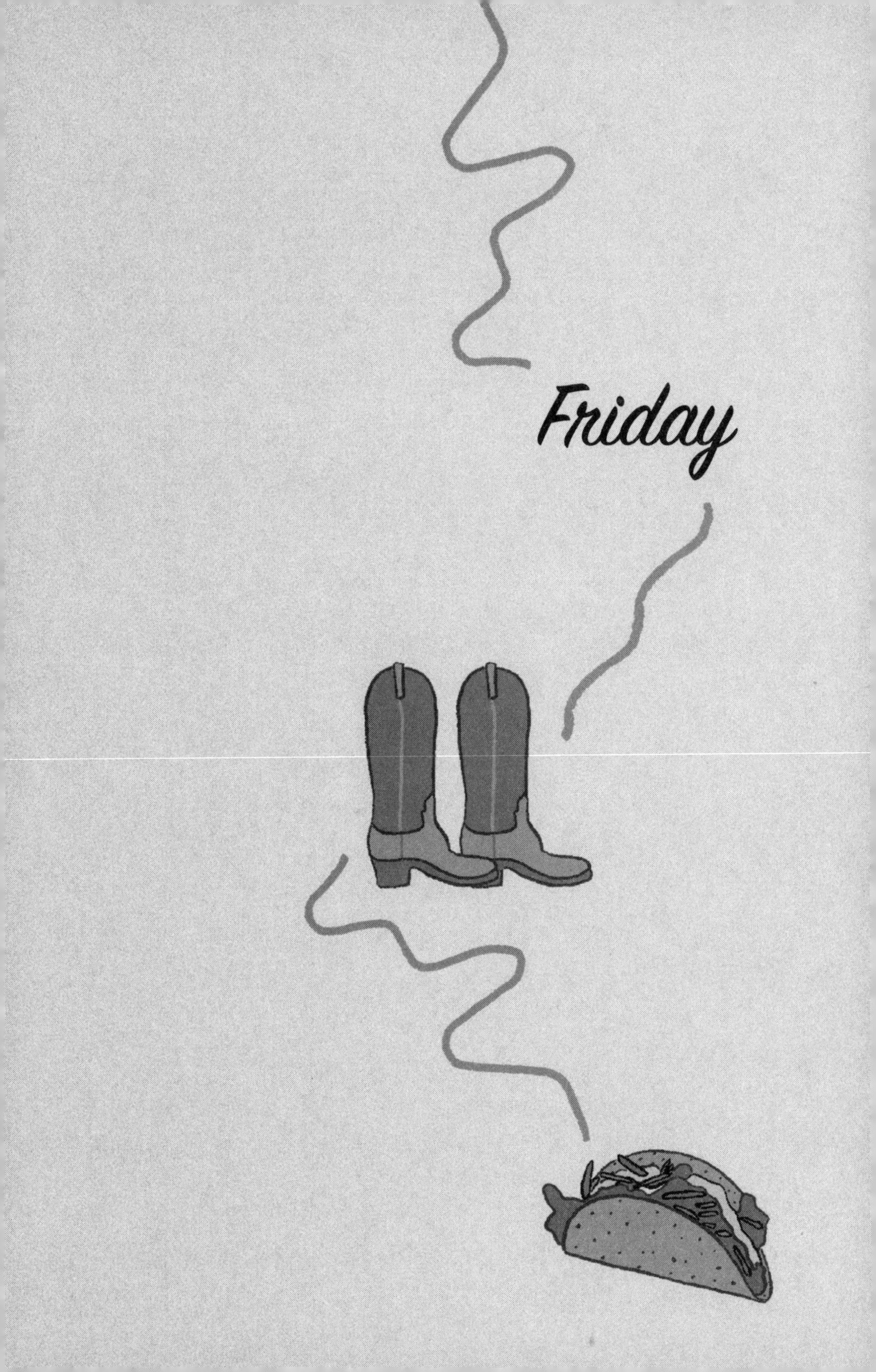
Friday

6:30 a.m.

My second alarm goes off.

I sit up fast. "Oh shit. Nooooo," I whine, running over to my dresser for clothes. I was supposed to get up on the first alarm at 5:45. I was supposed to be *leaving* at 6:30.

I just *really* wanted to catch him before his first run. I've done nothing but think about him all night.

I slip on a tank top from out of my dresser and blue jean cut-off shorts. I'm brushing my teeth while I put on my shoes when Vae's bedroom door opens. "You know it's spring break, right?" She's squinting at the bathroom light and hunching over, weak to her I'm Not a Morning Person syndrome. "I stayed up until two finishing that book, and now you're making all this noise—"

I spit out my toothpaste and say, "I'm *sorry.* I have to go see Mal," while I rinse my toothbrush under the faucet.

Vae opens her eyes all the way. "What are you gonna say to him?"

"I talked to him last night. He has some kind of surprise for me."

"Do you think he's asking you to move in with him?"

I'm about to rush out of the bathroom, but I pause. "We've only been dating for like three days."

"No, I know . . . but the circumstances are . . . special."

I pull down my tank top, as at some point it started rising above my belly button. "No, Vae, I don't think he's going to ask me to move in with him."

"Well, if he does, you should say yes. Don't be stupid—those people are rich. You'd be so comfortable and happy."

I frown slightly. "What happened to you needing me? You were begging me to stay two days ago."

"Yeah, well, I talked it out with Asher, and I realized how unhappy you were. How *unhealthy* living here can be sometimes. And I just want you to be happy, Nikki. You deserve to be happy."

My eyes are breaking my silence. "So, you and Asher, huh? Still whispering in each other's ears."

"Shut up, Nikki. Go see Mal or whatever."

I laugh, wanting to hug her but not quite knowing how. She starts closing her door. "Later, Nikki."

"Later, Vae."

She is definitely worth coming back for. She really hurt me last week, but I know why. I know where she learned how to act like that—where *I* learned how to act like that. As soon as I unlearn it, though, I'm going to teach my sister how to love.

She deserves that. She deserves genuine love.

On my way down the hall, with my sights on the front door, I accidentally kick some shoes on the floor. I turn on the hall light and almost jump out of my skin when I see I've stepped on Mama's shoes—you know the ones. They're just sitting in the middle of the floor. And I *know* they weren't there when I went to bed last night.

But then I see the rolled-up piece of paper sticking out of one of the toes:

Shaniqua,

I know you wanted to wear these for your audition. I'm probably never gonna wear them again anyhow. They're better off with you. Good luck at your audition!

Love, Mama

6:47 a.m.

I have accepted that I am not going to make it in time.

It's so dark. It feels like I should still be asleep. I absolutely hate Daylight Saving Time.

My car jerks forward suddenly, then sputters and jerks again. "Oh no! No!" The fuel gauge is stuck halfway between empty and full, like it always is—never moving. I was supposed to get gas immediately after I made it to New Mexico. But no, I turned around, distracted, watching my life make a total 180.

Of course this would be happening right now. Of course.

I grab my phone from my passenger seat, hurry to my favorite contacts, and pick Mal.

"Hey, baby," he answers.

"Mal," I whisper, my heart expanding, as well as my lungs, at the sound of his voice.

"What's up? You ready to meet up?"

I grin. "Funny that you ask . . ."

7:02 a.m.

It's seven o'clock and the sun hasn't risen yet. I'm sitting in my passenger seat, overthinking what to say when he gets here, when a pair of headlights slow to a stop behind me. My heart races.

I stare in my rearview at the bright blue headlights and watch as his door opens. He gets out wearing his running shoes, black joggers, and a bright orange T-shirt. An eighteen-wheeler flies past, ruffling the sleeves of his T-shirt. Then he jogs from his car to mine as I'm opening my door. "You know, I worry sometimes about how fast you get here."

He smirks, reaches down and cups my chin. "You know I'm always in a hurry to see you."

My breath jets and so do all those words I thought I might say to him.

He shuts the door for me while I'm situating my stuff in my pockets—completely oblivious. But then I look up and find his eyes close to my face. My back falls against the side of my car.

"I'm sorry, Nikki," he says. His hands land on either side of my head.

My eyes are closed, brushing the tip of my nose with his. "For what?"

"For everything. For not giving you the promposal you deserved the first go around. For getting with Cynthia just to make myself feel better. For not congratulating you about your audition."

Another eighteen-wheeler barrels past. The wind ruffles both of our shirts and the tiny hairs on my legs, but we keep our eyes closed and our faces close.

"I'm sorry that I hurt you," I say. "That I let you get tangled up in a relationship with me, knowing I wasn't planning to stay."

"Yeah, that sucked," he says. "Except . . . the part where we got tangled up in a relationship was the best part, so I'm not really complaining."

"Yeah, it was the best part for me too." I squeeze his hips closer. Then a car races past and honks their horn at us. "I'm sorry I couldn't say it back."

He shakes his head. "Don't be. Take your time and—"

"I love you too." The words clink, clunk up my throat and out of my mouth, sounding totally weak and weird, but he pauses at the sound—and then he releases a breath against my lips. It heats me from the top of my head down to the bottom of my vertebrae.

I clench his shirt and pull him the rest of the distance. Traffic gets heavier behind us, picking up wind against my forehead and my shins. He kisses me slowly and gently, like he's savoring every bit of me.

7:10 a.m.

"You wouldn't believe the conversation I had with my mom last night."

"Was it civil as fuck?' he asks, offering his hand.

"Considering the topic, yeah, it was pretty damn civil."

"I wanna know everything," he says, walking me to the passenger side of his car. "But first, I need to ask you something."

I freeze. "If it's truth or dare again, Malachai, then I'm out of here."

He laughs. "You already chose dare last night, so . . . are you ready for the surprise?" He pulls his phone out of his pocket and starts scrolling through it, about to show me something.

"Oh, shit. Here we go." When I look at the screen, the first thing I see is *American Airlines*. It's the only thing I need to see before I know what's happening.

I look up, eyes bucked.

"I bought two round-trip tickets to California before you called me last night—one for me and one for Vae, because I thought you were gone for sure."

"Wait, are you serious?" I grab on to his shirt, pleading for this to be true.

"The flight leaves this evening. . . . Wanna go?"

"Ohmygod!" I pull myself up and land on his lips. He laughs against my mouth, then picks me up and spins me around. "But what if they actually end up signing me?" When he sets me back on the ground, I look up at him, worried.

"Then my dad is going to look at every inch of that contract, and if it's a load of bullshit, we walk." He studies my eyes. "Whatever happens, Nikki, we'll get through it together. Promise."

I smile until it hurts. The energy between us burns like an inferno.

"But before we go . . . how about breakfast with my parents?" He looks truly concerned that I'll say no. "They've been begging to see you. It's getting sad."

"Yes, Mal. Of course. I need to—I need to talk to them. I owe them a lot."

"You don't owe them anything. Do you *want* to have breakfast with my parents?"

"Yes," I say confidently. "Especially since you started calling me your girlfriend. It's time to officially meet your parents."

He laughs again. "Oh yeah, I *did* say that last night."

"Yep, you did." I look up at him with a dazzling smile.

"Do you wanna be?" he asks, with his hand on my waist, like he already knows that I do.

"I mean, I guess."

"Yesterday, you couldn't get enough of me. But today you only *guess* you wanna be my girlfriend?"

"Okay, fine, I do. I really, really do."

7:33 a.m.

The closer we get to the front door, the more my stomach fills with nerves. I know Mal says I don't owe his parents anything, but it still feels like I do. Like whatever I walk into is going to be more than I can handle.

"Sorry, Dad may have gone a little overboard," Mal says as he opens the door. But when I expect to smell bacon and eggs, I smell something burning.

"I'm so sorry, Hutch!" we hear from the kitchen.

"Oh shit." Mal takes off and I take off after him. We hop over his parents' suitcases on the living room floor and run into a haze of smoke in the kitchen.

"I was just trying to help," Mrs. B says, then she spins around and spots us. "Kids! Oh God, you're not supposed to see this."

The "this" is a skillet on the stove messed over with a white powder—the same white powder that's all over the floor.

"Mom, what happened?" Mal asks with a face full of horror.

"You're not supposed to be anywhere near the stove."

"Malachai Brown," she snaps, "this is my house. I will go anywhere I damn well please."

"Anywhere except near the stove," Mr. B says with a scowl. "I had it under control, baby."

"Had *what* under control?" Mal asks.

"Just a teeny-tiny, very small . . . little grease fire," Mr. B says.

"Dad!"

I snort a laugh, and the whole family looks at me. They all look extremely embarrassed.

"There's still plenty of food on the table," Mrs. B says. "Son, take Nikki into the dining room—help yourselves."

He grabs my hand with a sigh. "Sorry about the mess, babe. My parents are weirdos."

"Your parents are awesome," I murmur as we enter the dining room. Case in point, the table is covered in food. Beautiful fresh fruit, pancakes with chocolate chips, waffles, bacon, breakfast sausage, and eggs. My mouth waters. "Holy shit," I hiss.

"Yep. Dad went *way* overboard."

My eyes are bigger than my stomach. Mal looks at the mountain of food that I pile onto my plate. I can tell he wants to say something, but he doesn't. He lets me pretend like I'm going to eat it all.

"Mal, can I ask you something?" I say while chewing a chunk of bacon.

"What's up?" He's working on a big pile of eggs.

"Those shoes you got me—did you pick them out yourself?"

He turns to me, looking caught. "Um. No. Riley picked 'em out."

"That's what I thought." I smile.

"Sorry, I don't know much about that shit. And I didn't know your shoe size."

"No, it's fine. I know. I bet Riley had the time of her life."

"I sent her to the mall with my debit card. She definitely didn't hold back."

I give him worried puppy-dog eyes. "Were they super expensive?"

"That's not for you to worry about. Eat, Nikki," he begs, motioning to my food. "We've got a six-hour drive to Dallas to catch this flight."

I take another bite of pancakes, chewing, trying to figure out how to say what's on my mind. "So . . . they're not super important to you, then, right?"

"What do you mean?"

"You won't care too much if I don't keep them?"

"You want me to take them back?"

"No, I want to give them . . . to my mom. She gave me her favorite designer shoes this morning. And she left me this note." I pull it out of my pocket and hand it to him. While he reads, I stop myself from trying to hide my emotion. So when he sees my face, his eyes melt.

"Nikki, this is . . . I'm so happy for you. No, I don't care if you give them to your mom. Sounds like a cool idea."

"Thanks, Mal." I smile, folding the note back into my pocket.

Then his parents walk in, holding hands. Their eyes fall to me and they both smile. "Thanks for having breakfast with us, Nikki," Mr. B says as they sit across from us.

"Thanks for having me." I shake my head at the delicious food separating me and Mal from his mom and dad. "You didn't have to do all this."

"We don't want any of that talk today," Mrs. B says, putting up her hand. "We love you like our own child."

That word. Before I can overthink it, Mal leans into my ear. "You don't have to say it back."

I smile, then turn to Mal and smile harder. He always knows exactly what I'm thinking. He just knows.

Breakfast with his parents is fun and comfortable. Our smiles light up the room. Our laughter blooms. Such a sunny day today.

After I decide to not overstuff myself, I still have half a plate of food left. Mal is cleaning his plate with his finger—"growing boy" and all. I'm pretty sure he went for a run before I called him this morning, so I'm sure he was ravenous.

Mrs. B. puts her elbows on the table, props her chin up on her hands, and looks across at me. It feels like a spotlight shines on me. "Nikki, we wanted to have breakfast with you to apologize."

My brow furrows. "For what?" What could they possibly have to be sorry for?

"We were a little rough on your mom yesterday. I might have yelled a little. I don't want it to ever feel like we're being overbearing, especially since we aren't your parents. If you ever want us to butt out, that's all you have to say. We will understand."

"I don't want that." I shift my gaze away. We're getting to that point I was afraid of—the uncomfortable shit. I'm starting to lose my handle on my emotions. I want to tell her how much I appreciate her and Mr. B. How they kept me sane during those nights when I just couldn't deal with my mama anymore.

But if I say it, I'm scared I'll start crying, like that night when the spouts wouldn't shut off. I'm scared that'll happen again.

"Well, if that's ever the case, let us know," Mr. B says.

"We'd love to be a part of your life, in any capacity you need," Mal's mom says.

"Thank you. Thank you . . . so much."

Mrs. B wipes under her eye. "You're so welcome."

"Thanks, Mom and Dad, for breakfast, and also for everything else," Mal says. "We're gonna head out to California today. That's okay, right?"

"Yeah, son," his dad says. "Just make sure to answer our calls."

"Yessir."

"Mal, are y'all checking any bags?"

"No, just carry-ons." We stand from the table, plates in hand. Mal leads me to the dining room doorway.

"Be sure you check the sizes of any liquids. Leave it in your car if it's not on the list of acceptable items. Want me to send you my list?"

"Sure, Mom. Thanks." He gives me an annoyed smile as we walk our plates to the kitchen.

"Oh!" she calls from the dining room. "Do you already have a hotel? I'll book you one and send you the reservation!"

NOTE TO SELF: People say chewing gum on flights helps with ear popping.

Never been on a plane before, because I've never had an opportunity.

But also, I've always been scared. Plane crashes just don't seem like something you survive.

So many firsts this week. I'm a little freaked out, but there's so much going on that I haven't quite grasped the magnitude.

8:49 a.m.

He helps me get my car back home. Parks behind me in the driveway.

I grab his hand on the way to the steps, welcoming him inside my house. And as soon as I get it unlocked with my new house key, Vae comes hot-stepping out of her bedroom, looking disheveled. "Nikki? I thought you were on a plane to Cali by now."

I narrow my eyes as Mal shuts the door behind us. "How do you know about that?"

Mal says, "I told Vae about the tickets yesterday, when we both thought you were gone. She happily conceded her ticket to you."

"So you knew he was going to surprise me this morning?" I give her a look. "Little sneak."

But then when I try pushing past her to go to my room, she blocks me. "Wait, where are you going? Why aren't y'all on the plane?"

"It leaves this evening," I say curiously. "Why can't I go down the hall, Vae?"

"No, I mean, you *can*," she says with shifty eyes, moving away so I can pass. "I just thought you were trying to bail on your dream or something."

The girl is a sneak. And she's a damn good liar, but not good enough. As I pass by her room, I push open the door. "Hi, Asher," I say before I even get a glimpse of him sitting on her bed.

"Oh, um, hi."

I keep going to my room, nonchalantly. Mal teases them behind me. "Ooooh, Vae's got a boy in her room! Ooooh, I'm telling!"

"Shut up, Mal! I hate you so much!"

I smile, turning on my bedroom light. It's good to see her living life—not just studying tirelessly in her room. She's sneaking boys into the house and shit. I can't believe it. "Be careful, Vae," I say as Mal walks into my room.

She's shutting her door back. "I'm always careful, Nikki."

"I swear, if I hear them having sex, I'm gonna lose my whole breakfast," Mal says, closing my door too.

"She would never."

With the assumption that I'm coming back home after the audition, I only pack as much as I need for the weekend. Plus Mama's shoes. Mal is exploring my walls, reading some of my lyrics from sixth grade. "Don't read those!" I push my way between him and the wall, covering the lyrics with my back.

“Why not? I’ve heard, like, every song you’ve ever made.”

“Yeah, well, these lyrics are really old and really bad, and I’d rather you didn’t read them. Try something on that wall.” I point to my bed. “Those are recent songs that I haven’t recorded yet.”

He puts his hands up, backing off. “These over here?” he asks, spinning on his heel. He goes to sit on the edge of my bed and looks over his shoulder.

One hand spread on my mattress, the other braces against his leg—he makes a pretty picture, sitting there. The image changes the whole context of my bed. Beds aren’t for sleeping anymore. They’re for all that other stuff.

When I don’t answer his question, he looks over and catches me staring. I like how bright his shirt is. Makes his dark skin really light up.

He smiles and licks his lips. “Come here.” Then he opens his arms to me.

8:59 a.m.

Before we leave, I tell Vae to send Asher home by one o'clock. She gives me attitude.

I tell Mal that I'll meet him in the car, hand him my much lighter runaway bag, then I walk the shoes he bought me to my mama's closed bedroom door. I leave them on the floor with a note rolled up in the toe:

Mama,

Never say never. I'm leaving these shoes for you to break in. They're brand-new. Go out dancing. Go to church. But they don't only have to be for special occasions.

Also, thanks for the shoes. Sorry I scuffed them.

Love, Shaniqua

9:00 a.m.

"You ready?" Mal asks when I join him in his car. The engine is rumbling, vibrating under our seats.

"Yeah, let's go."

"Are you scared?"

"Hell, yeah." I laugh. "Of course I am."

"Scared of what, exactly?" Once he starts us down the street, he offers his hand on the console.

I take it, gently closing my fingers between his. "Everything. The audition. The flight."

"Hmm." He pulls our hands up and kisses the back of mine. "Nothing to be scared of anymore, Nikki. Nothing but good is on the horizon. Regardless of what happens. Nothing but good." Then he smiles at me. "And the flight's gonna be fun. Trust me. *I know you.* You're gonna love it."

"Okay."

"Don't be worried," he says.

“Suddenly, I’m not anymore.” I turn into his reassuring gaze. “You’re right. Nothing but good is on the horizon.”

Whether I kill or bomb at the audition, at least I can come home. Mama seems to be really trying, and if it doesn’t work out with her, at least I have Mal and Mal’s parents. If LA doesn’t work out, Dallas will. My future is bright, regardless of which path I choose.

And whatever I do, I know for sure that I’m doing it for all the right reasons.

NOTE TO SELF: Don't forget where you came from.

Please don't lose yourself in California.

You grew up singing church songs. You grew up playing in the dirt, walking barefoot outside and slurping water from the water hose. You grew up poor, with never enough food stamps, eating peanut butter half sandwiches for breakfast, lunch, and dinner. You grew up in the hottest room in your trailer house.

No matter what kind of fame you find, no matter what kind of money you come into, never forget where you came from.

@AntTheProdigy: You fucking KILLED that shit, Nikki. Get ready to talk business.

Acknowledgments

This book has been the most difficult for me to write so far. It's the first book I've written since quitting my day job. With so much more time on my hands, why did I need so many extensions? I've come up with a lot of reasons for it, but I think the most accurate is simply *mental health*.

That's why the first person I have to thank is my editor. Aly, I am so lucky to have you and so grateful for the way you've worked with me on this book. Every time I turned in a draft, I hated it. And every time I needed to ask for more time, I felt sick to my stomach. But thank God I had you. Thank you for talking me down. Thank you for also giving me space and time to find my love for this story.

Thank you, Eva, for how you've helped me shape my books up until this point. I'm so excited for you and your new adventure! My books and I will wholeheartedly miss you. And thank you so much, Karina, for all that you do and all that you've done—I cannot wait to continue working with you! Thank you to everyone at Harper who has worked on my books—from the design team to marketing and everyone in between.

Thank you, Bri. My agent, my friend. Catching up with you is always so rewarding and your ideas are always so *good*. So grateful to have you on my team as well as everyone at HG Literary.

Thank you so much, Adriana Bellet, for truly capturing the essence of this story with your talent and creativity. I am so in love with the cover!

Big thanks to my team at Hot Key Books: Tia, Ella, Molly, and everyone. Thank you so much for the push you give my books in the UK and the care you put into everything you do.

And to my big sister—my very first best friend, my eternal best friend: You inspired me to read. You inspired me to write and to produce. Because I wanted to do what you did. I love you and I will always be proud of you.

Thank you, Mom, for being the best cheerleader a girl could ask for. Thanks for always coming up with names for half my cast and always encouraging me to do what I love. Your belief in me fuels me.

Thank you, Blake, for telling me to rest. For talking me through every rework and every new draft, and through all the times I absolutely hated everything I wrote. You are my sanity. You bring me so much peace. Thank you. I love you.

And lastly, thank you to all my readers. All those who share reviews, who reach out to me with praise and so much love. I am so grateful for everyone who picks up my books. Thank y'all so much for your time and encouragement and your community. I can't wait to share more with you.